A Mother's Fight

Libby Ashworth

W F HOWES LTD

This large print edition published in 2023 by
W F Howes Ltd
Unit 5, St George's House, Rearsby Business Park,
Gaddesby Lane, Rearsby, Leicester LE7 4YH

1 3 5 7 9 10 8 6 4 2

First published in the United Kingdom in 2022
by Canelo

A CIP catalogue record for this book is available from the British Library

ISBN 978 1 00412 257 8

Typeset by Palimpsest Book Production Limited,
Falkirk, Stirlingshire

BOLTON 1818

CHAPTER ONE

Hannah Fisher stared at the Reverend Brocklehurst. She'd come to his vestry in the parish church to ask him if she could be given more money to pay her rent now that the price had increased, and she wasn't sure that she'd understood his answer.

'Times are hard for everyone,' the vicar went on to explain. 'The parish must make the best use of the money it spends and the guardians feel that paying your rent is no longer necessary now that your children are old enough to work.'

'But there is no work,' she protested. 'Where will we go if we're turned out of our home?'

Hannah already knew what the answer would be.

'I can give you a letter for the workhouse,' suggested the vicar. 'I'm sorry,' he said when she didn't reply. 'I did press your case to the guardians, but I'm afraid I was overruled.'

Hannah could hear her heart thudding with fear at the thought of it. The workhouse was a prospect that terrified her.

'My childer?' she managed to ask after a moment.

'They'll be well cared for,' the vicar assured her.

'In the workhouse?'

He nodded. It was obvious that he was finding the conversation difficult, but Hannah had no sympathy for him. He would go home to his well-furnished vicarage and eat the ample dinner that his maid placed on the table in front of him. He would probably give no more thought to the matter as he tucked into his mutton chops or whatever tasty and nutritious meal had been cooked for him. It was so unfair. She'd done nothing wrong and yet she was being punished.

'Have you heard nothing from your husband?' asked the vicar.

Hannah shook her head. 'No,' she said. 'I did hope that Thomas Holden would bring me news of him, but he said that he never saw Jack again after they reached New South Wales. He said he thought he must have died.' She couldn't contain her emotions any longer and the tears flowed freely down her cheeks as she sobbed.

Hannah had been so hopeful when she'd heard that Thomas Holden was home that she'd run all the way to Hag End Fold to ask about Jack. The two men had been sentenced at the same time for the same offence – swearing an illegal oath at a secret weavers' meeting on the moors – and had been transported on the same ship the *Fortune*. But whilst Molly Holden had received letters from Thomas, Hannah had never heard a word from Jack after the ship had sailed. And now it seemed there was no trace of him.

'I'm sorry,' said the vicar again, as Hannah fumbled for a rag to wipe her face. 'But you must try to find the strength to bear it. At least you will be fed and clothed in the workhouse. You and your children won't starve.'

It was scant consolation, thought Hannah as she wiped her nose and pushed the rag back up her sleeve. If it hadn't been for her children she would probably have refused the offer and taken her chances on the streets of Bolton. But she couldn't allow her daughters and her young son to be homeless and hungry – even though the workhouse was a dreadful prospect.

'You'll need to go to the gatehouse and show this letter,' said the vicar as he handed her a sheet of paper folded into four. 'You have until Friday. If you stay in the cottage after that you'll be turned out by force,' he warned her. 'Don't let that happen.'

Hannah took the letter with trembling fingers. She didn't thank the Reverend Brocklehurst, but gathered her threadbare shawl around her shoulders and stood up to go. There was nothing left to say. Since the moment Jack had been arrested, she'd been at the mercy of others. And it wasn't that she was lazy or didn't want to work. She wasn't afraid of turning her hand to anything, but work was impossible to come by.

She walked down the stone-floored aisle of the church and let herself out of the heavy oak door into Churchgate. The sun was shining. Folk were going about their business. A man with a horse and cart was delivering barrels of beer to the Golden Lion; a woman was sweeping the street in front of her door and the chimneys of the mills were belching smoke and clouding what had been a clear blue sky earlier in the morning.

With a heavy heart, Hannah turned for home – to the cottage at Hill Fold where she'd lived for twelve years. Her children were sitting on the bare floor when she went in and they looked up expectantly. Ruth, her eldest, was eleven years old. At the same age Hannah had sat beside her own mother and learned to spin thread until her fingers became calloused with the work. At first, when her fingers had been painful and the summer sunshine had enticed her out to play, she'd been resentful of the tasks that had been set her, but she'd been well fed and secure and although she hadn't realised it at the time, she'd been happy. Now, no one wanted home spun cotton. It was all spun in the mills, on huge machines, and many women besides her sat idle in these troubled times. Some were lucky enough to have husbands or fathers to support them. Others, like Hannah, struggled on until the workhouse was their only option.

Her middle child, Kitty was nine years old. She was the frailest of the three with a bad cough that never seemed to get any better. Like the others, she was so thin that her sharp bones jutted through her pale skin and her lips had a bluish tinge, unlike the rosy lips and cheeks of the mill owners' daughters who strutted about the town in their fashionable coats and bonnets.

Her youngest was Edmund. Her boy. At seven years old he was too young to remember his father. She could see the hunger on his stark face and she was forced to hold back her tears as she shook her head and showed her empty hands. They would all go to sleep hungry again that night, huddled together for warmth under the one blanket she'd kept back from the pawnshop, lying on the thin straw mattresses she'd made after the beds had been sold to provide money for something to eat. It had only been after she'd sold everything she possessed, including all Jack's clothes and his looms, that the parish guardians had agreed to give her anything at all – and now even that was refused to them.

'We've been offered a better place,' she told the children, trying desperately to make it sound as if their move into the workhouse would be a good thing. 'We'll have proper beds to sleep in and three meals a day.' Hannah didn't tell them that they would be expected to work hard in return – dirty, tedious work picking oakum that would make their fingers twice as sore as hers had been when she'd learned to spin. And neither did she tell them the part that would hurt them most of all – that they would be taken away from her and only allowed to see her for a couple of hours of a Sunday afternoon.

Hannah knelt down on the hard floor that no longer had so much as a rag rug to soften it and gathered all three of her children as close to her as she could. 'It'll be all right,' she promised them, wondering how on earth it had come to this and whether there had been anything she could have done to prevent it.

CHAPTER TWO

It was hunger – not her own hunger, she could have endured that, but her children's hunger – that drove Hannah to pack up their few meagre belongings and leave home for the workhouse two days later.

She left the damp straw mattresses and the threadbare blanket. She left the four bowls and spoons and her kettle that hung from a chain in the stone fireplace, over a fire that only burned if she could scavenge enough wood and lumps of fallen coal to light it. She packed the few patched clothes they still owned into a sack and, with her threadbare shawl around her shoulders, she led her barefoot children down the track from the cottage towards Bolton. She saw a few faces at their windows, watching her go, but no one came to their doors to wish her well. They turned away if she glanced at them, maybe afraid that her misfortune would taint them as well if they came too close.

The workhouse had only been recently built, testament to the growing need in the town as more and more people were thrust into poverty by the slump in trade. Folk had said that things would get better after the war with France ended, but they'd grown worse instead. Even those in work had seen their wages cut again and again as the price of bread had risen so high that most families were no longer able to afford it and had to make do with oats.

When she reached Fletcher Street, on the edge of the town, Hannah hesitated outside the building. It was an imposing edifice. The red bricks shone vibrantly in the morning light; the walls too recent to have been rendered dark and sooty from the smoking chimneys.

Hannah felt the children's reluctance as they approached the main gateway. Their hands pulled on hers, resisting their fate.

'Name?' asked the porter as he stepped out of his little building at the side of the gate in his neat uniform with piping around his collar and cuffs.

'Hannah Fisher,' she told him. 'I have a letter.'

She held out the paper that the vicar had given her and the porter looked at it carefully. Then he nodded and told her to go through into the small yard beyond and wait. 'I'll tell matron that tha's 'ere,' he said.

Hannah heard him close the gate behind them and Edmund began to cry.

'Can we not just go home?' whispered Ruth.

'They'll not give us money for t' rent,' said Hannah. She'd already explained their situation to her elder daughter as best she could, but she knew how hard it was for her to accept it.

The high walls seemed to close in around her as she pulled Kitty to her side and held her tightly. 'It's for the best,' she repeated as if saying it enough times would make it true.

Hannah tightened her arm around Kitty as she saw a woman come out of a door and beckon them to go forwards. Her younger daughter was the one who concerned her the most. Ruth was strong and resilient and Hannah hoped that she would cope. Edmund too was a healthy boy and she hoped that because he was still young the work he would be set wouldn't be too onerous. But Kitty was the child who had always clung to her. She'd been a fretful baby and even as she'd grown Hannah had needed to give her close attention to keep her well. Hannah was afraid that she wouldn't receive the care she needed in this place and that the work would be too hard for her.

'Mrs Fisher?' asked the woman. Hannah nodded. 'I'm Mrs Cartwright, the matron. Follow me.'

They followed the matron up the four stone steps that led through a dark door and into a small reception room. There was an oak desk with papers carefully arranged on it. The man behind it sat in a comfortable chair.

'This is Mr Cartwright, the workhouse master,' the matron told them. 'He needs to take some details and then we'll get you admitted.'

'Thank you,' said Hannah, feeling anything but

thankful to have arrived in this place. The matron nodded and went out through another door. Beyond it Hannah glimpsed a room with rows of beds. It looked clean and each of the beds was covered with a white counterpane of the sort that Molly Holden wove. Molly had done all right, thought Hannah. After they'd all petitioned to go with their husbands to New South Wales and been turned down, Molly had picked up her husband's work and taught herself to weave. It had made Hannah wonder if she'd been too quick to sell Jack's loom, but she'd had no money to buy it back even if it had been possible and it had never occurred to her until it was too late that a woman could weave caddow quilts.

Molly had been lucky enough to get letters from Thomas Holden too. She'd known that her husband was alive and that he would come back – even though folk had told her that no one ever did. But Molly had believed in her husband and Thomas had come home, looking well fed and handsome – although now that trade had taken a turn for the worse Hannah wondered if it wouldn't have been better if Molly and little Annie had gone to New South Wales instead. Folk said that families could prosper there. She'd hoped that Jack was prospering. She'd waited and waited for a letter to come, sending money for their passage and asking them to join him. But she'd heard nothing, and when Thomas Holden had brought no news of Jack, Hannah had begun to fear the worst, that her husband was lost to her for ever – sent away to the other side of the world for repeating a few words that were of no consequence.

'Full name?' asked Mr Cartwright.

'Hannah Fisher.'

'Middle name?'

'None.'

'Married?'

'My husband was transported,' she replied. 'I've had no news of him.'

Mr Cartwright frowned. Hannah knew it wasn't a good start to have to admit that you'd been the wife of a criminal. She hoped it wouldn't go against her.

'I'll put widow,' said the workhouse master, making some marks on the paper in front of him. 'Age?'

'Thirty-two.'

'Any illness?'

Hannah shook her head. Her heart was broken, but she didn't think that Mr Cartwright would write that down on his admission form.

He went on to note the details of the children. Hannah explained that Kitty was unwell and Mr Cartwright said that they would all have to see the doctor and not to worry, Kitty would be taken care of. He seemed kindly in his brusque way and Hannah hoped that maybe things wouldn't be as bad as she feared, but it still seemed like a prison sentence – a sentence without end because she had no idea how she and the children could ever escape this place.

When all the forms had been filled in and Hannah had made her mark on them, Mr Cartwright told her that they were now workhouse inmates and he read out a long list of rules that they must obey. Hannah worried that she wouldn't remember them all and would get into trouble. And she was sure that the children wouldn't remember them, and she wouldn't be there to remind them.

Then, they were herded into another room and told to take off their clothes.

'All of them?' asked Hannah in alarm. She'd never stripped naked in front of anyone, not even her husband.

'Everything,' replied Mrs Cartwright. 'As long as the clothing has no vermin it'll be washed and kept for you. You'll get it back when you leave. If we find vermin we'll burn it,' she added. 'This is a clean place. We'll do the childer first,' she added, seeing Hannah's reluctance. 'They look like they could do with a good bath.'

Hannah wanted to reply that her children were clean, but the truth was that the best she'd been able to do for a long time was wash them down in cold water once a week – and less often in the wintertime when the water she fetched from the pump froze in the back kitchen overnight. She couldn't remember how long it was since they'd had clean clothing, and even if Mrs Cartwright did burn what they were wearing it would be no loss because the patches were holding together only a fraction of the garments they'd once been.

Hannah began with Edmund and helped him wriggle out of the jacket that he'd outgrown long since. The grimy shirt he wore underneath had to be peeled from his skin and he cried in protest as Mrs Cartwright became impatient with Hannah's attempts to be gentle and pulled it off him, making it disintegrate into a dust of broken fibres and frayed edges. The matron threw it down in disgust and wiped her hands on her apron. 'Let's get him into t' bath!' she exclaimed.

In an adjoining room there was a tin bath filled with steaming water. Another fierce-looking woman stood there with some shears in her hand.

'What are those for?' asked Hannah in alarm.

'To cut his hair. We don't want lice.'

Hannah wanted to protest that Edmund had no lice, but she suspected it wasn't true. She knew that he constantly scratched his head – they all did, and although she tried to comb their hair every day she knew it was impossible to keep the creatures away.

Edmund climbed into the bath eagerly and sat down, but his eagerness waned as the woman began to scrub at him with a flannel and a bar of something that stank so badly of tallow that Hannah thought it could never possibly improve on the worst of human stenches.

'Tha's hurtin' me!' protested Edmund as his

pale skin turned red under the woman's administrations.

'Let me wash him,' pleaded Hannah, but Mrs Cartwright put out an arm to hold her back.

'Nurse will wash him,' she told her firmly and Hannah could do nothing as she stood and watched her little boy sob as his hair was sheared close to his head and a jug of water poured over it, making him choke.

'Please,' she pleaded again, but Mrs Cartwright shook her head and ushered her back into the other room as Edmund was roughly dried.

Kitty, who had witnessed what had happened to her little brother was already sobbing and clinging to her. 'Don't let 'em do it me, Mam!' she pleaded. Hannah held her close and kissed her head, distraught that the girls would also have all their hair cut off. She would never have agreed to come if she'd known, she thought.

When it was her turn, Kitty clung hold of Hannah's skirts and wept.

'It'll be all right. Tha'll feel better when tha's clean,' Hannah told her as Mrs Cartwright prised the child's fingers away and carried her, howling and kicking, into the other room. Hannah tried to follow, but the door was firmly closed and she could only hold on to Ruth's hand as she listened to the screams of her younger daughter.

'Kitty always makes a fuss,' she said, trying to soothe Ruth. 'It's only a bath.'

Ruth went in silence when it was her turn and

although Hannah pressed her ear to the door she heard nothing more than the splashing of water and a few muted instructions. She had no idea what had happened to Edmund and Kitty. She didn't know if she would see them again or if they had already been taken away to the children's ward.

'Come along now, Mrs Fisher,' said Mrs Cartwright briskly when the door opened again. Hannah saw that the bath had been filled with fresh water and a clean towel and a bar of the pungent soap were laid out on a chair beside it. 'Leave tha clothes in t' corner,' the matron told her. 'I'll let thee wash thyself whilst I fetch thee a clean gown to wear.'

As Hannah undressed she saw that the nurse was keeping an eye on her from beyond the bathroom. She supposed that if she simply allowed her head to sink under the water and wash away her life the woman would rush in and pull her up. Not that she would do it. Not when she had her children to think of. She needed to survive to find a way of getting them out of this place.

Jack would have been horrified to see her reduced to this, thought Hannah as she carefully folded her threadbare clothing and stepped into the bath. It was so shaming. She'd heard the way that folk spoke about people who had gone into the workhouse. The old women would talk about them in whispers with their mouths hidden behind their hands. It wasn't a subject for open discussion, but something that was a shocking secret because it only happened to those who had fallen short of the standards expected of respectable people.

Hannah sat down in the bath and allowed the water to lap around her. It was comfortingly warm and in other circumstances she would have relished it. She picked up the soap and recoiled from its smell, but began to scrub at her skin with the flannel, watching in satisfaction as the grease and grime floated away.

As she washed, she glanced at the nurse in the other room. She was worried that she would come in and take the shears to her hair and although Hannah was aware of her head itching she didn't want to lose the thick brown locks that reached almost to her waist when her hair was unpinned. It had never been cut, not once, and to have it sheared off would be more than she could bear.

'Best let down tha hair and give it a good soaping,' called the nurse. 'I've a jug 'ere ready to rinse it.'

'I don't want it cut off,' protested Hannah as she took out the pins.

'I'll not cut it if tha can get it clean. We're only told to cut t' childer's hair,' the woman replied.

Hannah picked up the soap again. She made the best lather she could between her palms and began to rub it into every strand of her hair, working it into her scalp with her fingertips and hoping it was enough to kill any lice that were lurking there. When she was finished the nurse came in with a jug and told Hannah to put her head back whilst she poured it over her hair. Some splashed into her eyes, making them sting and her ears filled with water making her half deaf. She coughed and spluttered and the nurse handed her a cloth.

'Rub it hard to get t' water out,' she advised. 'Then tha'll have to come and sit by t' fire until it dries. I don't want thee catchin' a chill afore doctor's even seen thee.' She took the jug away and came back a moment later with some garments. 'Here's thy clothing,' she said. 'Mind tha takes good care of it.' She put the items down on the chair and handed a towel to Hannah. 'Come through when tha's dressed,' she told her.

Hannah stood by the bath and rubbed herself dry. The clothes she'd been issued with looked clean but were made of the coarsest of cloths. There was a calico shift, a petticoat, a gingham gown in pale blue with a white apron, a pair of worsted stockings, some slippers and a white cap. She dressed herself carefully. The shift felt itchy against her skin but she supposed it was a small price to pay for decent attire, and the uniform was in much better repair than the garments she'd taken off.

Her hair was still damp despite her brisk rubbing so she kept the cap in her hand and went through the doorway to find the nurse.

'Through here,' the woman told her and led into a dayroom with chairs arranged in a semi-circle in front of the hearth. She was relieved to see her children there. Her daughters were dressed in similar clothing, but she could see by the straggly ends poking out from under the edges of their caps that their hair had been cut short. Edmund was wearing trousers and a shirt of striped cotton. For the first time in his life he was shod and he was tapping the soles of his boots against the floor in fascination. Ruth was sitting upright on a chair looking bewildered and Kitty ran to Hannah as soon as she saw her and locked her arms around her waist. Hannah held her and kissed the top of her damp head, relieved not to be parted from her children just yet, although she knew that it was inevitable.

'Doctor'll be along to see you shortly,' the nurse told her. 'Sit next to t' fire until thy hair's properly dry,' she advised Hannah before going out and closing the door behind her.

Hannah sat down on a hard chair, although it was comfortable enough after having become used to nothing more than a stool. She pulled Kitty onto her lap and held her close.

'It's not so bad,' she told the children. 'I expect we'll get some dinner soon, and it won't be for long,' she promised. 'I'll find a way to make things right and then we can go home again.'

CHAPTER THREE

After the doctor had looked at their eyes and ears and taken their pulses and listened to their breathing, the nurse came for the children and bade them follow her. Hannah urged them to leave, saying that they were going to see the beds they would sleep in and that she would see them soon. She hoped it was true.

When the door had closed behind them, she turned to the doctor who was packing his instruments into his bag.

'Our Kitty's not a strong lass,' she told him. 'I'm worried they'll work her too hard.'

'She's undernourished. All your children are, Mrs Fisher,' the doctor accused her, as if she'd had any choice in the matter.

'I did my best. I weren't given that much to feed 'em,' she told him.

'Times are hard,' he agreed. 'But they'll be fed and cared for here. What happened to your husband?' he asked as he snapped the bag shut.

'He was transported.'

'A troublemaker,' observed the doctor.

'He was protestin' for fair payment,' replied Hannah.

'He'd have been better off looking after his family,' the doctor told her. 'Do you know where he is now?'

She shook her head. 'I was told he's probably dead.'

The doctor picked up his bag and went out. He was free to walk out past the porter, through the archway, over the bridge and back into Bolton. As she stared at the closed door Hannah wondered if she would ever be free herself.

Behind her the nurse returned. 'Come this way,' she said and Hannah followed her down a white-washed corridor to a green door. The nurse opened it to reveal a long room with dozens of identical iron-framed beds – two rows against the outer walls and two rows back-to-back down the centre. 'This one's thine,' the nurse said, indicating the one nearest to the door. 'There's a nightgown here and a shawl tha can put on when it gets cold. There'll be a change of under-wear once a week, after thy bath, and fresh sheets once a month.'

Hannah nodded. It seemed like heaven, but the loss of her freedom was a high price to pay for it.

'I'll leave thee to settle in. There'll be dinner at twelve. Bell'll ring. Someone'll show thee where to go. Tha'll be allocated work tomorrow.'

'What work will I have to do?' asked Hannah.

'Tha looks strong enough for t' kitchen or

laundry,' said the nurse. 'Better than pickin' oakum anyroad.'

Left alone, Hannah sat down on the side of the bed. There was nothing to see. The only windows in the room were high on the opposite wall and, as there was a high wall beyond, it was impossible to tell what the weather outside might be like. She looked around at the other beds but there was nothing to tell her about their occupants. There were no personal belongings of any kind.

She walked up and down the narrow gap between the beds, afraid to leave in case she was reprimanded. She was desperate to know where her children were and whether they were all right. She hoped that she would see them at dinner time as she'd promised them.

After a while she heard a bell ringing and went to the door. A woman who was passing, dressed in identical clothes to Hannah, paused.

'New?' she asked. Hannah nodded. 'Follow me,' she told her. 'And don't speak,' she warned her in a whisper.

They walked at a quick pace along a maze of corridors and up and down steps until they finally came to a hall, set with rows of trestle tables and forms.

Following the woman's lead, Hannah picked up a pewter basin and spoon and joined the queue of residents. At the front of the line, behind a table, a cook was ladling a spoonful of food into each bowl. The recipients then took it to a table and sat down, but didn't touch it. Hannah was puzzled. It smelled good and it was a long time since she'd eaten a proper meal. She certainly wouldn't turn her nose up at hers when she got it, she thought. She was more than eager to eat.

She nodded her thanks as her basin was filled with the boiled potatoes and meat – not much meat, but meat all the same. It was a long time since Hannah had been able to afford to buy even a cheap cut from the market.

As she walked to the trestles with her food, she looked across the room to where the children's tables were and was relieved to see Edmund sitting with some other boys and Ruth and Kitty waiting together in the line. She was thankful that Ruth was there for her little sister.

Hannah eased her way up a long bench and sat down. She was just about to plunge her spoon into the food and eat when the woman beside her nudged her arm and shook her head. Hannah put down her spoon, still wondering why no one was eating. They couldn't all be waiting for it to cool, she thought.

Then she saw Mr and Mrs Cartwright come in. They went to a separate table at the top of the hall and Mr Cartwright remained standing, waiting for the last person in the queue to take their place.

When there was complete silence across the hall, Mr Cartwright clasped his hands together and the women lowered their heads in prayer.

'Be present at our table, Lord. Be here and

everywhere adored. These mercies bless and grant that we may feast in fellowship with Thee. Amen.'

An answering, if muted, *amen* was repeated and as soon as Mr Cartwright sat down, the women grasped their spoons and began their dinner. The food was lukewarm and the potatoes were half black, but Hannah ate eagerly even though her stomach ached at the unexpected surplus. There was no conversation. The only sound was that of spoons clattering against the dishes and the chewing and swallowing of her companions.

Hannah kept glancing across the hall towards her children but her companion nudged her again and shook her head. It seemed that staring about was disapproved of too and she saw that everyone else kept their eyes and their attention firmly on their food.

Those who finished first put their spoons in their empty dishes and sat with their hands clasped on their laps and their heads lowered. Before long Mr Cartwright made a signal and the women stood and shuffled out from behind the trestles to take their bowls and cups to a table at the far end of the hall where they were placed to be taken away to be washed. Then the women filed out of the hall, presumably to return to their tasks.

Hannah lingered near the door, waiting for the children to come out, but after the last woman had left, the door was firmly closed. The children must have gone out another way. Hannah felt herself slump with disappointment and worry. She was glad that the children had been fed, but she knew that they would be frightened and alone. They had never been parted from her before and she longed to give them just a word of reassurance.

As the corridor fell silent again she wondered what she was expected to do. She doubted that she could find her way back to her room and she was afraid of getting lost. But she knew that she couldn't spend the rest of the day standing here.

'What are you doing there?' asked a voice. Hannah turned and saw a woman coming out from a doorway with some folded cloths piled in her hands.

'I'm sorry,' Hannah apologised. 'It's my first day. I'm not sure what I'm supposed to be doing.'

'If you have no work you should be in the day room, not skulking around here,' the woman replied. The irritation was clear in her voice and Hannah was alarmed. It was bad enough being sent to this place. She didn't want to get into bother.

'I'm sorry,' she apologised once more. 'I don't know the way.'

The woman sighed exaggeratedly. 'Name?' she demanded.

'Hannah Fisher.'

'Wait there,' she instructed. 'I'll go and ask where you should be.'

As she waited, alone and afraid of what might happen, Hannah felt an overwhelming need to sink to the floor and weep. Only a week ago, she'd been an independent woman bringing up her three children. It had been hard and she'd struggled, but at least she'd managed with the little help she'd had from the parish. Now, she was being treated like a child, reprimanded and admonished when it was no fault of her own. She began to wish that she'd never agreed to come. It had been a huge mistake and she must find a way of regaining the freedom for herself and her children that she hadn't realised was so precious.

CHAPTER FOUR

Although the thick straw mattress on the bed and the adequate quilt promised a comfortable night's sleep, Hannah lay awake for longer than she expected. As she listened to the snoring and muttering of her fellow inmates, she longed for the peace of her own home. Even if her own mattress had been thin and the blanket had barely covered her, it had at least been familiar and the bodies of her children, huddling close to her for warmth, had been a comfort.

She wondered whereabouts in this sprawling building her children were sleeping. She hoped that they were not lying awake too – or worse, sobbing because they were afraid. The pain she felt at being parted from them was tangible and she curled her body into a ball to try to ease it, whilst trying not to cry for fear of disturbing her sleeping companions.

The other women who slept in her dormitory had been welcoming and sympathetic when they heard her story. Their own experiences had been similarly harsh and unfair – tales of husbands dead or imprisoned for some trifling offence, families without work who were now split apart, and some who were simply too ill in body or mind to be able to cope with the world outside the workhouse.

Eventually morning came, and with the ringing of a bell, the women began to stir. One by one they pushed back their quilts and got to their feet, yawning and scratching as faint daylight crept down the walls from the high windows. Hannah watched what the others did, fearful of making any mistakes. She had quickly learned that she ought to have listened more carefully to the long list of rules that had been read out to her by Mr Cartwright when she arrived. Workhouse life was governed by rules for every small thing and nothing at all was left to the choice of those who lived here. Hannah's life was no longer hers to decide what she did with each hour. She was at the behest of the workhouse master every second.

The women began to dress themselves in their uniforms, combing their hair before putting on their caps. When the beds had been made, those who had used the chamber pots in the night retrieved them from under the beds and then they walked in a line down the wide wooden stairs to an outside yard. Here they queued to use the privy. The line was long and snaked around the perimeter of the yard in the shadow of the buildings. There was no cover and Hannah realised it would be a cold and wet experience on the days when the weather wasn't fine. She silently urged the women in front of her to be quick because although she was used to sharing, she wasn't used to waiting so long and her bladder ached. She'd held off using the chamber pot, not wanting to embarrass herself in front of strangers, but now she realised why most of the other women had decided not to hang on.

At last it was her turn. The privy was up two stone steps and there was no door. Inside there was a wooden board with four holes. Three were already occupied and the place stank so Hannah quickly relieved herself and moved on to the washroom next door where she rinsed her hands and face.

Then they lined up once more and matron took a roll call to ensure everyone was present – although, how anyone could have absconded in the night over the high wall or through the locked and barred entrance Hannah couldn't imagine. Next, they walked in single file up and down the confusing flights of stairs that led to the dining hall. The routine was the same at every meal and as Hannah waited for the gruel to be slopped into her basin, she tried to keep a surreptitious watch on the far side of the hall, hoping to catch a glimpse of her children to reassure herself that all was well with them, but the woman behind her dug a sharp finger into her ribs and Hannah moved forward without seeing them. Once she was seated at a trestle it was difficult to turn her head to look without attracting attention and all she could do was make her own supplications as Mr Cartwright lingered over the morning prayers whilst the meagre breakfast went cold.

After the meal had been cleared away Hannah was relieved to catch a glimpse of Ruth and Kitty in the girls' line, although the boys had already gone out and she wasn't able to see Edmund. What work they were to do she had no idea, but she hoped it wouldn't be too hard for them. At least today was Saturday, she thought, and held onto the thought that she would be able to see the children for an hour or two the next day and reassure herself that they had been treated well.

'Hannah Fisher,' said the matron. 'You'll be working in the laundry. This way.'

Hannah followed her across the exercise yard to a doorway where steam and heat were already billowing out to mix with the damp morning atmosphere.

'Tha'll be doin' scrubbin',' she was told by the woman in charge as she was given a coarse apron to wear. Then she was shown the barrels and soap, and the washboards against which she was expected to scrub the sheets or clothing, or whatever items were to be laundered that day.

The water was hot and, having rolled up her sleeves to above the elbows, Hannah was thankful for it as she plunged her arms into the suds and grasped handfuls of cloth to be pummelled against the wooden ridges. The work was hard but Hannah wasn't afraid of it, and even though her arms and back were aching long before the bell rang for dinner time, she didn't slacken or complain but did her best, determined to show that she was eager to earn her keep.

'Tha'll never keep it up if tha goes at it like that,' whispered an older woman who had been working beside her all morning. They were not allowed to speak as they worked and when Hannah had seen this woman glancing at her she'd thought it was in admiration for the progress she was making as she shifted each heavy, sopping sheet into the trough of water where it would be rinsed before being mangled and pegged out in the yard to dry. 'Take it easy,' she warned, speaking under the cover of the noise of the workers hanging up their aprons and rolling down their sleeves before moving to line-up at the door to march down to dinner. 'They'll give thee no thanks for exhaustin' thyself.'

As Hannah's stomach growled in hunger, she wondered if it was good advice. She knew that they would finish early today at four o' clock and that tomorrow would be a rest day, but her arms were already leaden with her efforts because the wet sheets were cumbersome and heavy. When the stew was ladled into her dish and her cup filled with beer, Hannah realised that those who had worked hard were given no preferential rations over the ones who had been slackers and she saw that she would still be hungry when her dinner was eaten.

CHAPTER FIVE

The next morning the rising bell rang once more at six o' clock. The Sabbath might have been a day of rest, thought Hannah, but it seemed that it was only the sinners in their own homes who were allowed another hour in bed to enjoy it.

She hastily used her chamber pot so as to avoid a painful wait in the yard and then dressed herself and combed her hair. She felt a fluttering excitement in her stomach. Today she would be allowed to see her children and she was counting down the hours until she could hold them in her arms. But first she would have to endure prayers in the chapel.

After breakfast, she joined the other women as they walked through the women's yard and out onto the street. As they crossed the road to the chapel, Hannah was beset by a sudden urge to break away from the procession and make a dash for freedom. But it would do her no good, she knew. Where would she go, and how could she possibly leave her children here?

On the far side of the ironically named Free

Street was the new chapel. The women filed inside and took their places on the rows of hard pews to the right. The children were brought in after them to sit at the front, and the men entered by a different door and sat in the pews on the left-hand side.

Hannah and Jack had never been churchgoers if they could avoid it. They'd been married in the parish church twelve years before. Hannah recalled it as a day when she'd been eager to pass through the huge wooden doors and walk up the aisle, as her footsteps, even in borrowed shoes rather than her customary clogs, echoed loudly in the stone-walled and stone-floored building. Jack had been waiting for her by the chancel steps and she could still see his face clearly as he'd stood and turned to gaze at her with a look of relief.

'Did tha think I wouldn't come?' she'd whispered when she reached him. He'd grinned at that and she'd put her hand in his. Hannah thought that it had been the happiest day of her life. She'd never imagined that they would ever be parted. She'd looked forward to them growing old together and sitting on either side of the hearth in their cottage with their brood of children and grandchildren gathered around them.

The workhouse chapel was different from the parish church. It was much plainer and devoid of any decoration apart from the religious texts that were painted on the bare walls. There weren't even flowers, and there was no organ to fill the space with resounding, thunderous tones. Just a small harmonium, played by Mrs Cartwright.

After the first hymn, the reluctant congregation shuffled and settled themselves on the hard pews to listen to the long and tedious prayers and readings. Hannah followed the lead of the women around her as they stood, sat and knelt for reasons she failed to understand. Then, after another hymn which Hannah couldn't sing because the words were unfamiliar and the hymn book pushed into her hand was indecipherable to her, the chaplain climbed up into his pulpit to preach to them.

Hannah took the opportunity to gaze at the heads of the children in the front pews. At first glance, the clipped heads of the boys and the identical bonnets of the girls seemed indistinguishable one from another. But Hannah was sure that she could recognise her own children. Edmund was on the front row. His head was the most recently shaved and she saw that he was staring around at the words written on the walls. He would be sure to ask her what they said and Hannah knew that she must ask one of the other women if they knew. Edmund was a clever boy and she wanted to encourage his curiosity. She'd wanted to send him to the Sunday School so that he could learn to read, but he'd been reluctant and she hadn't insisted. Perhaps she should have, she thought, as she studied the mysterious letters on the open page of her hymn book. Reading was a good skill for a boy to have, and if Jack hadn't been sent away he would have taught Edmund.

Hannah could see Ruth, but Kitty wasn't beside her and she felt distraught that her daughters had been separated. Kitty would never manage without her big sister to look after her and when Hannah couldn't see her in any of the pews she began to worry that her younger daughter was unwell and hadn't been brought to the chapel. Then she saw Kitty, sitting alone at the end of a row. Her little shoulders were shuddering and Hannah knew that she was trying not to cry. She longed to jump up and go to her to comfort her, but she knew that she must remain where she was for now, hemmed in by women on either side of her and the chaplain who was droning on from the pulpit.

After dinner, Hannah was told she might go to the day room and her children would be brought to her. The day room was where the elderly and infirm women spent most of their day. It had a fire in the hearth and cushions on the benches and chairs.

Hannah sat anxiously on the edge of one of the chairs by the table, and her eyes never wavered from the door. Every time it was opened she almost leapt to her feet in anticipation as other women's children ran in to hug their mothers. Then, at last, she saw Ruth and Kitty holding hands with Edmund behind them. She stood up and opened her arms and the children melted into her.

After she'd hugged them tightly she sat down again and scrutinised them carefully for any signs of harm.

'Have they been good to thee? Have you had food? What are your beds like?' The questions flowed from her without giving the children time to answer, but they seemed subdued and Kitty's eyes were red from crying. 'Ruth?' she asked her daughter.

'All the girls are in a big room,' she said. 'I share a bed with Kitty.' Hannah was thankful for that. 'Edmund sleeps in the boys' dormitory, up in the attic,' she explained.

'I've seen thee in the dining hall, and the chapel,' Hannah told them. 'I've not been able to come to thee, but I've thought about thee all the time.' She ran a hand over her son's head, feeling the prickliness of his scalp. She'd be glad when his thick fair hair grew back. He didn't look like himself at the moment.

Kitty climbed on to her knee and nestled against her with a thumb in her mouth. She seemed a lot younger than her nine years.

'What have you been asked to do?' she asked Ruth.

'We went to the classroom in the morning,' her daughter told her. 'We're to learn how to read.'

Hannah was pleased. 'That's good,' she said.

'Then after dinner me and Kitty have to untwist

ropes and get the fibres out. It makes our fingers sore.' Ruth showed her mother her reddened hands. 'And it makes Kitty cough.'

Hannah felt alarmed and angry at the news. She'd told the doctor that Kitty was delicate. She was terrified of the child becoming ill and breathing in the fibres from picking oakum was bound to affect her breathing.

'What do you have to do, Edmund?' she asked her son.

'Sums,' he replied. 'Adding up numbers. Then I have to help in the garden, pulling up weeds from between the vegetables. But I didn't know which was which at first and I pulled up the wrong one. The man hit me.'

Hannah seethed with indignation. 'Did he hurt thee?' she asked. 'I'll not stand for it. I'll complain to Mr Cartwright!'

She wished that she didn't feel so helpless. These children were her responsibility and she hated not being able to protect them and look after them. She was determined that she would say something to the workhouse master, although she doubted it would do any good. They were all here to work and the alternative was to be put out onto the street.

All too soon, a bell sounded and their hour was up. She kissed the children and told them that she would see them again soon. She promised that she would find a way to get them all out of the workhouse. But she found it hard to keep back her tears until they had gone out of the door; she didn't want them to see her cry. And she wasn't the only one. All across the dayroom, women were wiping their eyes on the corner of their aprons as they said farewell to their children for another week.

CHAPTER SIX

Hannah was working in the laundry when she was told that Mr Cartwright wanted to see her. She wiped her hands and arms on her apron and pushed strands of hair that were wet with sweat and steam back under her cap whilst she wondered what she had done wrong. She'd been living in the workhouse for a few weeks now and knew full well that a summons to see the workhouse master usually spelled trouble. Her attempt to complain to him about the treatment of her children had not gone well and Hannah knew that Mr Cartwright had marked her down as a troublemaker – just like her absent husband.

She rolled down her sleeves over damp arms. Perhaps it was one of the children, she thought. Her heart raced with fear that one of them might have had an accident, or be in some sort of bother. All manner of imaginings presented themselves in her mind as she hurried up the stairs to Mr Cartwright's office.

Approaching in consternation, she saw that the dark mahogany door stood ajar and Mr Cartwright was sitting at his desk facing it. He must have heard her footsteps because he glanced up and called to her to enter. He didn't seem angry or unduly concerned and Hannah hoped that the interview wouldn't be as intimidating as she feared. 'Close the door, Mrs Fisher,' he said. 'Come and sit down.'

The invitation took her by surprise. Workhouse inmates were normally expected to stand to attention with their hands clasped behind their backs whilst Mr Cartwright berated them. She perched on the edge of the upright chair and waited to hear why she had been sent for.

He removed his spectacles to look at her. 'I've been speaking with a friend,' he said. 'He's the minister at the chapel in Egerton. There's a member of his congregation there who's looking for a reliable woman to be his housekeeper and care for his young daughter.' Hannah didn't reply. She wasn't sure what she was expected to say. 'The child is currently in the care of a wet nurse,' explained Mr Cartwright, 'but she's ready to be weaned and Mr Duxbury is keen to take her home. But obviously he cannot raise a child alone.'

Hannah nodded, wondering if Mr Cartwright was suggesting that she might be employed by this man.

'I think you would be very suitable,' went on Mr Cartwright. 'You're a widow, but still young and experienced with children. Would you be willing to meet Mr Duxbury?'

‘I’m not sure,’ said Hannah. ‘Would it mean leaving here?’

‘Yes,’ replied Mr Cartwright. ‘You would go to live with Mr Duxbury. I’m told he has a pleasant house and he has work as the manager of a new spinning mill.’

‘What about my children?’ she asked.

‘They would remain here. Technically I can record you as being employed rather than having left the workhouse. It would be an irregular arrangement, but one I’m willing to make in the circumstances. I think you would be ideal for this position,’ he told her, and Hannah wondered if it was true, or if the real reason he wanted her gone was because she made too much trouble about the way her children were treated. She would have liked to once more raise the issue of Edmund being struck for not knowing weeds from plants when he had no opportunity to learn the difference, and she wanted to complain again about the way that Kitty’s cough was worsening because of her work in the oakum picking room. But she knew that such protestations would do no good. Mr Cartwright and matron always replied that the children were well cared for and she was not to worry.

‘I won’t leave without my children,’ she told him. Her decision was made and it hadn’t been a difficult one.

‘Don’t be so hasty, Mrs Fisher,’ said Mr Cartwright. ‘At least meet Mr Duxbury and hear what he has to say. He will come to see you this Sunday afternoon.'

Hannah knew better than to refuse, but she felt angry. It seemed that Mr Cartwright had already decided the matter for her, and now she would lose her precious hour with the children to meet some man she had no interested in knowing.

When Sunday came, Hannah dressed in her clean clothes and attended the chapel. All the while she sought a glimpse of her children as they sang and prayed and listened to the sermon. She was still furious that she would be unable to see them that afternoon.

After dinner, which was a lukewarm and greasy stew, she was told to go to Mr Cartwright's office where Mr Duxbury was waiting for her. Hannah felt cross and resentful as she climbed the stairs, knowing that other mothers were in the day room with their families. She knew that her children would be disappointed and upset not to see her.

Once again Mr Cartwright was looking out for her and ushered her into his room where a man stood up to greet her.

'This is Mr Ellis Duxbury,' the workhouse master told her. 'He's been very eager to meet you and explain what the position entails. I'll leave you to speak to him alone.'

Mr Cartwright went out and closed the door softly behind him and Hannah gave her attention to her visitor. He was a stockily built man, not much taller than her, with fair hair that was already thinning at his temples and abundant whiskers. He nodded his head towards her but did not offer his hand. Hannah was relieved. Her palms were slick with sweat and she wiped them surreptitiously on her skirt before sitting on the chair he gestured to.

'I'm pleased to meet you,' he said as he sat on the chair that had been placed opposite to hers. His eyes were blue, she saw, and his cheeks looked reddened, although by weather or agitation she couldn't tell.

She didn't answer him. In truth she didn't know what to say and she saw no reason to try to put him at his ease.

Mr Duxbury seemed unsure where to begin and there was an awkward silence before he spoke. 'Mr Cartwright told me you are a widow,' he said.

'Aye,' agreed Hannah, although the word tore at her heart like a knife. She would never think of herself as a widow, not until she had proof that Jack was no longer alive. But she had no reason to explain herself to this man. It was simpler to go along with the charade.

'You're still young,' he observed. 'What happened to your husband?'

'He was sent to New South Wales,' replied Hannah, hoping that having a husband who was a convict might put the man off.

'And you've brought up three children on your own?'

'Aye.' Hannah was determined not to make the interview easy for him. She just wanted to leave whilst there was still the chance she could spend some time with her children.

'I'm sorry,' he said. 'I'm sure it hasn't been easy for you.' He fidgeted with his hands. His fingers were short and stubby, like the rest of him she noticed, but they were clean. 'I have a child – a daughter – Florence. She's almost six months old now,' he told her. Hannah waited for him to explain what had become of the child's mother but he only bit his lower lip before going on. 'She's been fed by a wet nurse, but is ready to weaned. I need a kind woman to help me raise her,' he said. 'I hope that could be you, Mrs Fisher.'

'Have you no family who will help you?' asked Hannah. She heard the accusatory tone of her voice as she spoke and hated herself for it. The man was obviously trying to do his best for his child and it was not for her to judge him or his circumstances.

He shook his head. 'No,' he told her. 'I am forced to raise my daughter alone.'

Hannah was curious to ask about his wife, but she sensed it was something that Mr Duxbury didn't want to discuss. His loss must have been recent and his grief still raw, thought Hannah as she saw the expressions of anguish and sorrow flit across his face. It softened her a little and she began to feel sorry that she had been so sharp with him. She couldn't blame him for seeking help and he was not to know that she was unsuitable to assist him.

'I'm sorry to hear it,' she replied. Her voice was warmer and it seemed to encourage him. He smiled slightly. His teeth were crooked but not brown. She wasn't near enough to catch his breath.

'Will you come and work for me and help to raise Florence?' he asked, looking hopeful. But Hannah was shaking her head before he'd finished speaking.

'No,' she said. 'Mr Cartwright was insistent that I meet you, but it's not a task I can undertake.'

Mr Duxbury's face crumpled into disappointment. 'But you haven't heard me out,' he insisted. 'I have a large house. I can offer you a secure home. Surely you could consider that, rather than remain here?'

Hannah shook her head again. She wouldn't leave her own children in the workhouse to go and live in his house, no matter how pleasant it was. The guilt would be too much. Besides, when would she be able to see them? She saw too little of Ruth and Kitty and Edmund as it was.

'Perhaps you could think on it?' he suggested. 'I didn't expect you to give me an answer straight away. Although I did expect more enthusiasm – given your circumstances.'

'My mind is made up,' she told him. 'I hope that you find someone more suitable.'

He glanced up from under his long eyelashes and managed a rueful smile. 'I wish it could have been you,' he said and Hannah thought that he sounded sincere. It was a shame, she thought. He seemed nice enough and in different circumstances she would have welcomed the chance to work for him.

'You turned him down?' asked Mr Cartwright after Mr Duxbury had gone. He sounded astounded and far from pleased.

'I won't leave my children here alone. I won't have them raised as orphans,' she replied.

Mr Cartwright drummed his fingers on his desk and sighed. 'I thought you would see sense after you'd spoken to Mr Duxbury,' he told her. 'I thought you would realise that it was a good opportunity for you. Do you really want to spend the rest of your life in the workhouse?' he asked.

'No.' Hannah shook her head emphatically. 'I don't want to seem ungrateful, but I would leave here now – if I could have my rent paid – and I could take my children with me,' she told him. 'I would manage.'

'But you were not managing before,' Mr Cartwright reminded her. 'Here, your children are clean and clothed and fed. And they are being schooled. Soon they will be apprenticed and taught a trade. It will give them the opportunity to make something of themselves. Why would you deny them that?'

He seemed genuinely perplexed by her decision

and when he explained it he made it sound reasonable.

'But I'm their mother,' Hannah said.

'Well, I would advise you to go and think again,' counselled Mr Cartwright. 'Perhaps it is not too late for you to change your mind. Mr Duxbury seemed impressed by you and told me he was disappointed that you'd refused his offer.'

'I won't change my mind,' Hannah told him, even though she knew the workhouse master would never understand. He had no idea what it was like to be a mother – or even a parent. He and matron had no children of their own. And those strong bonds of love that she felt would for ever remain a mystery to him.

Mr Cartwright sighed as the bell began to sound for supper. 'You'd best go,' he told her. Relieved, Hannah hurried out and down the steps towards the hall where she would eat bread and a sliver of cheese and, if she was lucky, would catch sight of her children as they sat down. It would be all she had to sustain her through another working week until Sunday came round once again.

CHAPTER SEVEN

'Well, ain't thee the popular one?' asked the laundress when Mr Cartwright sent for Hannah again a few days later.

Hannah didn't feel very popular. She was slow to dry her hands and hang up her apron as she wondered what the master wanted with her now.

Her legs felt heavy as she climbed the stairs and knocked anxiously on the office door.

'Come in!' called Mr Cartwright and Hannah slipped inside, half-expecting Ellis Duxbury to be there again, but the master was alone.

He waved a piece of paper at her. 'Mr Duxbury has written to me,' he announced. 'He wants you to meet his daughter and will come for you at one o'clock on Saturday afternoon. You will be excused your work,' he said as if he were doing her some enormous favour. Hannah would have preferred her tub of water and the scrubbing board.

'Must I go?' she asked.

'Oh, yes, Mrs Fisher,' replied Mr Cartwright as he peered at her over the top of his spectacles. 'I think you must.'

Hannah stood before the master with her hands

clasped. It was clear that he was determined not to be thwarted from his plan to be rid of her from his workhouse and she asked herself if she could find the courage and determination to deny him his wishes. For a moment she doubted it. Her life was no longer her own and this man had power and authority over her, but that did not mean he could deny her the right to be the mother of her children. She would never agree to that.

'I'll ask matron if she can find you a warm shawl to wear,' continued Mr Cartwright. 'It's becoming rather chilly.' He rubbed his hands together as if he was cold, even though he had an ample fire burning in the grate behind him. 'You may go back to work,' he told her with a dismissive wave of his hand and Hannah went back down to the laundry feeling angry. She had no wish to go with Ellis Duxbury to meet his daughter. She suspected it was a plan hatched between him and the workhouse master to coerce her into agreeing to work as his housekeeper – and she was determined that they would never persuade her.

As she queued for her dinner Hannah searched the rows of children for her own. Ruth and Kitty were standing meekly in line, but she could hear Kitty coughing. She wished that she could speak to the doctor again about her. With the winter weather looming, she needed a poultice on that chest before it got any worse. Edmund was scratching at his scalp as he balanced his dish and cup in one hand. She wondered whether he had lice again despite having his head shaved. Hannah wished that she could do more for them, but at least whilst she was here she could keep an eye on them and see them on Sunday afternoons. If she was forced to leave then she would never know how her children were.

When Hannah went to the dormitory after dinner on the Saturday she saw that a clean gown and petticoat had been left for her along with a warm shawl. She picked it up to sniff it, but it seemed clean. She wondered whose it was. It was certainly better quality than the threadbare affair she had arrived at the workhouse in and she suspected that it belonged to the matron herself. Mr and Mrs Cartwright seemed determined to have her make a good impression. Still, she thought, she would be glad of it. The first real chill of autumn had struck her when she'd gone down to the privy first thing that morning.

She'd been instructed to present herself at the gatehouse at five minutes to one and as she had no idea how near that time it was and she didn't want to be late despite her reluctance to go at all, she walked briskly down the stairs and across the outer yard.

The porter who had greeted her when she first arrived stepped out to open the gate for her. Beyond it there was a small trap pulled by a dun-coloured pony. Next to it, holding the pony's reins stood Ellis Duxbury. He smiled when he saw her and held out a hand to help her up.

'I can manage, thank you,' Hannah told him as she put a foot on the step and pulled herself onto the cushioned seat. Mr Duxbury clambered up beside her and Hannah grasped onto the edge of the trap to steady herself as it swayed alarmingly. She'd never ridden in such a contraption before, always having relied on walking to get to where she needed to go, but she would never have admitted to Mr Duxbury that it was her first time.

His elbow nudged her arm as he gathered the reins in one hand and touched the pony's rump lightly with the whip.

'Is it far?' she asked as they trotted briskly through the streets of Bolton.

'Egerton,' he replied. Hannah had heard of the village but never been there.

As they passed the beginning of the track that led up to Hill Fold she turned to gaze at the familiar landmarks. She yearned to set off towards her home, except that she knew she would find it locked against her, or worse, rented out to some other family. Hannah found it hard to think of it.

Soon they were leaving the town behind and Hannah saw that the trees had turned to gold in the time she'd been in the workhouse. The leaves cascaded down onto their heads and shoulders as they drove past, and when she brushed them away they crunched under the wheels of the trap. She pulled the shawl more closely around herself, glad of its warmth and the way it covered her workhouse dress.

Ellis Duxbury made a few half-hearted attempts at conversation, but soon gave up when she didn't answer him. He gave his attention to the rutted road as he guided the pony around the worst of the dips and hollows. Before long they were out on the moorland that ranged around the town. It was even colder up here and there were rain clouds on the horizon. But Hannah drew in breaths of the fresh air, with its tang of heather and bracken and listened to the bleating of the sheep and the call of a curlew as it circled above them. It was a welcome respite from the workhouse and its tedious routines, and she wished that she could have brought the children with her. The fresh air would have done them good.

'Nearly there,' said Mr Duxbury after another mile and Hannah saw that there was a cluster of cottages, nestling along either side of the road ahead of them. He slowed the pony to a walk and drew up outside a neat terraced row. 'Here we are,' he said.

He jumped down and fastened the pony's reins to an iron ring on the wall and patted its neck.

'It's not mine,' he explained as he offered his hand to help her down. 'I've borrowed it from the minister at the chapel.' He waved towards a grey stone building some yards back from the road at the far side.

Hannah tried to stand but found it hard to keep

her balance in the trap. She had no choice but to put her hand in Mr Duxbury's to steady herself. His hand was warm and closed around hers firmly, allowing her to lean on him and reach out her foot for the step, although once she was down on the ground she snatched her hand back.

'This way,' he said and before they had reached the front door of the cottage it had been opened by a young woman with bright eyes who greeted them warmly and invited them inside. 'This is May,' Mr Duxbury told Hannah. 'She's been caring for my daughter.'

As soon as Hannah stepped over the threshold she heard the familiar sound of a handloom weaver at work in the room below them.

'That's my husband, Joseph, doing his weaving,' May told her as Hannah looked towards the stairs that led down to the cellar. 'Come and sit down,' she invited and Hannah took the chair by the hearth that had been made ready for her. A good fire was burning and a kettle sang on its hook above the flames. 'Would tha like some tea?' she asked and Hannah eagerly accepted.

It was a relief to spend time, no matter that it would be brief, in such a homely place. There was a rag rug that covered the stone floor, fresh floral curtains at the window, a small dresser with cups and plates, and stools around a scrubbed table. It was warm and pleasant, although Hannah kept her shawl around her. She guessed that May already knew that she was from the workhouse but she was still reluctant to show off her gown.

'Where is Florence?' asked Mr Duxbury.

'She's having a nap upstairs. I'll fetch her down in a minute. Sit thee down,' she told him.

Hannah watched as May set the tea to brew in a brown pot, then went to climb the narrow steps that wound out of view to the upper floor. She reappeared moments later with an infant in her arms.

Mr Duxbury gazed at the child but made no attempt to get up or take her into his arms. Instead, May carried the child to Hannah and placed her on her lap.

'Here she is!' she said. 'Isn't she a little beauty?'

The baby sat and stared at Hannah with solemn brown eyes. She looked healthy and a credit to May's care.

Hannah expected her to cry, but she didn't. 'Hello,' she said to her as she straightened the little cap that covered the baby's curls. 'Hello, Florence.'

She hadn't expected the rush of emotion she felt as she held the child, but the weight of the little girl and the smell of her reminded Hannah of her own children at the same age and she felt an overwhelming mixture of protectiveness and regret.

'She's a good little lass,' May told her. 'Tha'll have no bother with her. Truth be told, I'm goin' to miss her. But she needs to be with her father.'

Hannah looked up as the child grasped a fold

of her shawl in strong fingers. 'Nothing's settled yet,' she protested.

May looked puzzled. 'I thought it was. I thought tha'd agreed to it.' She glanced at Mr Duxbury again for confirmation.

'Mrs Fisher was unsure,' he admitted. 'But I think now that she's met Florence she'll be in agreement.'

'Mr Duxbury has a nice house,' May told her. 'Has he not shown it to thee yet?' Hannah shook her head. It was clear that she was being coerced by this man and that May didn't understand her reluctance.

'Would you like to see my home?' Mr Duxbury asked once May had taken Florence onto her own knee and was feeding her with small pieces of bread and butter whilst Hannah drank her tea.

Hannah wanted to refuse, but she was curious and the thought of returning to the workhouse made her want to cling to her afternoon's freedom for a little while longer.

'We can walk. It isn't far,' said Mr Duxbury when they stepped outside again.

Hannah wondered if he would offer her his arm, but he didn't. He walked slightly ahead of her as he crossed the road and took her to the door of a house at the end of the row. It looked well cared for. The windows were clean and the door painted in dark green. Mr Duxbury took a key from his pocket and let them in.

'That's the front parlour,' he said as they passed

the first door. He didn't open it or show her inside but led her to the kitchen at the back. Hannah looked curiously around. It was clear that it didn't hold a woman's touch. Everything was clean but functional. A fire was laid in the grate, but not lit; a wooden table had two chairs tucked neatly underneath it; and the shelves were tidily stacked with pots and pans that looked rarely used. A stone sink stood beneath the window and beyond it was a yard with a small garden.

'There are three bedrooms upstairs,' he told her, opening a door that led to the staircase, 'and a privy in the yard that isn't shared with anyone.'

'It's very nice,' she admitted, thinking that it seemed like a paradise to her. But a paradise she could never enter.

CHAPTER EIGHT

Mr Duxbury remained silent as they drove back to Bolton. It wasn't until he was leaving her at the workhouse gatehouse that he said, 'I would like you to come and care for Florence. She seemed to like you. Please say that you will.'

Hannah began to shake her head, but Mr Duxbury held up his hand before she could refuse him.

'At least promise that you will give it some more thought,' he asked. 'I'll come to see you again next week and you can give me your answer then.'

Hannah nodded. She knew that her answer would be the same and he would have a wasted journey, but she said nothing.

When she arrived back in the day room, the other women crowded around her asking where she'd been and what she had seen. They were hungry for news of the outside world and devoured everything that Hannah told them.

'So will tha go?' said one.

'I think tha should go,' said another. 'Is he handsome?' she added.

Hannah shook her head. 'He's a plain looking

man, but kind – or seems so. But it's a housekeeper and someone to care for his daughter that he wants, not a wife.'

The woman grinned. 'I wouldn't be too sure,' she warned. 'Men have an eye for a pretty woman and tha's fetchin' enough.'

Hannah smiled at the compliment. 'I have my children to think of,' she said. 'I can't leave them here alone.'

The advice she received was mixed. Some of the other mothers agreed that she couldn't leave her own children to care for this man's daughter, but others pointed out that it was a rare chance to escape the workhouse and one they wouldn't hesitate to take if it was offered to them.

Hannah lay awake for a long time that night as she weighed up her decision, but it always came back to her children. She wouldn't abandon them.

At dinner the next day, Hannah was called over to the top table by Mr and Mrs Cartwright.

'I'm surprised you are still keeping Mr Duxbury waiting for an answer, Mrs Fisher,' the master observed. 'It doesn't reflect well on me and my wife when we recommended you so highly for this opportunity. He has said he will come again next Sunday and I have told him that you will be ready to leave with him.'

'But I've decided not to go,' protested Hannah, realising from the tone of the master's voice that he was determined to force her hand. 'I won't leave my children,' she told him again, looking across the room to search for their familiar faces. 'I wish I'd never come here,' she told them and regretted her words immediately as she saw the anger cloud the faces of the master and the matron.

'Would you have preferred your children to starve on the streets?' demanded Mrs Cartwright. 'Perhaps you are not such a caring mother as you claim,' she added. 'I would advise you to think carefully about what you have been offered and appreciate its value.'

The master dismissed her with a wave of his hand and Hannah returned to the empty table where only her dish and cup remained. Without any appetite she pushed the last of the cold food into her mouth and cleared her pots away.

When her children were brought to her that afternoon, she hugged each one of them closely to her and told them that she loved them. How could she bear to leave them here? Yet she feared that the decision was being made for her and that if she evoked the wrath of Mr Cartwright by thwarting his wishes he could make her life very unpleasant, and there would be no prospect of escape.

All week long, as Hannah scrubbed sheets and towels and hauled them to the troughs to rinse, her mind chased around and around as she tried to decide what she would do when Sunday came. She knew that the Cartwrights were determined that she should go. They had made it clear that her reluctance was a personal insult to them and she feared that she might simply be bundled out into Mr Duxbury's care and the gates closed behind her.

On the Friday, Mrs Cartwright called her out of the laundry to speak to her in the yard. 'I've been speaking to Mr Cartwright about your situation,' she told her, 'and we may be able to allow you to make some visits to your children – provided Mr Duxbury is in agreement. It would be an irregular arrangement, but we would make an exception in your case. It really would be for the best,' she added when Hannah didn't reply. 'Please think about it,' wheedled Mrs Cartwright.

Hannah promised nothing and went back to her work wondering if she should simply leave and take the children with her. But where would she go? She no longer had a home. She would receive no help from the parish if she left the workhouse, and if she went to another town she would simply be sent back to Bolton. If she left, she would condemn her children to a life of vagrancy and begging on the streets. It would be worse than leaving them here where they were at least fed and clothed. Was she being selfish, she wondered. Might it be for the best if she agreed? Maybe she would be able to save some money and come back for the children later.

When Sunday came Hannah found that the clean clothes put out for her were the threadbare ones in which she'd arrived. She fingered the petticoat, which was so thin as to be transparent, and the gown that had been patched at the elbows with mismatched material. The other women were getting ready for chapel in their workhouse dress and Hannah realised she was the only one who had been issued with her own clothing.

She dressed slowly, taking care not to tear the fragile material.

'Are you leaving?' asked the woman who slept in the next bed.

'I haven't agreed to,' Hannah told her, fearful that, in the end, she would have no choice in the matter.

She felt odd and conspicuous as she queued in the yard and then joined the line for breakfast. In the workhouse dress she was just one more inmate, but in her own clothes she looked different and everyone noticed her and passed a whispered comment. Some of the women nodded and smiled, thinking that she was fortunate, others expressed surprise.

All through breakfast and prayers in the chapel Hannah fretted about what the afternoon would hold. She didn't listen to a word of the sermon, but focused her eyes on the bowed heads of her children in front of her. She hoped that she would be allowed some time with them, but before they were brought to the day room after dinner, Mr Cartwright sent word that Hannah was wanted upstairs and she climbed the steps to his office with a sense of resignation.

Mr Cartwright was seated behind his desk. When she came in he pushed a sheet of paper towards her, then dipped a pen into his inkwell and proffered it.

'Just make your mark here,' he told her, pressing his finger to the place where she was to sign.

'What is it?' she asked, wishing that she could read the words. If Jack had been there he would have been able to tell her what they said.

'Just a formality so that you may go with Mr Duxbury.'

Hannah shook her head. 'I haven't agreed to it,' she told him.

She saw the look of irritation pass across Mr Cartwright's face as he tapped at the paper again with his finger. 'Here!' he insisted.

Hannah hesitated, but she was afraid. She didn't want to sign his paper, but she knew that if she made a scene Mr Cartwright would lock her in the small attic room where troublemakers were left alone with nothing to eat but bread and water for days at a time.

'I haven't seen my children today,' she protested, alarmed that she might be forced to leave without even being allowed to say goodbye to them.

'Best not to upset them,' said Mr Cartwright. 'Emotional partings rarely do children any good.' He tapped the sheet of paper again. 'Make your mark here,' he instructed, 'and then you will be free to go.'

Hannah knew that it was useless to argue with

Mr Cartwright. His mind was made up and, not knowing what else to do, she took the pen in her hand and scratched a cross on the parchment.

'Good,' said Mr Cartwright. 'Now I will take you down to the gatehouse where Mr Duxbury is waiting for you.'

CHAPTER NINE

Ellis Duxbury had borrowed the trap from the minister again and Hannah wept as he drove her away from the workhouse to his home at Egerton. He said nothing as they went along. He offered no comfort and seemed either embarrassed by or indifferent to her grief. With every mile Hannah's pain at her separation from her children seemed to increase and she kept glancing back as she clung to the seat of the trap until the town behind her disappeared as they climbed the hill to the village on the moors.

Eventually Mr Duxbury reined the little pony in outside his house and Hannah managed to clamber down before he had chance to come around the trap and offer her his hand. She was unsure what to expect. She knew that she'd been employed to look after the child, but she was uncertain what else would be expected of her, or if she would be given any sort of wage above the cost of her keep. Somehow she doubted it and suddenly Hannah felt a growing anger at what had been forced on her. She'd never felt so alone as she did at that moment staring at the place that was to be a home to her for the foreseeable future.

'Come inside,' said Ellis Duxbury as he pushed open the door and stood back for her to go first. Hannah walked down the narrow lobby to the kitchen. May was waiting for her with Florence on her lap.

'There you are,' she said as she stood up and held out the child for Hannah to take. 'She's all thine now – although I'm only across the street,' she added with a smile. 'Come and visit. I'll miss this little one,' she added as she put a kiss on the baby's soft head before going out.

Immediately the little girl began to cry. It wasn't surprising, thought Hannah as she tried to shush the baby by jogging her on her shoulder. As far as Florence knew, May was her mother – the woman who'd fed and nursed her, probably since her birth. And now she was left with a stranger.

The screams filled the room and the child became puce in the face. Hannah walked about the room with her, trying to calm her. It reminded her of the occasions when her own children had cried from colic and she'd tried to soothe them – and unbidden her own tears threatened to chorus with those of the child. Hannah knew that it wasn't a good beginning.

'She's missing May,' she tried to explain to Mr Duxbury when she saw his anxious face. 'Perhaps you could hold her?' she suggested, thinking that the baby might take some comfort in the familiarity of her father. But his face took on the expression of someone who had been asked to hold fire in his bare palms. He shook his head.

'No,' he protested. 'I don't know what to do with her.'

Hannah wondered how much interest he'd taken in his daughter up to now. Not much, she guessed. He seemed perplexed by the child's crying, as if he thought it was Hannah's fault. Perhaps it was, she thought as she struggled to contain her own emotions. It wouldn't be surprising if it was her own grief that was making the child upset.

'Perhaps you should take her upstairs,' suggested Mr Duxbury. 'I'll show you where you'll be sleeping.'

He picked up the bundle of her meagre possessions and Hannah followed him up the steep steps to the back room. Someone had made it ready for her. May probably, she guessed. There was a caddow quilt on the bed and the cot beside it had been made up with a mattress and blankets.

Hannah put the child down in it and began to take off her tattered bonnet and shawl. She saw Mr Duxbury looking at her clothes, but he made no comment about them.

'I'll let thee get settled,' he said. 'I must take the trap back to Reverend Jones. I eat at half past five. I think May has left the food. I have bread and ham for tea on a Sunday.' She nodded. It seemed that she was expected to prepare it for him.

After Mr Duxbury had gone back down the stairs

and she'd heard him close the front door, Hannah crossed to the small window and glanced out into the yard. Like the house, everything was neat with some late beans tied up to canes and some empty beds already dug over ready for the winter vegetables.

She explored what little furniture was in her room. The chest was filled with clothes for the child so she put her own things into one drawer of the dresser and hung up her bonnet and shawl on the hooks behind the door. It closed with a latch, she noticed, but there was no lock.

The child's cries were lessening and Hannah left her in the cot to fall asleep whilst she took the opportunity to look around. Across from her room, Mr Duxbury's bedroom was at the front of the house. The door stood ajar and she peeped inside. There was a bed with a similar quilt to hers, a chest of drawers with a brass candlestick, and a cupboard. The floor was bare boards apart from a small rug on one side of the bed. The curtains were drawn back to give a view of the cottages across the road and she could hear a few voices speaking in the street below but she wasn't near enough to hear what they were saying without going further into the room. Feeling a little guilty for prying, she turned away and opened the door to the third room. It contained a small iron framed bed and a chest that was empty. Neither room revealed anything about Mr Duxbury or his late wife.

Hannah returned down the stairs. In the kitchen, May had left the kettle on its hook over the fire and a teapot stood on the table with tea leaves spooned into it. On the shelves she found the bread and butter and ham, but she had no idea what the time was or whether it was near to half past five. There was no clock and even if there had been, Hannah would have struggled to read the dial. At home with Jack, there had been no need to know the time. They had not been governed by anything other than their own needs, and the distant chimes from the church tower had been enough to remind them of the hours of the day.

The table, she noticed, was already set with two plates, cups and saucers. It seemed that she was expected to eat with Mr Duxbury even though she would have much preferred to eat alone.

Whilst she had the chance, curiosity drove Hannah to take a look at the parlour. She gingerly pushed open the door and peered in, feeling guilty that she was trespassing on Mr Duxbury's private space. But she hoped that it might reveal something about him.

There was a cast-iron hearth that was cold, although a criss-crossing of sticks and a few lumps of coal were laid out ready to be lit. On either side of the hearth were two easy chairs. The rest of the parlour was filled with a large polished table on which stood an oil lamp alongside some pens in a jar and a neat pile of notebooks. It seemed

Mr Duxbury used the room as a study as well as a sitting room. There were some cheerful floral curtains at the window and a rag rug on the floor that echoed the same colours. But there were no ornaments or pictures of any kind – nothing of a personal nature that might have given her some clues about her new employer.

'What are you doing in here?' Hannah jumped at the sound of Mr Duxbury's voice. She hadn't heard him come in. 'The parlour is mine,' he told her. 'You must stay out!'

Hannah was shocked and perturbed by the tone of his voice and a chill ran through her at the sight of his angry face.

'I'm sorry,' she apologised. 'I didn't know.'

She hurried past him and into the kitchen. 'I was looking for a clock to tell the time,' she lied, trying to excuse herself.

'Is Florence upstairs?' he asked, as he closed the parlour door firmly and then followed her.

'Aye. She's sleeping now.'

He nodded. 'We may as well have our tea then,' he said, and as Hannah busied herself slicing the bread and ham and putting it on the table she wondered how her children were coping without her. They must have been so disappointed not to be able to see her that afternoon and she hoped that the Cartwrights might keep their promise and allow her to visit them, though it would be a long walk there and back and whether Mr Duxbury would agree to her going she had no idea.

CHAPTER TEN

After they'd eaten their tea, Mr Duxbury told Hannah that he was going to the chapel for the evening service as he'd missed the one that morning. She was glad when he went out again. The food she'd eaten was good and better quality than she'd had in a long time, but it had stuck in her throat because of her anxiety and she'd only managed to swallow the fine white bread down with copious drinks of tea.

Alone, she washed up the plates and cups and put them away. Then she went upstairs to wake Florence. She'd kept back some of the bread, cut into small portions and coated with plenty of butter for her. The child ate eagerly, taking each piece from Hannah and sucking it into her mouth. Hannah watched her carefully, wary that she might choke, but Florence was used to some solid food and after she'd finished she drank some milk from the little boat-shaped glass bottle that May had left for her. At first she coughed and began to choke as the milk poured, uncontrolled, into her mouth. Hannah sat her up and rubbed her back as she studied the bottle, only noticing too late that there were some small holes in it. She experimented covering them with her fingers and tipping up the bottle until she learned how to control the flow of the milk. Then she fed the rest to Florence, who sucked and drank happily until she turned her head away, wanting no more.

Hannah sat beside the fire that Mr Duxbury had stoked up before he went out and held the child on her lap for a while until she was sure that she was winded. Then she found a bowl to wash Florence's face and took her upstairs to change her napkin and put her into a nightgown.

All the while Florence watched her with wary eyes. She was obviously puzzled to have been abandoned to a stranger. Hannah could empathise with the little girl's distress and she spoke soothingly to her as she tucked her up. Thankfully she didn't cry again and as Hannah rocked the crib, the old habits of childcare came back to her. She remembered how she'd done the same for her own children in turn. Ruth, her first born, had been such a good baby that Kitty had been somewhat of a shock. Ruth had hardly ever cried, but Kitty had seemed to do little else and she'd always been a sickly child. Hannah felt her own tears rise again as she thought of her. The workhouse was no place for Kitty. She wasn't strong and Hannah worried that she would fall ill again now that she had no way of keeping an eye on her. It was all very well for Mr Cartwright to say that she would be cared for, but Hannah wasn't sure that she trusted the man.

It grieved her to have to leave Edmund there too. The boy had never known his father because Jack had been sent away so soon after he was born, and now he was deprived of a mother too. Hannah's feelings of resentment at what had befallen her surged up and overwhelmed her as she sat on the edge of the bed. She hated all these men for what they had done – from Colonel Fletcher, who had sent Jack to the court in Lancaster, down to Ellis Duxbury who was using her misfortune to his own advantage.

Hannah stared down at the sleeping child. She was rosy-cheeked and healthy. She had a privilege that Hannah's children would never benefit from and for a moment Hannah resented the child. She glanced at the bolster on the bed and saw how easy it would be to rid herself of the baby. But the unbidden thought horrified her. She was shocked and surprised that such a thing had crossed her mind even for a moment. Of course she would never harm Florence.

Although she was very tired and longed to lie down on the bed and sleep, Hannah decided that Mr Duxbury might not approve and so she went back down the stairs and sat by the hearth, waiting for him to come home. He wasn't late and at least he didn't smell of drink when he did come in. It was some consolation, thought Hannah as she brewed a pot of tea.

'You can get off to bed,' he said as she handed him the cup. 'You look all in.'

She was grateful that he'd noticed and after visiting the privy which she found reassuringly clean, she bade him goodnight, lit a candle, and went up to her bedroom, closing the door behind her. She drew the curtains across the window, stepped out of her clothes and folded them carefully on the chair and got into the bed. The sheets smelt fresh and the mattress was stuffed with flock. Hannah thought it was the most comfortable bed she had ever slept in.

She hoped that Florence wouldn't wake in the night. Hannah didn't relish the idea of being kept up by a screaming infant and longed to lose herself in the anonymity of sleep. But, tired as she was, sleep still eluded her long after she had blown out the candle. She lay awake and listened as she heard the doors being locked and Mr Duxbury's footsteps on the stairs. His bedroom door squeaked as he opened it and the floorboards creaked as he closed it behind him. Her ears strained for each sound. But all she could hear was the soft rhythmic breathing of the baby and two tawny owls calling to each other somewhere in the trees.

Sleep eventually overwhelmed her and she woke to a cock crowing nearby and sat up in alarm, unsure where she was for a moment. Florence was still asleep and she was thankful that the baby hadn't cried in the night. She listened hard for any sound that would give her a clue as to the time. She was unsure if she should get up and make a breakfast for Mr Duxbury. He had given her no detailed instructions as to her tasks.

After a while she decided that she might as well get up because she was too anxious to sleep again or even remain in the bed, comfy though it was. She knew that the back door was locked so she scrabbled under the bed and was thankful to find a chamber pot. She put on her clothes and tidied her hair, then gently unlatched her door and crept down the stairs.

Early morning sun was peeping over the edge of the wall that surrounded the yard. Hannah found a pail filled with water and after poking the embers of the fire into life she added more coal and set the kettle to boil. Then she looked at the food that was arrayed on the shelves, unsure what Mr Duxbury would want to eat. There was some bread left over from the day before, a sack of oatmeal too and half a jug of milk – although some of that she would need to keep back for Florence. She wondered where she would get more. There was so much that she didn't know and worry tore at her.

She put cups and plates on the table and brewed the tea. Jack had always enjoyed oatmeal for his breakfast so she mixed some oats with water and a little milk in a pan and stirred it until it thickened. She was wondering whether to butter some bread as well when Mr Duxbury came down the stairs.

'It smells good,' he told her as she spooned the

porridge into his bowl and then reached down the jar of treacle for him to sweeten it.

'I didn't know what you would want,' she told him.

'I don't mind,' he said as he dipped a spoon into the dish and blew on it. 'You'll find I'm easy to please. Is Florence still sleeping?'

'Do you want me to fetch her down?' asked Hannah.

He shook his head. 'No. Don't wake her. I'll see her when I come home for my dinner. There are some potatoes you can cook with the leftover ham. It'll make a good meal. We might have eggs for tea,' he added. 'Go across to see May and she'll tell you where to get them and more milk.'

He scraped the bowl clean and drank his tea, then put on his jacket and cap as the first of the morning footsteps began to sound on the street outside.

'I'll be back around twelve o' clock,' he told her. 'Here are keys for the doors.' He laid them on the table and added a few coins for her to pay for the shopping. 'Lock up when you go out,' he said.

Hannah breathed more easily when she heard the front door close behind him. It was a relief that he would be out for most of the day.

CHAPTER ELEVEN

When the baby had been fed and dressed, Hannah locked the front door of Ellis Duxbury's house and with little Florence on her hip and a basket over her arm, she crossed the street to May's cottage. She knocked tentatively on the door and a moment later it was flung wide open.

'Oh Florence!' May opened her arms for the little girl and Florence reached for her eagerly, a smile lighting her serious face. 'I missed thee,' May told the child, holding her close as the baby snuggled her head into the woman's neck. 'Has she been all right?' she asked Hannah. 'She hasn't cried for me, has she?'

'She's been a good lass. Slept right through the night,' Hannah reassured her.

'Come in. Come in,' said May stepping back from the doorway. 'Come through.'

Hannah followed her into the back kitchen where May invited her to sit down. She made no move to return the child to Hannah, but clung to Florence possessively. She was obviously finding it difficult to be parted from her and

Hannah knew just how she felt. She wished that she could gather her own children in her arms and hold them close.

Watching her, Hannah wondered why Ellis Duxbury hadn't simply left the child in May's care. She was obviously very fond of her and had no children of her own, although there must have been a baby, reasoned Hannah, for her to be able to nurse Florence.

'Here,' said May at last and put the child down on Hannah's lap. 'I'll make some tea.'

As she busied herself with the kettle and the teapot, Florence's eyes followed her every move and more than once she wriggled on Hannah's knee and reached out for May, wanting to be picked up.

'She's bound to find it confusing,' said Hannah as the child began to whimper. 'She thinks of thee as her mother.'

'Aye,' replied May as she poured the tea. 'I suppose she does. Has she eaten?' she asked. 'I could nurse her for a while.'

Hannah shook her head. 'I don't think that's a good idea,' she said gently. 'She's weaned now and tha should let thy milk dry up, otherwise it'll stop thee bearing another child of thine own.' She fell silent, wondering if she'd said the wrong thing. 'Tha's done a good thing nursing Florence,' she added. 'Mr Duxbury owes you a debt of gratitude.'

'It were the Reverend Jones that asked me – the

minister at t' chapel,' May told her as she sat down and handed Hannah her tea. 'I'd given birth to a little lass, but she didn't live more than a day. Mr Jones asked me if I'd be willing to nurse another child that had lost its mother. And what could I say? It would have been unchristian to refuse.'

'Did tha not know Mr Duxbury before then?' asked Hannah curiously. It seemed odd when the man lived so close and attended the same chapel.

'Not well. He only came here a few months ago,' explained May. 'He came to work as manager at t' new spinnin' mill. I think the child had been with another woman down in Darwen where he lived afore, but Mr Duxbury wanted her nearby where he could visit her.'

It seemed a reasonable explanation, but it was one that disappointed Hannah. She'd been hoping that May would tell her more about what had happened to the child's mother, but it did explain why there was no trace of his late wife in Ellis Duxbury's house.

'Mr Duxbury said tha could tell me about where to get the fresh milk and eggs,' she said.

'Aye. I'll walk up to t' farm with thee shortly and introduce thee. There's a chap who comes around with bread and pies too. I'll ask him to call. Everything else is got at t' market.'

Florence cried when Hannah parted from May and went back to Mr Duxbury's house to cook his dinner. She was still red-eyed and fretful when he came in.

'What's wrong with her?' he asked Hannah, and she worried that he thought she hadn't been taking proper care of the child.

'We went to visit May this morning and she's upset to be parted from her again,' explained Hannah. 'She'll settle down when she gets to know me.'

He nodded and sat down at the table waiting for Hannah to put his meal in front of him.

'Are you not eating?' he asked her when she retreated to the chair at the hearth.

She shook her head. 'I'm not hungry,' she replied. The truth was that she didn't want to sit at the table with him and thought that she would have her dinner after he'd gone back to work.

At last, he pushed away his plate and stood up. 'I'll be back about seven for my tea. Listen out for the chime of the clocks to tell you the time,' he told her. 'Stay out of yonder parlour.'

Hannah nodded and waited for the sound of him closing the front door behind him before she relaxed. The man was an enigma. From what May had told her he kept his background a closely guarded secret. He seemed to have no family or friends to speak of and although he had told them he came from Darwen and had worked as a cotton spinner there it was as much as anyone knew about him.

'He attends chapel every Sunday. He's a good

man,' May had said as they parted earlier, but Hannah was still puzzled by him. It was as if he'd sprung from nowhere and she wondered how much the Reverend Jones and Mr Cartwright really knew about Ellis Duxbury.

CHAPTER TWELVE

Gradually Hannah became accustomed to her new routine. Florence began to accept her and even though she still reached out for May whenever she saw her, she seemed less fretful and had begun to smile at Hannah when she went to lift her from the crib in the mornings. Her pleasure was something Hannah found hard to resist even though she'd never considered that she would become fond of the child. She'd tried to distance her emotions from the baby, thinking that she was betraying her own children, but Florence's gurgling little laugh was infectious.

Hannah had learned that Mr Duxbury rose early, ate breakfast and went to his work. He returned to eat his dinner at midday, then left again until the evening – and when he'd had his tea he went into the front parlour and closed the door. Then Hannah tidied up the kitchen and went to bed, and often it was late before she heard him coming up the stairs to his own room.

He gave her money each day to buy food, but made her account for every penny. She had nothing of her own even though she was desperate to buy some material to sew new clothes for herself. What she had was almost falling from her as the material grew thinner and the holes and rips more difficult to mend.

She'd hoped that Mr Duxbury would take her with him when he went down to the market, so that she could look at the stalls, but he left her in the house with Florence and returned after an hour or so with sacks of oatmeal and potatoes which were stored in the kitchen.

He rarely engaged her in conversation except to ask about the day-to-day running of the household. He didn't even seem particularly interested in his daughter and rarely interacted with her. He seemed entirely wrapped up in his own thoughts and whatever it was that kept his attention in the parlour.

The only day he didn't go to the mill was Sunday. In the mornings they went to the chapel. Mr Duxbury made it quite clear from the first week that Hannah and Florence were expected to go with him.

'I've nothing decent to wear,' she'd protested on the first Sunday, wanting to avoid sitting through the long service and being forced to listen to the Reverend Jones preach at her. She'd had enough of sermons whilst she'd been in the workhouse.

He'd glanced at her and replied that she looked suitably dressed as she was. 'We don't hold with finery and fancy clothes,' he'd told her. 'It's not like the parish church where the mill owners' wives compare bonnets.'

In the chapel she sat beside him on one of the hard pews. She held Florence on her lap and Mr Duxbury frowned every time the child made a sound. Each week she hoped that after she'd sat through the service Mr Duxbury would tell her that she might go to visit her children, but every time, after they'd returned to the house and eaten their dinner, he told her that he was going out to walk on the moors; sometimes he didn't return until long after dark when Hannah had begun to worry that some trouble might have befallen him.

After four weeks had passed Hannah was so desperately worried about her children that she dared ask him about a visit.

'Mr Cartwright said it would be allowed,' she reminded him as she tried to prevent him going into the parlour without hearing what she had to say.

He hesitated in the doorway and seemed unable to make up his mind, but at length he nodded. 'Very well,' he said. 'If it will ease your mind, I will ask Mr Jones for the pony and trap after chapel tomorrow. I'm sure May will be willing to look after Florence for a few hours.'

'I can walk. I'm used to walking,' she told him. She would have preferred to go alone and didn't want to put him to any trouble. All she needed was his permission.

He shook his head. 'It would take you too long. I'll borrow the trap,' he said and Hannah realised that he'd made his decision and it was no use her arguing.

The next morning, Hannah woke with excitement fluttering in her stomach at the thought of the visit. For once, she got out of bed eagerly and after preparing breakfast she washed and dressed herself in the best of her meagre clothes. All through the chapel service she could barely sit still and she wished away the time until they could set off for the workhouse.

Although the weather had turned chilly and she was very cold as they travelled down into Bolton, Hannah was thankful that at least it was fine. Mr Duxbury said little as he drove the trap along, but Hannah had grown used to the prolonged silences between them and they no longer made her feel uncomfortable.

They left the pony in the care of the porter at the gatehouse and Mr Duxbury accompanied her through the yard and up the steps to Mr Cartwright's office. He and Mr Duxbury shook hands and Mr Cartwright asked him how the arrangement was going. Mr Duxbury told the workhouse master that he was satisfied with Hannah and her work and it wasn't until then that Mr Cartwright even acknowledged her presence.

'I knew it would work out well for you, despite your reluctance,' he told her.

'Can I see my children?' she asked.

'Of course. If you go through into the reception room they will be brought up to you.'

Hannah pushed open the door. The room was empty and there was silence, except for the quiet murmur of the men's voices in the office behind her. She wondered if they were talking about her.

She paced the room anxiously as she waited, listening for approaching footsteps. She hoped that she would find her children well, and that they hadn't been mistreated whilst she was unable to make her complaints to Mr Cartwright. But it was so long since she'd seen them that she'd also begun to worry about how they would greet her. She'd had no chance to explain to them before she left that she was being forced to go away, and she hoped that they wouldn't blame her for it or think that she'd deliberately abandoned them for an easier life. Nothing was further from the truth. She'd missed them so much and she hoped that they would understand and forgive her.

At last they came. The far door was opened and Ruth and Edmund rushed into her arms. She hugged them both, kissing their heads.

'Are you well?' she asked them, not wanting to relinquish her hold on them to look at their faces in case she was overwhelmed with emotion. She'd promised herself that she would be strong and not cry – for the children's sakes.

'Where's Kitty?' she asked suddenly, realising that only two of her children had been brought to her. 'Why has she not come with you?'

'She's poorly,' Ruth told her mother. 'They've put her in the infirmary.'

‘What’s to do with her?’ Cold terror struck at Hannah as she waited for her elder daughter to tell her more. Kitty becoming ill was her worst fear. ‘Why has no one told me?’ she asked, glancing back at the closed door behind her. Mr Cartwright hadn’t mentioned it. ‘I want to see her,’ she said, her anxiety turning to anger at the thought that her younger daughter was lying ill in bed and no one had sent a message. ‘Which way is it?’ she asked, realising that she’d no idea where the infirmary ward was.

She pulled open the far door that led to the bathrooms where they’d been scrubbed and shorn when they first arrived and out through the small admissions ward to the corridor beyond. She looked this way and that. ‘Which way?’ she asked again, before setting off towards the stairs that she knew led down to the women’s yard, with Ruth and Edmund shadowing her footsteps.

She paused in the yard and looked around. She saw the privy and the doorway to the dining hall and a small door at the far side where she’d never been. Perhaps that led to the infirmary she thought, setting off towards it with determination. She pushed open the door and stepped inside to be met by an overwhelmingly putrid stench of human detritus and rotting waste. She turned and put her hand to her mouth as she retched.

‘Wait there!’ she told Ruth and Edmund. ‘Don’t come in,’ she said as she pushed them back out into the open air, away from the dangerous miasma.

‘What’s tha doin’ in ’ere?’ demanded a voice and Hannah turned to see a woman in a workhouse dress covered by a filthy apron come out into the small hallway. Hannah covered her nose as she realised the smell was coming from a chamber pot that the woman held in her hand.

‘Is this the infirmary?’ Hannah asked.

‘Aye. What of it?’ replied the woman eyeing her suspiciously. ‘Tha’s not one o’ them do-gooders come to visit, is tha?’ she asked. ‘Tha doesn’t ’ave a look of one,’ she added as she noticed Hannah’s threadbare clothes in the gloom.

Hannah wished that she would move away with her stinking pot. ‘I’m here to see my daughter, Kitty Fisher,’ she said.

The woman looked unconvinced. ‘Tha’s not an inmate,’ she pointed out. ‘How come tha’s a daughter in ’ere?’

‘Move out of the way!’ retaliated Hannah, giving the woman a shove that made some of the contents of the pot slop out over the bottom of her dress and her shoes.

‘Oy, no need for that!’ she said as Hannah pushed past her and went into the ward, where there were two rows of identical beds. It was the familiar sound of Kitty’s coughing that drew Hannah to the right one.

‘Kitty?’ Hannah sat down on the edge of the thin mattress and cradled her daughter’s face in her hand.

‘Mam? Is it really thee?’

Her daughter's breathing was shallow and laboured and even speaking a few words seemed to leave her breathless and exhausted.

'I'm here. I'm here,' she said as she pushed Kitty's sweat-darkened hair back from her face.

The sheets on the bed seemed damp and looked like they hadn't been changed in a while. When Hannah eased back the bedding to straighten it, she saw that her daughter looked thinner than ever and every cough seemed to shake her fragile body with convulsions.

'How long's tha been poorly like this?' she asked.

Kitty shook her head feebly. 'I don't know.'

Hannah turned as she heard someone come in behind her. It was the matron.

'Mrs Fisher, you can't be in here,' she said.

'Why wasn't I told she was ill?' demanded Hannah, determined not to give up her place beside her daughter. 'Has the doctor seen her?'

'No need for that,' replied Mrs Cartwright. 'It's only a bad cold. She'll be better in a day or two.'

Hannah glanced down at Kitty and doubted that was true. The child was as ill as she'd ever seen her.

'I told the doctor she was delicate. He promised me she would be taken care of.'

'And so she is being taken care of. That's why she's been moved here,' said Mrs Cartwright impatiently.

Hannah looked around the infirmary ward. It was filled with old women who looked as if they were living on borrowed time. She doubted any of them would last the week out. It was clearly a place where inmates were sent to die rather than to get better.

'You must leave her now,' insisted Mrs Cartwright.

Hannah shook her head. 'I'll not go,' she said. 'I'm her mother. I'll look after her.'

'Please don't be difficult,' said the matron. 'There are nurses here to care for her.'

Hannah remembered the woman with the chamber pot. She was just one of the inmates. She didn't want to leave Kitty in her care.

'I want to look after her myself. I'm her mother,' repeated Hannah, wishing that she had some fresh water and a cloth to bathe her daughter's face. She clasped Kitty's hand in hers as the child began to cough again, her chest wheezing and her breath gasping.

Hannah heard a noise behind Mrs Cartwright and the matron turned to speak to someone. 'She won't leave,' she heard her say.

Mr Cartwright came into the room and Hannah could see the anger on his face. 'Mrs Fisher, you must leave at once!' he told her.

'No!' Hannah was surprised at her own vehemence. She'd never thought that she would dare to stand up to this man, but her desire to protect her child gave her the courage she needed. 'Kitty needs to see a doctor. She needs a clean bed and careful nursing!'

'She's getting all the care she needs here,'

Mr Cartwright told her. 'It's time for you to go. Mr Duxbury is waiting for you.'

Hannah began to shake her head in defiance of him but he strode up towards her through the narrow gap between the rows of beds and clamped his hand around her upper arm. 'You must leave!' he repeated.

Kitty had begun to cry and Hannah held onto her hand. 'I'll not leave thee!' she told her daughter. But Mrs Cartwright began to prise their hands apart as Mr Cartwright hauled Hannah to her feet and dragged her out.

'Kitty!' called Hannah as she tried to grasp hold of the rails on the beds as she was pulled past them.

'Mrs Fisher, you're distressing the child!' Mr Cartwright told her. 'Show some sense, woman!'

The only thing that made any sense to Hannah was to remain with her daughter, but as Mr Cartwright pulled her, Mrs Cartwright began to push her and moments later she was back out in the yard.

Ruth and Edmund were still there and their faces filled with fear at the sight of their mother being physically restrained.

'Take those children away,' muttered Mr Cartwright to his wife.

'Ruth! Edmund!' called Hannah as the matron ushered them across the yard. 'It's all right,' she called, trying to reassure them, although it was clear that things were far from being well.

Mr Cartwright had hold of both of Hannah's arms and even though she struggled, she was helpless in his grasp as he propelled her back up the steps and along the corridors to his office, where he pushed her through the door to the astonishment of Mr Duxbury who rose from his chair with a look of alarm.

'Is something wrong?' he asked as he stared from Hannah to Mr Cartwright and back again.

'Nothing of consequence,' muttered Mr Cartwright. 'You'd better take this woman home – unless you'd rather leave her here.'

'Why would I do that? What's wrong?' he asked. 'Mrs Fisher?'

There was a tone of concern in his voice that took Hannah by surprise. And when he reached for her elbow and guided her to the chair she was completely overwhelmed and began to sob, unable to speak for her tears to make any attempt to explain herself.

'Mrs Fisher has caused quite a scene,' Mr Cartwright told him. 'This is the last time she will be permitted to visit her children. I can't allow this sort of behaviour to disrupt my workhouse.'

'No!' Hannah was distraught at his words. 'You can't stop me seeing them! I'm their mother! I want to take them out of here!'

'Do not talk such nonsense, Mrs Fisher!' replied Mr Cartwright. His tone was icily cold. 'You cannot take your children. Not if you wish to keep your job.' He turned to speak to Mr Duxbury.

'Would you like me to make enquiries about an alternative housekeeper?' he asked. 'I wouldn't blame you if you no longer wanted this woman under your roof.'

'I have no problem with Mrs Fisher,' he replied.

'I hope you won't regret this decision,' Hannah heard Mr Cartwright say to him. 'I can only apologise. I truly thought that Mrs Fisher was a suitable person to care for your daughter.'

'She is suitable,' Hannah heard Mr Duxbury tell him. Then he took her arm, gently, to help her up from the chair and led her out of the office and across the yard to the gatehouse. 'I don't know what transpired in there,' he said as helped her up into the trap, 'but I'm sorry that you are so distressed.'

Hannah buried her face in her hands as they left Bolton. Kitty so ill, and her other children so alarmed and afraid was all she could think of. She knew that she couldn't just abandon them. She had to find a way of getting them back, but she had no idea how it could be achieved.

'Do you want to tell me what's wrong?' asked Mr Duxbury after a while, breaking the silence.

Hannah glanced at him. He didn't seem angry with her, only concerned.

'Kitty's very ill,' she whispered after a moment.

'Is Kitty your daughter?'

'Aye. My younger daughter. She's always been delicate. The workhouse is too hard for her.'

'What happened?' he asked.

'I wanted to stay and nurse her. Mr Cartwright dragged me away. And now he says I can't visit them again. I can't bear it,' she said. 'I should never have left them. I didn't want to.'

Mr Duxbury fell silent again and all Hannah could hear was the clop of the little pony's hooves and the creaking of the wheels as they ascended the track to Egerton.

'If you want to return to the workhouse to be with your children, I will understand – although I would be sorry to lose you,' he said at last.

'I don't think Mr Cartwright would allow me back after what happened today,' Hannah replied. She realised that she had no other option than to return to Mr Duxbury's home. She had nowhere else to go. And even if she went back to the workhouse and demanded the return of her children, how could she care for them? The thought of Kitty in the infirmary bed grieved her with a physical pain, but how could she care for a sick child on the streets? Hannah felt desperate, but she could see no solution to her troubles.

CHAPTER THIRTEEN

Florence smiled as soon as she saw Hannah. Hannah knew it should have gladdened her, but it didn't. She felt angry and resentful because it was her own children she wanted to hold in her arms.

'I think she missed thee,' said May as she handed the child over. Hannah thought she sounded a little jealous that the baby no longer clung to her. 'Were thy children well?' she asked.

Hannah shook her head as she fought with her tears. 'My Kitty's poorly,' she managed to say.

'I'm sorry to hear it,' said May. She hesitated as she saw how upset Hannah was. 'Is there owt I can do?' she asked. 'I've had t' kettle on to boil. Shall I make tea?'

'No. I'd best go,' said Hannah. 'Mr Duxbury will be back in a minute. He's just returning the trap.'

'Then come across to visit tomorrow,' said May and Hannah managed to smile and nod at the younger woman. She was trying her best to be kind and Hannah appreciated it. She knew that she was lucky to find a friend here.

When she got back to the house, Mr Duxbury had already returned and was sitting by the hearth to kindle the fire. Hannah settled Florence in her little chair and began to get the tea ready. Mr Duxbury watched as she sliced and buttered the bread and set it out on the table. It was unusual for him to stay in the room with her unless he was eating and Hannah sensed that he wanted to discuss the events of the afternoon but was unsure what to say.

'I am sorry about what happened today,' said Mr Duxbury at last. 'What ails your daughter?'

'It's her chest,' explained Hannah. 'They have her picking oakum and the fibres get into her lungs and make her cough. I told the doctor she wasn't a strong child, but I don't think they've had him out to see her again even though she's so poorly.'

Hannah choked back a sob. All she'd been able to think about since leaving the workhouse was Kitty's frail face and her look of despair as Mr Cartwright had forced her mother away from the bedside. It had played over and over in Hannah's mind until she could bear it no longer.

'I'm sure Mr Cartwright would arrange for the doctor if he thought it was necessary,' Mr Duxbury told her and Hannah felt angry that the man was defending the workhouse master, but she said nothing. It would do no good to make an enemy of her employer. 'I'm sure Mr Cartwright is doing what he thinks is best for you,' persisted Mr Duxbury.

Hannah shook her head. 'It's wrong,' she told him. 'Children shouldn't be kept separate from their mothers, especially when they're so poorly.'

'How old is your daughter?' he asked.

'Kitty's nine,' she told him.

'I've children younger than that working in my mill,' he replied.

'She'd work willingly if she were well,' Hannah told him. 'Ruth and Edmund too. But there was no work at Hill Fold. That's why we ended up having to go in t' workhouse when the parish wouldn't pay my rent any longer. I'm not afraid of work,' she reminded him.

'Mr Cartwright didn't tell me much about you except that you were a widow and experienced with children,' admitted Mr Duxbury. 'He said you were happy for your children to remain in the workhouse.'

Hannah shook her head. 'I never wanted to leave them there,' she told him. 'It was only the promise that I could visit that made it a bit easier, but if I'm not allowed to see them I don't know what I'll do.'

The tears were running down her cheeks now and she wiped at them with the back of her hand. She could see that her grief was making Mr Duxbury uncomfortable.

'I don't want you to be unhappy here, Mrs Fisher,' he said. 'Perhaps I could speak to Mr Jones. He knows Mr Cartwright well and might intervene on your behalf and persuade him to let you visit again.'

A flicker of hope ignited in Hannah. 'Would you?' she asked, grateful for his consideration.

'Yes, I'll try,' he promised.

CHAPTER FOURTEEN

Despite Mr Duxbury's promise to speak to the Reverend Jones, he went about his work as usual the following week and each evening declared that he thought it was too late to disturb the minister and that he would speak to him on Sunday morning.

With every passing day, Hannah felt more desperately worried about Kitty. She even wondered whether to leave Florence with May and walk down to the workhouse and demand to see her children. But she doubted it would do any good. The more she shouted and raged, the more reason she would give Mr Cartwright to refuse her. She wondered about going to a magistrate, although the only magistrate she knew of was Colonel Fletcher in Bolton, the man who had been responsible for Jack being sent away to New South Wales. She didn't think he would hear her pleas with any sympathy.

Finding it impossible to shoulder her worries alone, Hannah took Florence across the street to visit May.

'I'm sorry,' Hannah apologised after she'd told

the younger woman how desperate she was to know if Kitty was any better. 'I have no one else to talk to.'

'It seems rum to me,' said May. 'But I don't know anything about this Mr Cartwright.'

'Mr Duxbury doesn't seem to know him that well either,' said Hannah. 'I thought they were well acquainted, but it seems it was Mr Jones at the chapel who made all the arrangements. Mr Duxbury thinks he can help to sort it out, but I'm not so sure. I'm scared I might never see my childer again.' She began to cry and May came to put an arm around her shoulders.

'I'm sure it's all a misunderstanding,' she said. 'Perhaps Mr Cartwright will think again and change his mind.'

Hannah didn't reply. She just hoped that May was right.

Hannah counted every minute as she sat beside Mr Duxbury in the chapel the next Sunday morning. She was in agony in case he forgot his promise to speak to the minister on her behalf, but after the service was finished Mr Duxbury kept his place by the door until Mr Jones had finished talking to the rest of his congregation.

'Good morning!' the minister greeted them when they approached him. Hannah thought that he looked smaller outside the chapel. Inside he seemed to fill it with his powerful voice and personality. His preaching was loud and formidable. No one dozed off whilst he was in the pulpit. And when they sang the hymns, his rich tones reverberated from the stone walls, encouraging his congregation to lift their voices in praise with no hesitation. But now he seemed to be more gently spoken, and she could hear the lilt of his Welsh roots in his speech.

'How are you settling in, Mrs Fisher?' he asked her.

'Mrs Fisher is worried about her children,' Mr Duxbury answered for her before she could speak.

'Is that so? What's the problem?' he asked.

'My daughter Kitty is very poorly in the workhouse infirmary,' explained Hannah. 'I wanted to stay and nurse her, but Mr Cartwright dragged me away and then he became angry and said I couldn't visit any of my children again.' Hannah could feel her bottom lip quivering as she spoke even though she was trying desperately to keep her composure.

Mr Jones raised an eyebrow in surprise. 'Is there any truth in this?' he asked, turning to Mr Duxbury.

'Mr Cartwright did say that Mrs Fisher was no longer welcome at the workhouse,' he confirmed.

'I'm surprised,' said the minister. He looked accusingly at Hannah, as if she was the one at fault. 'I've always found Mr Cartwright to be a reasonable man,' he said. 'What exactly happened to prompt his decision?' He looked to Mr Duxbury rather than Hannah for an explanation.

'I'm not certain,' said Ellis Duxbury. 'Mr Cartwright brought Mrs Fisher back from her visit sooner than I expected. She was very upset and he was very angry and said that she had caused a scene.'

'I only wanted to care for my sick child!' interrupted Hannah, unable to remain silent any longer. 'But Mr Cartwright is keeping my children from me! It isn't fair! I was told that I would be able to visit them!'

Mr Duxbury put out a hand to restrain her outburst. 'Mrs Fisher is obviously worried about her children,' he explained. 'I wondered if you could speak to Mr Cartwright and clarify the situation.'

Mr Jones turned back to Mr Duxbury. 'I'll ask about this the next time I visit Mr Cartwright,' he promised him. 'I'm sure there will be a simple explanation, but I can understand Mr Cartwright changing his mind about the visits if Mrs Fisher made a scene and upset the children.' He glanced at Hannah but gave her no chance to speak. 'It will have done them no good, and we need to consider their welfare,' he went on. 'If you are not satisfied with the arrangement, perhaps someone more suitable could be found,' he suggested.

'No, no. Mrs Fisher is suitable – and Florence likes her,' replied Mr Duxbury.

The minister nodded. 'Women can be quite unpredictable, you know,' he said.

Hannah was about to tell the minister exactly

what she thought of his views but before she'd drawn breath he had bid them *Good morning* and walked away. Hannah followed Mr Duxbury furiously back to the house. She hated the way the men had spoken about her and not listened to anything that she'd said.

'I'm sure Mr Jones will bring a satisfactory answer from Mr Cartwright,' Mr Duxbury told her when they were inside the house and the door had been closed.

'But what if he still refuses to allow me to visit?' asked Hannah. She felt desperate as well as angry. 'I will not abandon my children in that place!'

Mr Duxbury frowned and Hannah turned away to settle Florence in her chair and then began to set the table. They always had a cold dinner on a Sunday as her employer was keen to set out on his walk as soon as possible after returning from the chapel. So Hannah had got into the habit of roasting a joint of meat on a Saturday afternoon, which they ate hot when Mr Duxbury returned from work and then she cut slices from it the day after. She buttered bread to go with it and made a pot of tea.

Mr Duxbury ate quickly and then put on his jacket and hat. 'I'm not sure what time I'll be back,' he said. 'Lock the door if you go to bed. I have my key.'

Then he was gone, closing the door quietly behind him. Left alone, Hannah cleared away the pots and wondered how to pass her afternoon. All she could think of was Kitty in that filthy infirmary bed, and Ruth and Edmund sitting alone when the other children were allowed to spend time with their mothers or fathers. She wiped away tears on her apron then picked up Florence to change her and put her down for a nap.

What would she do if Mr Cartwright wouldn't change his mind about the visits? It would be impossible for her to stay here and do nothing. She was certain of that. There had to be a way of having her children with her and still earning a living.

She sat down on the chair by the hearth feeling too restless to settle to any of the tasks that were waiting to be attended to.

After a few moments she stood up and walked up the lobby to the parlour. She was confident that Mr Duxbury wouldn't catch her this time so she opened the door and went in.

Everything was as it had been before. The fire was still unlit even though the room was cold. The pens and notebooks remained on the table and the cushion on the chair looked undisturbed. Hannah wondered what Mr Duxbury did in here every evening when he could have remained in the snug warmth of the kitchen. Was it because he didn't want to be in her company? Still, it could have been worse. He could have sent her up to her room where she would have shivered in the chill whilst he sat by the fire.

Daringly she opened one of the notebooks to

look inside. It was covered in small, neat writing that she was unable to read, but the drawings were clear enough. They were of a large building, but not a church or a house. It had row upon row of windows, a waterwheel to one side and a tall chimney. Hannah carefully turned more pages and found drawings of machinery that looked like spinning jennies, only much bigger as if they could spin hundreds of threads at a time. The drawings must be for one of the new spinning mills, thought Hannah as she carefully closed the book and put it back on the pile it had come from, taking care to make it appear undisturbed. She wondered if it was Ellis Duxbury who had drawn them and why. She was certain now that he was hiding a secret although she still had no idea what it might be.

After finding nothing of further interest she came out and closed the door behind her. She wished that she could visit May, but she knew that she had gone with her husband, Joseph, to visit his mother and that she would find no one in.

Hannah was in bed, though not asleep, when Ellis Duxbury returned. She heard him come in and climb the stairs with his flickering candle. The light lingered outside her door. She could see it in the narrow gap around the frame and she half-expected him to knock. Then it moved away and he closed his door quietly. It had been dark for hours and Hannah wondered where he had been.

Surely not walking on the moors in the pitch blackness? His absences every Sunday made no sense to her. But it was none of her business, she thought as she turned over and settled to sleep, relieved that he was safely home.

'I hope I didn't disturb you when I came in last night?' Mr Duxbury asked Hannah as she put his breakfast on the table in front of him the next morning. 'I was very late. I'm sorry if I woke you.' He looked at her. 'You don't seem well,' he added.

She was about to ask him why that should surprise him, but she simply said, 'I'm quite well. There's no need to trouble yourself about me.'

'I'm sure Mr Jones will bring an affirmative answer from Mr Cartwright,' he said. 'I know you are troubled about not being able to visit your children.' He ate quietly for a moment. 'I know how important it is to you that you see them and reassure yourself that they are well. I . . .' Hannah thought that he'd been about to say more, to open himself up to her, but he frowned as if he'd thought better of it. Once again, she wondered what secrets he was harbouring. Perhaps he went to visit his wife's grave every Sunday, she thought as she washed up. He never took flowers, but these non-conformists didn't seem to like them. They had none in their chapel.

He pushed back his chair and reached for his cap and jacket. 'I'll be back at twelve,' he said and went off to his work at the mill, eager to be there before his workers.

Hannah poured herself another cup of tea and sat down by the fire. She yawned. She felt exhausted and she wasn't surprised Mr Duxbury had commented on her appearance. A glimpse in the little mirror as she'd pinned up her hair had confirmed her pale face and red-rimmed eyes.

Florence was still in her cot and Hannah knew she ought to go and fetch the child down, but she craved a few minutes peace before her morning work began. She sipped at the tea and was overcome with guilt. Here she was, sitting in a cosy house, by a warm fire, with tea in her hand and able to do as she pleased, for the moment at least, whilst her children were still subject to the tough regimes of the workhouse. She wondered what they were doing. Were they in the schoolroom? Or had they been set to work. And was Kitty any better? Surely someone would have told her if the child was worse or if she had . . . Hannah pushed the thought aside. She couldn't even bear to consider that Kitty might die without her in that infirmary bed.

Her desire to see her daughter or at least check on her health was overwhelming and she wondered if she would have time to walk into Bolton and back between making Mr Duxbury's dinner and his tea. She could ask May to mind Florence for a few hours. She was sure she would agree. Hannah knew she missed the child and there was no sign of a new baby of her own to fill the ache in her heart. But what would Mr Duxbury say? Should she ask his permission? He had given her no rules to abide by, but she didn't want to incite his anger because she was beginning to think that he might be an ally. He had asked Mr Jones to intervene and had expressed some sympathy that morning. She decided that she would not go behind his back but would seek permission before she set off.

'I don't think it's a good idea,' said Mr Duxbury at dinner time when Hannah suggested her plan to him. 'Let Mr Jones speak to the Cartwrights first. I know you are worried,' he added when she didn't reply, 'but I think it's for the best to wait.'

'But what if Mr Cartwright still refuses?' she asked.

'Let's wait and see,' said Mr Duxbury. Hannah nodded. She didn't tell him that she had already made a plan. If she wasn't allowed to visit the children she would go back to the workhouse and demand that they were released into her care. She would leave little Florence with May, and when she had her children she would take them far away from here. How they would manage Hannah had no idea, but at least they would be together and that mattered to her more than anything.

All through that day Hannah hoped that the minister might call with the news that Mr Cartwright had agreed to another visit, but he didn't come. Neither did he come on the Tuesday. On the Wednesday evening, she was about to go up the stairs to her bed when there was a sharp rapping on the front door. She heard Mr Duxbury come out of the front parlour to answer it and she strained to hear who it was. Elation and terror coursed through her as she recognised the voice of the minister, and Hannah said a silent prayer that he had brought good news.

She stood to greet him, but Mr Duxbury took him into the front parlour and she could only hear the rumble of their voices despite pressing her ear to the wall to try to discover what was being said. After what seemed a long time, the door opened and Hannah hoped that Mr Duxbury wasn't going to show the minister out. She was fearful that he might have come on some entirely different business and that he hadn't been to the workhouse on her behalf at all.

She moved back to the table and grasped its edge as the door from the passageway was opened and the men came in. She could see that Mr Duxbury's expression was grim and a sudden terror gripped her that they had come to tell her that her daughter was dead.

'Kitty?' she whispered.

'Sit down,' said Mr Duxbury as he hurried towards her and pulled out one of the chairs from under the table. He took her elbow as she swayed slightly and guided her down. 'All is well with Kitty,' he reassured her. 'She has not . . .' He stopped and looked to the minister for confirmation. 'Mrs Fisher's children are well?' he asked.

'Yes.'

'Did you see them?' Mr Duxbury asked him.

The minister shook his head. 'It was not necessary. Mr Cartwright reassured me they are in good health.'

'Can I see them?' asked Hannah eagerly.

'I have spoken at length to Mr Cartwright,' he told her. 'He has agreed, albeit reluctantly, that you may go to say goodbye.'

'Goodbye? Why goodbye?' asked Hannah. She didn't understand what she was being told, but she could feel her heart racing and her fingers shook as she reached to gather her shawl more tightly around herself.

'Because Mr Cartwright has good news,' the minister continued as he came to sit at the table opposite to her. 'He has found apprenticeships for them.'

'Apprenticeships?' repeated Hannah, feeling a wave of panic wash over her.

'Yes. I'm sure you must be grateful to him for his efforts. Your daughters are to go to Quarry Bank, and your son will be apprenticed to a coalminer at Colonel Fletcher's pit. It seems very satisfactory to me,' said Mr Jones, looking immensely pleased with himself. He was almost preening.

'But . . . but he can't do that! Surely he would need my permission?' protested Hannah.

'It is what you agreed, Mrs Fisher.' The minister seemed genuinely puzzled at her reaction. 'You made your mark on the papers before you left the workhouse,' he said.

Suddenly a queasy feeling overcame Hannah as she remembered the papers that Mr Cartwright had pushed in front of her. 'Mr Cartwright made me sign something and never told me what it said,' she admitted. 'I hope he hasn't tricked me.'

'No one has been tricked,' the minister told her. 'Perhaps you simply didn't understand what was said.'

'I'm not stupid,' Hannah told him. 'I would never give my children away – never!' she added for emphasis. 'Where is this Quarry Bank anyway?' she asked. She'd never heard of the place and knew it was not nearby.

'It is in Cheshire,' the minister said. 'It's in the countryside and it was agreed that it would be the ideal place for your daughters, especially the younger one who has been poorly. The fresh country air and the good food will do her good. And Mr and Mrs Greg also provide medical care for their apprentices. They are fortunate to be given a place.'

Hannah looked up at Mr Duxbury who was standing with his back to the fire. 'It can't be right, can it?' she appealed to him, hoping that he would do something.

'Mr Jones assures me that Mr Cartwright discussed this with you and that you were in agreement,' Mr Duxbury told her, although his expression revealed that he was dubious.

'I never agreed to it!' Hannah protested. 'I would never have agreed to my children being sent off to some place far away where I can't visit them. I'll go to the workhouse tomorrow and demand that they are given back to me!'

'And what will you do then, Mrs Fisher?' reasoned the minister. 'If Mr Cartwright were to agree to release the children into your care, where would you go? How would you live? You cannot bring them back here. Mr Duxbury cannot be expected to feed and house your children for you. You knew that you could not bring three children with you when you came to care for little Florence.'

'No, but I was told I would be allowed to visit them!'

'And you did visit, did you not? I lent my pony and trap so that you could go. And I'm willing to lend it again this Sunday so that you can say your goodbyes. It is for the best, Mrs Fisher,' he added. 'You are unable to care for your children yourself. Mr Cartwright tells me they were very malnourished and hardly clothed when they were admitted to the workhouse. This way they will be cared for and taught to work for their living. It is a good opportunity for them and you are ungrateful if you prevent them having a better life than the one they had with you!'

Hannah could not have felt more shocked if Mr Jones had physically slapped her face. She stared at him. Unable to speak, not knowing what to say. And it was clear that there was nothing she could say that would make a difference. Once more these men had forced her hand and left her helpless. They had stolen her children and there was nothing that she could do.

Mr Jones stood up to leave and Mr Duxbury escorted him to the door. Hannah heard them exchange a few words in the lobby and then the door closed. Mr Duxbury turned the key and drew the bolt across then came back into the kitchen and sat down by the hearth. He was silent for a few minutes before he eventually said, 'I'm sorry.'

'I never agreed to it,' Hannah told him. 'Why can't my childer stay in the workhouse?' she asked. 'Why are they sending them away? Why do they want to punish me? I've done nothing wrong.'

'It is a matter of money,' Mr Duxbury explained. 'The parish guardians know that it costs less to pay the fee for an apprenticeship than to keep children in the workhouse for years – especially the younger children. The children sent away are usually orphans but in some cases it happens when they are abandoned.'

'But I never abandoned them! I never wanted to leave them. I was given no choice.'

'I'm sorry if you feel you were forced to come here,' said Mr Duxbury. 'You are under no obligation to stay. You're free to go, if you choose. But it's a joy to have my daughter at home and we would miss you if you left us now. I wouldn't be able to care for her alone,' he went on. 'I know nothing about babies.'

'Could May not care for her again?' Hannah asked. 'I know she misses her.'

'May has her own home and her husband,' said Mr Duxbury. 'In time she will have more children of her own. She cannot live here and be a mother to my daughter.'

'Perhaps the workhouse will find some other poor woman for you,' replied Hannah. 'There are enough of them.'

'But they would not be you,' he replied. 'Please don't make any hasty decision, Mrs Fisher,' he asked her. 'I don't want you to leave. And Florence would be upset.'

'But what about my children?' she replied. 'Do you not think they are upset to lose their mother?'

'I'm sure they are,' he agreed. 'But I cannot see what can be done. If you made your mark on the papers it cannot be argued with.'

'But I didn't know what I was signing!' she told him once more. 'I was told a lie – and there was no witness.'

Mr Duxbury frowned. 'It may be worth asking the advice of the magistrate,' he agreed after a moment.

Hannah took no consolation from the suggestion. 'Colonel Fletcher will do nothing to help me.' She almost spat out the sound of the man's name on her lips, her hatred of him was so intense.

'Let me at least try,' said Mr Duxbury. 'Allow me to speak to him to see if anything can be done – to see if there can be some justice. It grieves me to see you so unhappy,' he told her, 'and I feel as if part of the fault is mine.'

There was nothing Hannah could do for the moment but agree. It was late and she couldn't go to the workhouse and bang on the gates in the middle of the night, no matter how much she wanted to.

'And I will take you to see your children on Sunday,' he promised. 'Mr Cartwright has at least agreed to that.'

With a brief nod of her head, Hannah took her candle and went upstairs to her room. Florence was sleeping soundly so Hannah sat on the edge of the mattress and tried to make sense of what she'd been told. Perhaps, when Mr Duxbury took her to see her children on Sunday afternoon, he would help her explain to Mr Cartwright that she didn't want her children to be apprenticed and that she had made a mistake by signing his papers. Surely he would be reasonable? But when she remembered how he had treated her last time, she wasn't so sure. And even if he did agree, Hannah knew that he would not allow the children to remain in the workhouse. It was clear that the parish guardians were intent on saving money and they would not help her unless she agreed to their terms. It seemed hopeless. She was left with a choice of allowing them to have their way and losing her children, or taking her children to beg on the streets and maybe starve. She would have to explain it to them as best she could when Sunday came, she decided, and ask them to help her choose what was the best thing to do.

CHAPTER FIFTEEN

Hannah sat restlessly through the chapel service on the Sunday morning. She was convinced that the Reverend Jones was preaching the longest sermon in his life just to spite her, and even when the worship was finished, Mr Duxbury lingered to check on the arrangements for the pony and trap. Hannah thought they would never get back to the house to eat their cold meat sandwiches so that they could go to the workhouse.

It must have been after two o'clock in the afternoon before they left Florence with May and set off towards Bolton. The weather had turned even colder and there was a fine drizzle in the air, sweeping down from the misty moorland. Hannah pulled her meagre shawl up over her head and tried to stop her teeth chattering together as they drove along.

'You should have dressed in your warm shawl,' said Mr Duxbury when he noticed that she was shivering.

'This is the only shawl I have.'

'But when you came to visit, the first time, you

had a much better one.' He glanced at her with a puzzled expression.

'It wasn't mine,' she explained. 'It was lent to me by Mrs Cartwright so that I would make a good impression.'

He said nothing for a moment then glanced at her again, his eyes lingering on her patched petticoat and the hole in the toe of one of her shoes. 'Mr Cartwright told me that you would come with all you needed and that all you would require was food and a bed,' he told her. 'He said that you would be grateful and that there would be no need for wages.' He reined the pony in to the side of the track to allow some men on horses to pass by in the opposite direction. 'But you must have something warmer before the winter comes. You can't go out in the rain and snow in that thin shawl and shoes that let in water. Come with me on market day and we'll see what can be bought.' He urged the pony on. 'I presume you have no money?'

She shook her head. 'What little I had was given to the workhouse,' she said. 'I was issued with clothing there, but had to make do with what I owned when I came to work for you.'

'I will buy you some better clothing,' he said.

'I don't want to put you to expense,' protested Hannah.

'Think of it as wages,' he said. 'Besides, I don't want people to say that I keep my housekeeper in rags.'

The rain was coming down steadily before they reached the workhouse and they were both wet. The gatehouse keeper said he would find some shelter for the pony and Hannah and Mr Duxbury squelched across the yard to the entrance, Hannah trying to avoid the puddles that would flood her feet with water.

Mr Cartwright didn't seem to be expecting them. He came hurrying up the stairs, breathless and with an agitated expression. He did not look welcoming.

'Mr Duxbury! Please, step into my office.' He went to sit behind his desk and waved Mr Duxbury to a chair, but ignored Hannah and left her standing with the rain dripping off the fringes of her shawl on to the floor.

'I can only apologise,' he told Mr Duxbury. 'I did not expect you to come today.'

'Can I see my children?' asked Hannah. Mr Cartwright continued to ignore her.

'I'm sorry this tedious affair has caused you so much trouble and I cannot blame you for bringing this woman back to us. As I explained to the Reverend Jones, these women rarely understand what is explained to them, but I can assure you that the arrangements I made for Mrs Fisher's children will benefit them.'

'Can she see them?' asked Mr Duxbury.

Mr Cartwright frowned. 'Did you not receive my note?' he asked. 'I sent word to explain that I'd had second thoughts after making my promise to Mr Jones. I had to consider the children. It would have done them no good to be subjected to the sort of scene I witnessed on Mrs Fisher's last visit. And Mr Greg was keen that their arrival should not be delayed.'

'Where are my children?' demanded Hannah. 'I was promised that I could see them!'

'Calm down, Mrs Fisher,' said Mr Cartwright before turning back to Mr Duxbury. 'This is what I wanted to avoid,' he said. 'Excuse me whilst I find my wife and she will take the woman to a ward.'

'No!' Ellis Duxbury stood up and moved protectively towards Hannah. 'I have brought Mrs Fisher to visit her children.'

'They are not here.' Mr Cartwright spread his hands in a slight shrug.

'But . . .' Hannah looked from one man to the other. 'I was told I could see them,' she said again as all the hope drained from her and made her feel weak. The room began to darken around the edges and she felt a hand on her elbow as someone helped her to a chair.

'Mrs Fisher was promised she could say goodbye to her children. I find it cruel that she has been denied that.' Hannah could hear the cold fury in Mr Duxbury's voice.

'I sent a note,' protested Mr Cartwright.

'I did not receive it!'

Hannah's senses had rallied enough for her to see the two men glaring at one another across the desk.

'It is unfortunate,' said Mr Cartwright. 'I'm sorry you have had a wasted journey. Perhaps I can offer some tea as your coat is dried by the fire,' he suggested.

'But what about Mrs Fisher?'

Hannah saw the workhouse master glance down at her. 'She may have some tea as well,' he conceded.

'But she cannot see her children!'

'Mr Duxbury, please, sit down. I will bring another chair.' He hurried around the desk as the door was opened.

'Whatever is the matter?' asked Mrs Cartwright from the doorway. 'I can hear the shouting from downstairs.'

'Mr Duxbury did not receive my note and his afternoon has been wasted. Ask someone to bring tea and cake, and another scuttle of coal for the fire.'

'I see Mrs Fisher has returned to us,' observed the matron. She didn't sound surprised.

'Mrs Fisher has come to see her children, but I am told they are no longer here!' interrupted Mr Duxbury.

Mrs Cartwright looked stunned at his outburst. 'We decided it was for the best,' she told him. 'It would have been too distressing for the children. They have gone to good places where they will be cared for. You can be assured of that.'

'I was promised I could say goodbye,' insisted Hannah. She'd been counting down the hours and the minutes all week and she couldn't believe that her children weren't there after all. 'I just wanted to see them.' She could contain herself no longer and her tears flowed no matter how much she tried to compose herself and hold them back. She'd been determined to remain dignified and not be accused of causing another scene, but now she no longer cared.

'Mr Duxbury,' said Mrs Cartwright, 'you cannot continue to have this woman care for your daughter. She is clearly hysterical. Please, allow us to find you someone else. We will care for Mrs Fisher. It is clear that she needs the help of a doctor.'

Ellis Duxbury moved so that he was standing between the matron and Hannah. 'Mrs Fisher needs no help from you,' he told her. 'She will return to my house with me. And I will not let this matter drop,' he warned both the Cartwrights. 'It seems clear to me that Mrs Fisher has been tricked or duped. She says she never agreed to her children being apprenticed, and I believe her.'

'Mr Duxbury,' said Mr Cartwright coming out from behind his desk to take his arm and lead him towards the fire. Mr Duxbury shook him off. 'You do not have the experience of these kinds of women that we do,' continued Mr Cartwright. 'Their minds are not strong and they suffer from all types of delusions. They can be cured with the right treatment and I think Mrs Fisher may benefit from some treatment at the insane asylum—'

'No!' Even Hannah jumped at the furious

response from Mr Duxbury. 'I will not hear of such a suggestion! Mrs Fisher is my housekeeper and she shall remain in my employment until I choose that she is dismissed!'

He reached for his damp coat and his hat. 'Come, Mrs Fisher. Let's go,' he said.

'You do not have authority over her,' warned Mr Cartwright.

'Do you?' he challenged. 'Mrs Fisher tells me she signed papers that released her from your workhouse.'

'She signed papers that agreed to the apprenticeship of her children. Mrs Fisher is still an inmate here, although she is released to work for you.'

'Mr Duxbury,' pleaded the matron. 'Think of your daughter. Do you want her cared for by a mad woman?'

Hannah watched as he hesitated. He looked at her and she took a deep breath and wiped away her tears, striving to look in control of her emotions so that he wouldn't change his mind. She'd heard talk of the insane asylum and it was terrifying. He held out his hand to her. 'Come,' he said again. 'Let's go home.'

Hannah was shaking uncontrollably as Ellis Duxbury guided her down the steps to the gatehouse. She kept glancing over her shoulder, convinced that Mr Cartwright would come after them and force her back inside to await goodness only knew what fate.

Mr Duxbury asked abruptly for the pony and

trap to be brought round and he helped her up without a word. Then he shook the reins and urged the pony to a brisk trot. His face was stony and he was breathing hard. Hannah could feel the fury exuding from him.

It was raining hard and their clothes were soon soaked through, but Hannah was oblivious to the discomfort as she tried not to break down completely. It would do no good to prove Mr Cartwright correct by giving in to the torrent of fear and anguish that writhed through her. Where were her daughters and Edmund? They must think that she'd abandoned them without a care when she didn't return for them. The thought almost undid her and she began to cry again, hoping that her tears would be disguised by the raindrops that were stinging her face.

At last they reached Egerton and Mr Duxbury pulled up outside his house. He tied the pony to the tethering ring on the wall and came to help her down. Hannah felt the water squelch in her damaged shoe as she reached the ground.

'Go inside and get dry,' Mr Duxbury told her. 'I will return the trap. Florence will be safe with May for a while longer. We need to talk,' he added as he unlocked the door for her to go in.

Hannah dripped rainwater through the lobby and into the kitchen where she took off her shawl and hung it up. She stoked the fire and then found a towel, wishing she had some dry clothes to change into. She didn't think she'd ever felt so miserable – not even on the day that she'd learned Jack was to be sent to New South Wales.

She cried as she filled the kettle with water and put it to boil, then fetched the teapot and the cups. All the while she felt as if she was moving in a dream. The kitchen swam before her but none of it seemed real, and she wondered if she would wake with a pounding heart and discover that it was just one more nightmare to add to the bad dreams that had beset her since Jack had not come home from that weavers' meeting on the moors.

She sat down on the chair at the hearth to try to dry her petticoat and rubbed her fingers as they throbbed now that some warmth was starting to return to them. What was she going to do? It was clear to her that she could not remain here. She had to go and find her children and rescue them. There was no other choice.

She was still sitting, staring at the growing flames and trying to make a plan, when she heard Mr Duxbury come in. He took off his coat and shook it, making the fire sizzle, then put it on a hook behind the door. He threw his drenched hat carelessly to the floor and sat down to pull off his boots. His shirt was damp at the shoulders and around the collar, and his breeches were soaked to the knee.

He stood the boots side by side to dry and ran a hand through his damp hair. 'We need to talk,' he said again. Hannah nodded. She knew that he was usually a man of few words and that he was also perturbed by what had transpired. 'I'm as shocked as you at the behaviour of Mr Cartwright,' he said.

'I want my children,' replied Hannah. She could hear the tremble in her voice and hoped that Mr Duxbury would not notice it. 'I need to know that they're safe.' She wanted to add that it was not madness to desire such a thing, but she was aware that she must be careful to do nothing that would alarm him about her mental state.

'I will speak to Colonel Fletcher,' he promised her. 'He may know where your son is. The other place – Quarry Bank – I've heard it's a good place for apprentices and I think you should be reassured that your daughters will do well there.'

'But Kitty was so poorly.'

'Mr Greg would not have taken a sick child,' he told her. 'She must have been recovered. That is some consolation.'

'But how will I get them back?' she asked him.

'I don't know,' he admitted. 'Unless Colonel Fletcher will intervene.'

'Do you think he will?' asked Hannah hopefully, but her hopes were crushed when she saw Mr Duxbury shake his head.

'I think he will say that the arrangements will benefit your children. Looking at it dispassionately that's how it seems. Your feelings as a mother are not considered in matters regarding workhouse children. Mr Cartwright will simply say that you agreed. He has the papers. I don't really know what can be done. I'm sorry,' he apologised again and Hannah felt the desperation rising in her. If Mr Duxbury seemed defeated by what had been done, what hope did she have of undoing it?

'I cannot simply stay here and abandon them,' she said.

He didn't answer straight away. He was looking at his hands and seemed lost in his thoughts.

'I fear what will become of you if you leave,' he said at last. Hannah knew that he was recalling what Mr Cartwright had said. 'If you are found begging on the streets they will surely send you to the asylum,' he warned her. 'And if you thought your life was bad in the workhouse . . .' His words trailed off as he looked blankly towards the wall. 'They are unpleasant places,' he said, 'if you have no one to protect you.'

'What other choice do I have?' she asked.

'You could marry me,' suggested Mr Duxbury.

She stared at him, not sure that she had heard aright or understood his words.

'Marry?' she asked. He nodded. 'But I can't do that,' she told him. 'Jack. My husband . . .'

Ellis Duxbury was shaking his head. 'You are a widow,' he reminded her. 'But if you were my wife I could protect you from the magistrates and the parish guardians. I could ensure that you are never sent to an asylum. And I promise that I will help you find your children.'

'But how would it benefit you?' she asked, puzzled by his suggestion and suspicious that she was once again being coerced into something that would prove to be an unwise choice.

'It means you would stay,' he said. 'Hannah,' he continued, surprising her with the use of her name, 'I want you to stay.' He leaned forward and clumsily reached for her hand. 'I was so lonely before you came,' he told her, 'and I've grown used to your company.'

She was about to say that he saw little of her because he was either at work, or in his parlour, or out walking, but she kept silent.

'I don't know,' she told him, pulling her hand from his. 'It isn't something I was expecting. I'm not ready to marry again. Not yet. Not until I'm sure that Jack isn't coming home.'

'No one comes back,' he told her.

'Thomas Holden did,' she said. 'He was sent away with Jack and he came back.'

Ellis Duxbury moved away from her. 'It was only a suggestion,' he said. He looked disappointed and embarrassed as he averted his eyes. 'I won't mention it again. I'm sorry.'

'It was a kind thought,' she said. She didn't want to seem ungrateful, but she knew that his words had shifted something in their relationship and that it would never be quite the same. It made her feel uncomfortable and she wondered if it would be better to leave and take her chances on the streets.

They were interrupted by a knocking on the door. Ellis Duxbury got up to answer it and Hannah heard May's voice in the lobby.

'Is everything all right?' she asked. 'I saw you come back but you haven't been for Florence and I was worried something might be wrong.' She came into the kitchen with Florence in her arms and looked at Hannah. 'What happened?' she asked her. 'What's upset you so badly?'

'They've sent my children away. I didn't have the chance to say goodbye.'

'That's not right!'

May turned and thrust Florence into her father's arms. The child squirmed and began to cry as Ellis Duxbury grasped her awkwardly, as if he was holding a sack of flour. May crouched down and put an arm around Hannah's shoulders. 'That was so cruel,' she sympathised. 'Is there nothing to be done?'

'I'll see the magistrate,' said Ellis Duxbury.

'Can Mr Jones not help?' asked May.

'I've already explained it to him – when I returned the trap. He didn't think there was much he could do.'

'I was tricked into signing some papers,' explained Hannah. 'I was stupid. Jack would never have let me sign something I couldn't read.'

'Jack?' asked May.

'My husband,' explained Hannah.

'He was sent to New South Wales,' Ellis Duxbury told May. 'No one has heard from him,' he added.

'What can I do to help?' asked May. 'Shall I keep Florence a while longer?'

'No,' said Mr Duxbury. 'She's home now. We'll care for her.'

His tone made it clear that he expected May to leave and she got reluctantly to her feet. 'If you want to talk to me, come across,' she said to Hannah.

'Thank you,' said Hannah as her friend patted her shoulder before going to the door. Florence cried and reached out to her, but Mr Duxbury shifted her onto his other shoulder and held the door open. When he came back, Hannah expected him to drop the wriggling child on to her lap, but he kept hold of his daughter.

'I think she's hungry,' said Hannah. 'I'll make the tea.'

'No,' he said. 'I'll do it. I'll put her in her chair.'

He bent to put Florence down, but she was crying and kicking her legs and Hannah thought that she might have laughed at his struggle if things had been different.

'Give her to me,' she said at last and saw the look of relief on his face as Florence held out her arms and fell silent as she nestled on Hannah's lap and put a thumb in her mouth.

Hannah watched as Ellis Duxbury placed a loaf of bread on the table and wielded a knife. She expected that she would have to take over that task as well, but he seemed proficient and soon had the meal prepared. He must have been used to fending for his own needs since his wife died, she thought as she watched him, impressed that he was not totally helpless.

She put Florence down on the rug with a finger of bread and butter and took a sip of her tea. The warmth comforted her but she struggled to eat any of the generous portion of bread and butter that Mr Duxbury had made for her, although she tried when she saw him watching her anxiously.

He ate his own sitting in the chair opposite to her. To any onlooker it would have seemed cosy – the young couple on either side of the hearth and a child on the rug between them. Hannah expected him to finish his meal and go to the parlour but he lingered by the fire and then took the pots and began to wash them up.

'I'll do that,' she protested.

'No. Stay there,' he told her. 'I can manage.'

She knew that he was trying to be kind, but she wished that he would leave her alone. His presence was awkward, especially after his earlier mention of marriage. She would have to leave now, thought Hannah. He had made the situation impossible.

'I will go to see Colonel Fletcher tomorrow,' he told her when he'd put the cups and plates back on the shelf.

'What about your work?' she asked.

'They will manage without me for an hour or so,' he said. 'Don't decide anything until I come back.' She could hear the pleading tone in his voice. He was obviously concerned that she would simply leave Florence with May and disappear. 'I promise I will do everything I can to help you,' he added.

Hannah nodded. 'I'd better put Florence to bed,' she said, eager to be in her own company so that she could think about what she should do. But he followed her up the stairs and watched as she washed the child's face, changed her nappy and settled her into the cot.

'She's grown to love you,' he observed as he watched Hannah bend to kiss the child's head and tell her to sleep well.

'She hasn't known me long. She would soon grow to love someone else,' said Hannah as she watched the child's eyes flutter and close as she gently rocked the cradle with her hand. She said it to convince herself as much as the child's father because it was true that she'd grown to love the little girl as well, and she would miss her if she went away. But, she reminded herself, this child was not her own and it was her own children who were far more important to her.

'Is she asleep?' he whispered after a moment.

'Aye. She is.'

'Come back downstairs for a moment.'

'No. I'm tired out,' she replied, wishing he would leave her room. 'I think I'll go to bed myself.'

Hannah thought he was going to ask again, but he nodded and accepted her choice.

'Good night then,' he said. 'I hope you sleep well.'

She closed the door firmly behind him, wishing once again that it had a lock or a bolt, and listened as his footsteps went down the stairs. She heard him moving about in the kitchen for a while then he went into his parlour. He would be cold, she thought; he never lit a fire in there. But even though she listened for him coming out again she must have fallen into a restless sleep long before he came up the stairs to his own bed.

CHAPTER SIXTEEN

Hannah woke early and memories of the previous day soon beset her with their horrors. She dressed quickly intending to make the breakfast before Florence woke, but when she came out onto the landing she saw the door to Mr Duxbury's room was slightly open and his bed was empty. She went down the stairs expecting to find him asleep in his parlour, but when she gently opened the door and peeped inside there was no sign of him.

In the kitchen the water in the kettle was hot and the fire was burning well. He must have risen early without waking her and gone to see the magistrate. As Hannah brewed herself some fresh tea she felt grateful that he was trying to help her. It was so long since she'd had a man to turn to – and she knew how important it was when all the rules were made by men, and women were rarely listened to. Perhaps Colonel Fletcher would pay more heed to a mill manager than to the wife of a convict.

She wondered whether to go and see May, but there was the weekly wash to get on with and she was reluctant to shirk her tasks. Besides, she was eager to hear what Mr Duxbury had to say when he came back.

It was mid-morning when Hannah heard the front door open. She hurried in from the wash-house in the back yard where she had been mangling the towels and pegging them up to dry. She gazed at Mr Duxbury's face, trying to discern from his expression what sort of news he'd brought.

'Well?' she asked when he didn't immediately speak. 'What did the magistrate say?'

Mr Duxbury took off his hat before replying to her. 'It was as I thought,' he said as he sat down. 'Colonel Fletcher says that he cannot see any wrong has been done and that your children have good positions as apprentices. He said that your son has been sent to live with a family who work in his colliery and he will ask if you can visit him to be reassured of his welfare. But it will only be with their agreement, and they may not agree.'

'Is he to work in the coalmine?' asked Hannah. The prospect worried her. She hated to think of him spending his days deep underneath the earth, never seeing the sunshine or breathing any fresh air into his lungs. The mill would have been preferable, she thought, although that too had its dangers and she knew families who'd had children killed or badly maimed in both places. If Jack had been here, he would have kept the lad at home and taught him to weave. It didn't pay much these days, but it was an honest living and one where a man could rule himself rather than being beholden to the new factory owners whose only concern was making money so they could live in big houses and eat the meat that poor working people could never afford.

'He'll probably be employed opening and shutting the doors of the tunnels at first,' said Mr Duxbury. 'It's not too difficult.'

'He was learning to read and write in the workhouse,' said Hannah as she dried her hands on her apron. 'He was always keen to learn. He could have done better than be a coalminer.'

'I'd best get back,' said Mr Duxbury, picking up his hat from the table. 'I'll have to work through dinner time so don't expect me.'

Hannah felt guilty that she'd put him to any trouble. 'I'll bring you something,' she told him.

He nodded. 'Thank you,' he said with a glance at his daughter. He put on his hat and went back out, leaving Hannah alone in the kitchen. She wasn't surprised that Mr Duxbury had met with no help from the magistrate. All she could hope was that she would be allowed to see Edmund and find a way of getting him back into her own care.

At dinner time Hannah wrapped a dish of stew in a cloth and with Florence in one arm she took the path that led down to the spinning mill that looked almost the same as the drawings she'd seen in Ellis Duxbury's notebook. The stone building stood at the side of the Eagle Brook that cascaded down from the moorland to turn a huge wooden waterwheel. Florence laughed at the sound of the groaning wood and the splashing water as Hannah paused to watch for a moment before going inside, where she was taken aback, first by the familiar aroma of unspun cotton, and then by the noise of the machinery. She stood transfixed and watched as the huge machines rolled back and forth across the floor, spinning bobbin after bobbin of cotton as they went. It was incredible to her. She knew how long it took to fill a bobbin on a spindle, but these machines were filling dozens of them at once. She watched as the children working there ran in under the retreating machines with dustpans and brushes to sweep away the fluff that was being left on the floor and then ran quickly out again as the machines began to move towards them. Other children were exchanging filled bobbins for empty ones, while others took away the filled bobbins and brought in the cans of raw cotton to feed the hungry jennies.

'Can I help thee?' asked a man, turning momentarily from his work to fix her with a curious stare.

'I've brought some dinner for Mr Duxbury,' she shouted above the din.

'Up there.' He jerked his thumb towards some steps at the far end of the room and Hannah hurried away. At the top of the steps she found a room with a window that overlooked the workers. Mr Duxbury was sitting at a desk with papers spread across it, seeming engrossed. He looked up in surprise.

'Mrs Fisher!'

'I've brought your dinner,' she said wondering where to put the dish down.

'I'd forgotten that you'd said you would come,' he admitted as he cleared a space in front of him. 'And I'd lost track of the time.'

Hannah turned to look down at the workers as the noise suddenly stopped and the machines rolled to a halt.

'Dinner time,' he said as Hannah watched the workers reach into the pockets of their coats that were hanging on the wall and take out packages of food. They found stools or upturned cans to sit on and began to eat. The children sat down on the floor, amongst the cotton fluff that covered their clothes and their caps. Hannah thought they looked pale and exhausted and many of them coughed. She thought of Kitty and Ruth, but especially Kitty with her wheezing chest.

'Is it like this at Quarry Bank?' she asked.

'I expect so,' he said as he began to eat.

Hannah frowned as she imagined her daughters working around such machinery, which seemed to move of its own volition.

'It seems dangerous.'

'Only if you're careless,' replied Mr Duxbury.

Hannah shifted Florence to her other hip, wondering if he would allow his own daughter to work in such conditions. She doubted it.

'You'd better go,' said Mr Duxbury and Hannah realised that he was aware of some of the workers talking and glancing up at the window. 'I'll be back for my tea at seven o'clock,' he told her. 'Don't put Florence to bed until I've seen her.'

Hannah agreed. She knew that the child would be tired and fretful by that time and would probably cry, but it pleased her that Mr Duxbury was beginning to show some interest in his daughter.

She went back down the steps and her footfalls echoed on the stone floor of the quiet mill. It made her self-conscious and she was aware of the men's eyes following her as she walked to the door. She was glad to get out and walk back to the house.

As Hannah had feared, Florence was crying when Mr Duxbury came home.

'Is she unwell?' he asked, anxiously.

'No. She's just tired,' explained Hannah. 'You could try picking her up,' she suggested as she set plates out on the table.

Ellis Duxbury reached tentatively for the child and held her in his arms. Florence seemed so surprised that she fell silent and he sat down with her on his knee looking pleased. Hannah was glad. The baby needed to know her father. It would make Hannah feel less guilty when she left. And leave she must, she'd decided as she spent the afternoon changing the beds and dusting the rooms. After what she'd seen that morning, she had no intention of leaving Kitty or Ruth working in a cotton spinning mill or allowing Edmund to spend his days underground.

'Colonel Fletcher sent up a note to say you can visit your son on Sunday afternoon,' he told her. Hannah almost dropped the pot she was holding. 'Perhaps May will look after Florence again.'

'I'm sure she won't mind,' said Hannah eagerly. 'I'll go and ask her tomorrow.'

'I have to go into Bolton tomorrow on business,' he said. 'I thought you could walk with me and we could go to the market to buy some warm clothes and new boots for you.'

Hannah was grateful that he hadn't forgotten his offer. It would be a relief to have a shawl thick enough to keep her warm and boots to keep her feet dry – especially if she had to travel all the way to Cheshire to find her daughters.

Mr Duxbury had to go into the mill first thing the next morning, but he soon returned and Hannah was waiting for him with her basket and with Florence warmly dressed. They set off walking down the hill, the rising sun red on the horizon promising inclement weather to come.

'Let me carry her,' said Mr Duxbury after they'd covered the first mile, lifting his daughter from Hannah's arms. The child didn't protest and seemed happy enough to be with her father. And Hannah was glad to be relieved of her burden.

'I have some time before my meeting,' he explained. 'So we'll go to the market first. I'll arrange a cart for the heavier things. Maybe you could take some dinner with me and then ride back on it?' he suggested.

Hannah was happy at the thought of a ride home. She'd been wondering how she would walk back with her purchases and Florence to carry as well. But she felt uneasy about him asking her to eat dinner with him, although she wasn't sure how to refuse without seeming ungrateful and difficult.

The market was busy when they arrived. It was a familiar sight to Hannah and the familiarity of the stalls and the stallholders gave her a taste of normality – of the life she used to have before all her troubles began.

'I know the woman who deals in clothing,' Hannah told Mr Duxbury as she led the way through the crowded spaces between the stalls.

'I've not seen thee in a while,' said Mrs Holt as Hannah approached to look at what was available. She eyed Hannah's ragged appearance and then looked at her companion with the child in his arms. She was obviously intrigued but Hannah decided not to give her an explanation. It was none of her business.

'I need a warm shawl and some shoes,' Hannah told her as she began to rummage through the garments stacked on the wooden boards that constituted the stall.

'This one's lovely,' said Mrs Holt. 'New in. Looks hardly worn.' She held up the shawl. It was woven from good quality wool in a plaid pattern of muted colours that wouldn't show the dirt. Hannah thought that it was ideal. 'It's not even been patched,' said the stallholder as she spread it out for Hannah's inspection, all the time glancing at Mr Duxbury. 'I have some boots too. Came from the same place. I've put them on one side for a special customer.'

Hannah doubted that Mrs Holt thought she was a special customer. It was a long time since she'd been able to afford to buy any clothing and Hannah knew that she would say the same thing to anyone who came along, trying to make them think they were receiving some preferential treatment.

The boots were well soled and looked a good size. They were pretty too, with new laces and she hoped they would be comfortable if she had a long way to walk. Hannah knew that they and the shawl had probably belonged to someone who had died, but as long as they were clean and serviceable, Hannah knew that she must put the thought from her mind.

'What else does tha need?' asked Mrs Holt. 'I've some good gowns and petticoats,' she tempted her.

Hannah glanced at Mr Duxbury. She was reluctant to take advantage of his generosity and ask for too much.

'Choose whatever you need,' he told her. The stallholder raised an eyebrow and smirked. It was clear what she was thinking.

'Mr Duxbury is my employer,' Hannah said.

'Oh, aye,' grinned Mrs Holt as she laid out some gowns for perusal. 'Tha'll not get better anywhere. And I'll give thee a good price an' all,' she encouraged.

In the end, Hannah chose just one petticoat and two gowns. She was desperate for a some undergarments too, but was embarrassed to ask whilst Mr Duxbury was standing beside her. She hoped she might be able to ask for some red flannel from a different stall so that she could stitch herself a winter shift.

'Mrs Fisher will wear the shawl,' said Mr Duxbury as the woman began to parcel up the purchases with brown paper and string. He passed it to Hannah who gladly put it around her shoulders. The fierce wind predicted by the sunrise was circling the stalls and flapping the canvas covers, threatening rain.

Mr Duxbury continued to carry Florence who gazed around at all the stalls with curiosity in her big dark eyes. Hannah asked to buy some material to make new clothes for Florence.

'She's growing so fast now that she's eating solid food her things are getting a tight fit,' she explained.

Mr Duxbury was more than eager to make more purchases for his daughter and Hannah had no trouble getting sufficient linen and red flannel for her own needs as well. Afterwards they bought candles and soap and sacks of oatmeal and flour that were to be delivered to the carrier.

'Now,' said Mr Duxbury. 'I think it's time for

something to eat. You both look hungry,' he observed, smiling down at Hannah who was taking her turn to carry the baby.

'I can buy a pie and wait for the cart,' protested Hannah. She'd rarely been to an inn. Jack had never been much of a drinking man and the thought of it made her anxious.

'Nonsense,' said Mr Duxbury. 'I'm to meet a merchant in the Golden Lion at two so we've time to eat before then. The carrier won't go until three so there's no point you hanging around in the cold. Besides, we've little Florence to think of. We don't want her catching a chill.'

Hannah couldn't argue with his last point so she walked beside him, away from the stalls and onto Churchgate. The last time she'd walked down here it had been to see the Reverend Brocklehurst, the day he'd told her the parish would no longer pay her rent. It had only been a few weeks, yet it seemed an age ago, and the days when she'd had her own home and her children around her seemed like another lifetime.

The Golden Lion was crowded, noisy and smoky. There were men sitting around the tables, laughing and talking, but there were some women as well which made Hannah feel better. The landlord quickly found a table for them. 'Under the window,' he said. 'I've saved it for thee,' he told Mr Duxbury. 'What will tha have? There's mutton pie today, with cabbage and potatoes.'

'That sounds good. Two portions please. And

some bread and butter for the baby. Bring me a jug of ale and two cups,' he added.

Hannah sat down with Florence on her knee and tried to ignore the curious glances of the other diners. She couldn't remember ever having a cooked meal brought and set in front of her, and despite her misgivings she was determined to enjoy the treat.

CHAPTER SEVENTEEN

'I hear tha's causing a bit of talk,' said May when Hannah went across the road to see her the next morning.

'What dost tha mean?' she asked, puzzled.

'Visitin' Mr Duxbury down at t'mill,' replied May. 'Then goin' off to market together and him buyin' thee clothes, and then goin' in t' Golden Lion. Folk are sayin' as how he's got himself a fancy woman.'

'Do they not know I'm his housekeeper?' asked Hannah, feeling annoyed and wondering who May had been talking to.

'They say tha's too young and pretty for a housekeeper,' May told her.

Hannah felt uncomfortable and wondered if May gave the rumours any credence. 'Folk must be short of summat to talk about if they want to gossip about me,' she said.

'So there's nowt in it?' asked May.

'No. I needed some clothes and Mr Duxbury paid for them. It was wages,' she said. 'Nothing more. And I only took him his dinner down to the mill because he was workin' through after he'd done a favour for me.' May raised her eyebrows. 'He went to see Colonel Fletcher on my behalf about my children. And I'm grateful for it. I can see my Edmund on Sunday if tha'll have Florence for a while.' She paused. 'Or I'll take her with me if it's not convenient,' she added.

'There's no need to be sharp wi' me,' protested May. 'Sit thee down and I'll make some tea. I were only tellin' thee what were bein' said,' she grumbled as she filled the kettle.

'I'm sorry,' apologised Hannah. 'It touched a nerve.'

'I can see that,' said May. 'He's not been makin' advances has he?'

'No, of course not. He's a gentleman,' Hannah replied. She wondered whether to admit to her friend that Ellis Duxbury had suggested marriage but she decided to say nothing. He'd never mentioned the matter again, although Hannah was aware that he had treated her more as a friend than a housekeeper whilst they'd been in Bolton. It was no wonder people were speculating. She realised that she must be more careful.

When Sunday came Hannah dressed in her new clothes to go to the chapel and tried to ignore the glances and arm nudging that she noticed as she and Mr Duxbury sat down in their usual pew. Folk liked a bit of gossip, she thought. She was guilty of listening to similar stories about other people in the past, but it felt different now that she was the one who was being gossiped about.

Ellis Duxbury seemed oblivious to it all and Hannah hadn't repeated to him what May had said. She didn't want to admit that it had troubled her and she didn't want to elicit another proposal of marriage from him.

Florence was restless on her knee and after a while, Mr Duxbury took her onto his own lap to try to distract her and keep her quiet as the sermon went on at length. Afterwards as they came out of the church door and Mr Duxbury shook hands with the minister, Hannah groaned inwardly when he asked Ellis to wait a moment because he wanted a private word with him.

Hannah knew that it wasn't concerning the pony and trap. Mr Duxbury had already told her that she would have to walk down to Tonge for her visit with Edmund.

'I can't come with you,' he'd said. Hannah had nodded. She guessed that he would be taking his usual moorland walk that afternoon.

'Shall I go ahead and get the dinner ready?' asked Hannah now, eager to get the meal over with and set off to see her son. Every day of the week had seemed endless as she'd counted down the days to Sunday and she wanted to get there as soon as possible to spend time with Edmund.

'Yes, take Florence,' he said, handing her the child. 'I won't be long.'

Hannah hurried back and made the cold meat

sandwiches. She wondered if she should wait for Mr Duxbury but once the tea was brewed and he still hadn't come, she decided that she and Florence should eat.

He let the door slam behind him when he came in, making her jump. Florence began to cry, but Ellis Duxbury hardly looked at either of them. He sat down at the table and watched in silence as Hannah poured his tea. It was clear that whatever Mr Jones had said had annoyed him and Hannah worried that the minister might also have heard the gossip about them.

'I may be late back. Don't wait up,' he told her when he'd gobbled down a sandwich and drained his cup of tea. Hannah was glad when he went out. The atmosphere had been difficult.

She quickly tidied the table and took Florence across the road. May took the child in her arms and planted a kiss on the baby's cheek, making her chuckle with delight and an unexpected moment of jealousy swept through Hannah when she saw that the child was still so fond of May. She pushed the emotion aside. She mustn't become attached to the child, she told herself, not when it was clear that she must leave her behind to look for her own children.

'Don't worry about rushing back,' May said. 'She'll be just fine with me.'

Hannah strode out as she went down the hill. She could barely restrain herself from breaking into a run she was so eager to see her son, but it was a long walk into Tonge and she knew that she would be exhausted if she ran all the way.

Hannah found the cottage easily enough in the middle of a row of miners' cottages rented out to the workers by Colonel Fletcher. She could see the colliery wheel from the end of the street, but it was overhung by silence for the Sabbath day – the only time of the week it paused its work.

Hannah knocked on the door of number fifteen with her heart beating wildly. It was opened by a small man whose features were darkened by permanent lines of coal dust in the creases of his neck and forehead.

'I'm Mrs Fisher. Where's Edmund?' she demanded.

'Come in,' he said without a smile. 'He's in 'ere.'

Hannah stepped over the threshold of the cottage into a small room that was gloomy and lit only by an ample fire that blazed in the hearth. She supposed that working in the mine supplied a plentiful amount of fuel for the workers.

'This is t' wife, Mrs Grundy,' he told her.

Hannah barely glanced at the woman who was rocking in a chair by the hearth. All she could look at was her son. He was sitting on a low stool and had been employed polishing two pairs of boots with some dubbin and a rag. Hannah had expected him to rush straight into her arms but he didn't move and looked warily at Mr and Mrs Grundy. The woman gave a slight nod and it wasn't until then that he dropped the rag he was clutching in his hand and got up to cling to Hannah.

She put her arms around him and pressed him to her, bending to kiss his head. His short hair prickled her lips and her tears anointed him as she closed her eyes and breathed in the scent of him.

'Edmund,' she said. 'Oh, Edmund.' She released him to take his face between her palms and study him. His face too was grubby around the hairline and he was still thin and looked desperately pale as the flickering firelight emphasised the hollows of his cheeks.

'Hast tha come to take me home?' he asked hopefully.

'Oh Edmund.' Hannah bent to press her lips to his forehead. 'Not today. But soon,' she promised. 'Come outside,' she said, grasping his hand. She could see from his wariness that he would never tell her the truth about how he was being treated whilst he was in the same room as the Grundys.

She drew him to the door and led him away from the house to a patch of grass where she sat down and wrapped the shivering child under her shawl.

'Are they kind to thee?' she asked.

He shrugged slightly. 'They feed me,' he said. 'And I've a mattress to sleep on.' It was something, thought Hannah.

'What work's tha doin? Hast tha been down t' mine?' she asked him.

'Aye. We go down in a bucket,' he explained. 'It's a long way and very dark. It's hot down there an all. I work just in my pants. I have to push the cartloads of coal that Mr Grundy hacks from the wall and take it to the bucket that lifts it to the surface. It's very low and it makes my back hurt – and my legs,' he told her. 'And we're not even allowed a drink o' water. Sunday's th' only day I don't go down, but I have to go to Sunday School in the morning.'

'I'm so sorry, Eddie,' she told him, holding him close to her and feeling him flinch as she rubbed his back. 'I never agreed to this. I'd never have taken thee to t' workhouse if I'd known they were going to trick us like this. But I'll find a way to get thee away from here. I promise I will.'

They sat, locked in each other's arms until it began to go dark and, reluctantly, Hannah took Edmund back to the Grundys' cottage.

'I'll come to see him again,' she told Mr and Mrs Grundy.

'I dunno,' said Mr Grundy doubtfully. 'We were told it were just for today.'

Hannah didn't argue. She was determined that she would come again the next week and take Edmund away with her, whatever they said. She'd never agreed to this apprenticeship and she was determined that it shouldn't continue.

* * *

Hannah didn't sleep at all that night. In the end she gave up trying and sat up with the bolster propped behind her and her new, warm shawl around her shoulders. The images of Edmund's face would give her no peace. The child had been clearly frightened and confused, and she felt a failure as a mother because it was her role to protect him and she'd been unable to do that.

When she got out of bed to face the day she found that her legs were aching from her long walk and the new boots had made her toes sore. She dressed herself and went downstairs to wash her face, hoping that it might revive her. She wasn't looking forward to her long day caring for Florence and wondered if she might permit herself the luxury of a lie down when she put the baby for her nap after dinner. No one would know, she reasoned. Mr Duxbury never questioned her about the household affairs, and as long as his meals were on the table when he came home and he had a clean shirt to wear he seemed content.

'You look tired,' he observed when he came downstairs.

'I didn't sleep well,' she said.

'I hope I didn't wake you when I came in.'

'I wasn't asleep,' she said, remembering that it had been well past midnight before he came home. She'd wondered if he'd been drinking, but his footsteps had been steady and this morning he showed no signs of having imbibed too much. It was her with the thumping head and aching eyes.

'How was your son?' he asked as he picked up a spoon to eat his oatmeal.

'He . . .' Hannah felt grief overwhelm her and she fought down the urge to cry. 'He was tired and upset. He wanted me to take him away from there.'

Mr Duxbury nodded. 'I can understand it. It's hard – for both of you,' he said. Hannah turned away to wipe her eyes. How could he possibly understand?

When he had gone, she dressed and fed Florence and washed the dishes. She knew she should be getting on with the laundry but she hadn't the energy for it, and she was debating whether she could get away with leaving it until the next day when she heard the knock on the front door. Hannah groaned. A visitor was the last thing she wanted. She rolled down her sleeves before she went to answer it and found the Reverend Jones standing on the narrow footpath with his hat in his hand and a ponderous expression on his face.

'May I come inside, Mrs Fisher?'

Hannah stood back for him to enter and he closed the door behind him and followed her through to the kitchen.

'Sit down,' she said. 'Would you like some tea?'

'I don't want to keep you from your work,' he said, as he settled himself, 'but I do have some concerns that I feel I must discuss with you.'

Hannah spooned some tea into the pot and filled it from the kettle she kept on the hob. She suspected that she knew what this was going to be about.

'I spoke to Mr Duxbury yesterday,' said the clergyman, 'about some of the rumours that are circulating in the village.'

'I wouldn't give any credence to rumours,' Hannah told him as she set the tea to brew.

'Yes, that's what Mr Duxbury said. But as I told him, there's no smoke without fire, so to speak, and I wonder if, perhaps, there needs to be more care taken over your behaviour.'

'My behaviour?' she asked him.

'I heard that you've been visiting your employer at his place of work.'

'I took Mr Duxbury his dinner one day.'

'And that you were seen dining with him in a public house.'

'He bought us some dinner after we'd been to market.'

'To buy you clothing?'

'Yes,' Hannah agreed. 'All I had were rags.'

The minister frowned and Hannah turned to arrange the cups and saucers. She was sorry that she'd offered him tea and was hoping that he would refuse and say that he had to go on his way, but he accepted the cup she poured and stirred in the sugar.

'The trouble is, Mrs Fisher,' he went on, 'that these sorts of things can be misinterpreted. And no matter how innocent they may seem to you, others view them differently.' His spoon clattered on the saucer and he raised the cup to take a sip. 'You need to be careful of your reputation, being a woman alone, living in the same house as a single man. It is bound to cause talk if you are seen to be overfamiliar with your employer.'

Hannah, who had remained standing, grasped at the back of one of the chairs at the table to steady herself.

'There is no overfamiliarity between me and Mr Duxbury,' she assured him.

'I'm sure there isn't. I didn't come to accuse you of anything, Mrs Fisher, only to point out the necessity for you to take more care of your conduct.' His words made Hannah's temper flare. He sounded as if he were accusing her of doing something wrong. 'The temptations of the flesh are strong,' he went on. 'You must pray to be delivered from them.'

It was on the tip of Hannah's tongue to ask if he had asked Mr Duxbury to pray as well, but she choked back the words. She knew that if she spoke she wouldn't be able to hold back the tirade of anger she was feeling.

The minister put his cup down and reached for his hat. 'I've kept you from your chores for too long,' he apologised. 'But I hope you will take note of my advice. Do nothing to draw attention to yourself and stay out of public houses. They are not suitable places for a woman, or a child,' he added, nodding his head towards Florence.

He settled the hat onto his head and bade her

a good day. Hannah followed him up the lobby and shut the door firmly behind him before turning to rest her back against it for a moment. The last thing she needed today was an extra sermon, she thought. And the sooner she left this house the better.

CHAPTER EIGHTEEN

Hannah fretted about Edmund all week, imagining him toiling under the ground with Mr Grundy and not returning home until very late, tired and thirsty. She doubted that he was receiving much care from Mrs Grundy either. The woman had seemed morose and unused to children. To them, Edmund was nothing more than a means to help them earn more wages.

She'd longed to go and rescue her son straight away, but she knew that her best chance would come on Sunday when Edmund was sent to the Sunday School at Tonge Fold.

When the morning came she sat down at the breakfast table and told Mr Duxbury that she was feeling poorly.

'I can't go to the chapel today,' she moaned, feigning a stomach ache with her hand clutched to her belly. 'You'll have to take Florence and go alone.'

She felt guilty at the look of concern on Mr Duxbury's face. 'Shall I send for a doctor?' he asked.

'No. I'll be all right shortly. It's just a belly ache.'

'If you're sure.' He hovered beside her and Hannah thought that he was going to put a hand on her shoulder, but he drew back.

'I'll lie down for a bit,' she told him. 'Florence is washed and dressed.'

As soon as Mr Duxbury agreed, Hannah hurried up to her bedroom and closed the door. She sat on the edge of the bed and waited until she heard him go out, then she picked up the bundle of clothing that she'd packed the previous night and crept back down the stairs. She felt guilty about taking the new clothes. She would have paid for them if she'd had any money to leave, but she knew that she would probably freeze to death without the shawl and boots.

She went to the shelves in the kitchen where the food was kept. She'd put a little aside from each meal during the week and she packed the oatcakes, the bread, some cheese, and apples from the trees in the yard into her bundle. Then she left her door key on the table, went out of the house onto the deserted street and set off down the hill towards Tonge.

The little schoolroom was familiar to Hannah. She'd passed it many times. She pulled the shawl closely around her head, to conceal her face and clutched her bundle close. Although there were only a few people about, she didn't want to draw attention to herself. She thought the class would finish about half past eleven to allow the children time to go home for their dinner. The church clock had already chimed eleven so she hoped she wouldn't have long to wait.

She walked up and down the street, trying to look as if she was on an errand, and every time she passed the schoolroom she looked at the red painted door, willing it to open. At last, she heard a sound and Hannah watched as the children came out. None of them ran like healthy children should. They stumbled and shuffled, some limping, some bowed over and many coughing. They were small and pale and malnourished and their clothing was mostly rags. Edmund looked no better than the rest when she caught sight of him. He wandered away from the others and sat down on a low wall.

'Eddie! Edmund!' she called urgently to attract his attention. He looked up at the sound of her voice and she gestured him to come to her. With a wary glance around he stood up. 'Quickly!' she urged him. 'We must go.'

Once he realised that she'd come to take him away, a wide smile lit his face and he hurried to her and she hugged him.

'Come on,' she said, 'before someone sees us.'

They bent low as they made their way past the stone wall that surrounded the churchyard, so that they wouldn't be seen. When they were clear, Hannah grasped hold of Edmund's hand and they began to run until he pleaded with her to allow him to rest.

He was clutching at a pain in his side and breathing fast as they stopped to catch their breath for a moment on the road that led south out of Bolton towards Manchester. It was Hannah's intention to get well clear of the town before nightfall and try to find some shelter so that they could continue their journey to Quarry Bank Mill the next morning to rescue her daughters.

'Come on,' she urged, glancing behind them. 'Just a bit further.' The Grundys would surely have missed Edmund by now and might come searching for him or even alert the constable that he had run away.

They walked on for a while longer until Hannah judged that they were well clear of the town. There were fields around them now and the houses were fewer. They trudged on down the lane until it began to grow dark.

'Are we going to walk all night?' asked Edmund.

'No,' Hannah reassured him. 'We'll lose our way in the dark. We'll find somewhere to rest soon. I've brought some food,' she told him, hoping to tempt him to go a bit further.

At last she saw that he was exhausted. He could barely take each step and he seemed unsteady on his feet. Hannah looked around for a safe place to wait until morning. There was a farmhouse nearby, but she didn't dare approach it so she led Edmund away from the track into a field of sheep. It was surrounded by a hedgerow and she found a place where the branches overhung the grass. It would shelter them a little if it began to rain.

They sat down on the damp ground and Hannah

wrapped herself and Edmund in the shawl as best she could. She took some of the food from her bundle and they both ate until Edmund fell asleep with his head in her lap.

The branches of the hedge were poking into her back and she thought that she would never get comfortable, but after a while she must have dozed off herself. She woke with a start when a tawny owl answered its mate with a familiar *twoo* call. She could hear a sheep nearby, tearing at the grass and she hoped it wouldn't come too close.

Edmund shifted in his sleep but didn't wake as she tried to find a more comfortable position. The sky above them had cleared and she could count the stars, but there wasn't enough moonlight to continue. She would have to wait for first light, she thought, and then they would press on.

As soon as Hannah was able to distinguish the features of the hedges and distant houses, she woke Edmund and they shared the rest of the food she'd brought. Then she stood up and brushed down her wet skirts. Edmund was shivering and she wished that she had a jacket for him. The best she could do was to shelter him under her shawl as he walked close beside her.

It was still quiet when they set off but as they walked on she met one or two carts coming towards her, laden with goods for the market. She kept her eyes down and wished that she could have concealed her face but that would have meant taking the shawl from around her son.

'Is it far?' asked Edmund.

'It's a good walk,' she told him. She wasn't sure how far it was herself, or what she would do when she got there, but having one child with her gave her the determination to find the others.

Hannah pulled Edmund into the side of the road as she heard hooves approaching from behind, but rather than passing her by she heard the hoofbeats slow as the trap drew level with her.

'Hannah!'

She looked up in alarm at the sound of Mr Duxbury's voice. Her heart was beating wildly and she held Edmund even closer. How had he managed to find her?

'Hannah!' he repeated. 'Where are you going?'

She didn't stop, but kept on walking with her eyes downcast, thinking that if she didn't answer he might think he had mistaken some other woman for her.

'Hannah! Please stop!' he called again as he matched the pony's pace to hers. 'Climb up into the trap. I need to talk to you.'

Hannah kept walking, wishing that he would go away and hoping that he wasn't going to tell her that she was a thief to leave with her new clothes and the food from his kitchen.

'Hannah, I'm not going away,' he warned her. 'Get into the trap. I'll take you home and we can talk about this.'

Hannah shook her head.

'See sense, woman!' he called to her. 'Where do you think you're going?'

Hannah pressed her lips together and glanced ahead of her, hoping that she might see a path that led across the fields so that she could get away from him.

'Hannah. Please stop. Let's talk,' he said.

'There's nothing to say,' she replied at last. 'Leave me alone.'

'Where are you going?' he asked.

'Quarry Bank.'

'But it's nigh on twenty miles away,' he warned her. 'And what will you do when you get there?' Hannah didn't reply. He must realise that she was going to find her daughters. 'The lad can't walk that far. He looks exhausted. Get in the trap,' he urged her again.

Hannah glanced down at her son, who was watching Mr Duxbury.

'Is he going to take me to prison for running away?' Edmund asked.

'No. Of course not,' she said. 'Just keep walking. He'll go away in a minute.'

'I'm going nowhere,' said Mr Duxbury as he reined in the pony and jumped down. He took hold of the bridle and the pony broke into a trot as he hurried to catch her up and fall into step beside her. 'I'll walk all the way with you if I have to,' he warned.

'There's nowt tha can do to help me,' she told him, 'except leave me alone.'

'Don't be stupid!' She was startled at his tone. 'You can't survive like this!' he said. 'The constables are already looking for your son. And when they find you, you'll be charged with child stealing. What do you think will happen when you come before the magistrate?' he demanded. 'Fletcher will send you to the prison in Lancaster for certain. Do you want that to happen?'

Hannah met his eyes and saw for the first time how concerned he was for her. She was surprised by the intensity of the feelings evident in his worried face.

'Get in the trap. Please,' he added. 'I'll take you home and I'll do everything in my power to protect you and make things right. I promise.'

'You can't,' she told him. 'It's nothing to do with you.'

'I'll not see you go to prison!' he told her. 'I'll take you back by force rather than allow that to happen.' His eyes were blazing with determination as he grasped hold of her wrist.

'Mam?' said Edmund. He looked terrified.

'It's all right,' she reassured him. 'This man means us no harm.'

'Then you'll come with me?'

Hannah realised that Ellis Duxbury was not going to be thwarted. She wasn't sure what his reasons were for pursuing her, but it was clear he was not going to give up and there was no way that she could get away from him. Left with no choice, she nodded her head and allowed him to help her up onto the seat. Edmund climbed up beside her and she wrapped her shawl around them.

Mr Duxbury turned the pony and then got up beside her. The miles she'd travelled on foot were quickly recovered, and as the sun rose in the winter morning sky they reached Bolton and then headed towards Egerton with Hannah worried and unsure about what the future might hold.

Ellis Duxbury said nothing more as they drove back. When they reached his house, he tied up the pony and unlocked the door.

'Is Florence with May?' Hannah asked as she walked into the empty kitchen.

'Yes. You can fetch her in a minute,' said Mr Duxbury. He hesitated. 'You won't go, will you?' he asked. 'You won't run off again whilst I take the trap back?'

'No,' she said. She thought that even if she'd wanted to, she would never summon the energy.

'Good. I won't be long.'

Hannah sat down and wondered what he would tell the minister about her. And what would May think? If she'd been the subject of gossip before then this could only have made it a hundred times worse, she realised. So why had Ellis Duxbury brought her back? It was his own reputation that was being damaged as well, she realised.

'Is this where we're to stay?' asked Edmund as he looked around the kitchen.

'For the time being,' said Hannah as she roused

herself to add coal to the fire and put the kettle on to boil. For now at least she could ensure that her son was warm and well fed.

When Ellis Duxbury came back, Edmund had fallen asleep, curled in the chair by the fire.

'What did Mr Jones say?' she asked him.

'He lectured me that if you were to remain then I must do the right thing.'

'Right thing?'

'He says we must be married before any more scandal is caused.' Ellis Duxbury looked at her. 'He's right, Hannah,' he said. 'You must marry me. It's the only way I'll be able to protect you.'

Hannah was about to protest that it wasn't possible, but all she could do was shake her head.

'Listen to me,' said Ellis Duxbury as he drew up one of the chairs from the table rather than disturb Edmund. 'If you marry me, I can protect you and your children. Your son can stay here. I'll go to see the Grundys and I'll pay them off if necessary. They will have received a generous payment from the workhouse to take Edmund on, so they'll not be out of pocket and I'll get them to sign a paper to say that your son wasn't suitable.'

Relief flooded through Hannah as she listened to his words. He was a good and generous man and she was lucky to have found him, she thought, but she couldn't marry him.

'And I promise that I will take you to visit your daughters,' he went on.

'Will you let them come here as well? Hannah asked.

'If Mr Greg agrees to let them go. But I'm sure he will see reason when we explain that it was not your choice and you signed the papers without knowing what they said.'

He made it sound so tempting, thought Hannah. The prospect of living in this warm and well-furnished house with her children around her and all the food and clothing they needed was something she could only have dreamt of a few months ago. She knew that she ought to be thankful for her good fortune, but still she couldn't overcome her doubts.

'Why?' she asked him. 'Why do you want to do all this for me?'

He looked uncomfortable. 'I . . . I want to help you,' he said. 'I want you to stay and care for Florence – and for me.'

Hannah watched his face. He looked uncomfortable and there were no words of love or even affection in his proposal. He made it sound as if it was one of his business deals. It was very different from when Jack had asked her to marry him. They'd been walking home from the summer fair at Tonge. Hannah had been holding his hand and carrying her bonnet in the other. Her hair had fallen loose around her shoulders and she'd been laughing at some story he'd told.

'I love thee,' Jack had said. 'Let's get wed.'

'Aye, let's!' she'd replied and he'd picked her up and swung her round in his arms until they were both dizzy and fell in a heap on the grass, kissing and spinning.

Hannah looked at Ellis Duxbury. He was brooding on the chair and studying his hands as if something troubled him. After a moment he looked up and met her eyes.

'Say you'll marry me, Hannah,' he said. 'Otherwise what will you do?'

It was the question that was troubling her. She'd tried to help herself and her children but it seemed that everything was set against her, and his warning that she might be accused of child stealing frightened her. And he might not keep his promise to pay off the Grundys if she didn't agree to his proposal. He had no reason to.

'You'll not be able to stay on otherwise,' he continued. 'I don't think the Reverend Jones will stand for it – and the man has influence in the village. I don't think I could go against his wishes.'

Hannah thought that Ellis Duxbury could. She thought he was a man who knew his own mind, but she also knew he was using every wile he could think of to persuade her to agree.

'I couldn't love you,' she said. 'I still love Jack.'

'I know,' he said. 'I'll not press for an answer now,' he conceded. 'I'll leave you to think about it. But you will need to decide quickly.'

He reached for his hat and went off to the mill and after Hannah had given Edmund some bread and jam, she tucked him into her bed upstairs to rest and went across the road to collect

Florence. She could see that May was curious but she didn't confide in her friend, simply telling her that she'd been to collect her son.

'Tha must be glad to have him back,' said May. 'It were generous of Mr Duxbury to allow it, and for him to miss his work to take out the minister's trap to collect thee.'

Hannah could see that her friend was suspicious about what had happened, but she didn't want to say more. 'Aye,' she agreed. 'I'm grateful to him. I'd best get back.'

She picked up Florence and left May to ponder on what had really happened that morning. She was well aware that folk would talk even more now and that the only way she could stop them, and get her children back, was to agree to marry Ellis Duxbury.

That night, as she lay awake listening to the familiar sound of her son asleep beside her, Hannah weighed up her choices for a long time after she heard Mr Duxbury come up the stairs and close the door to his room. Would he expect her to sleep in his bed with him if they were married? Could she respond to his demands? She shuddered at the prospect, but then she thought of Ruth and Kitty working in the cotton mill and of Kitty, pale and coughing. Hannah realised that she was being selfish. Agreeing to marry Ellis Duxbury was the least she could do to protect her children. She must put her own feelings aside and tell him in the morning that her answer was yes.

CHAPTER NINETEEN

When Hannah had told Ellis Duxbury that she would marry him he'd smiled briefly and said that he would speak to the minister to make the arrangements. Then he'd gone to work. Hannah had felt it was an anti-climax after her fretful night. But now that the morning of the wedding was here, just a week later, she wished that there was a way she could avoid it.

Her wedding to Jack had taken place on a warm summer's day at the parish church in Bolton. She'd had a cotton gown with flowers printed on it, a straw bonnet with blue ribbons and a posy picked from the hay meadow. Today she was dressed in a dark-brown gown over a blue petticoat with a plain white neckerchief and the laced boots Ellis Duxbury had bought for her at the market. He'd given a warm, red, woollen cloak with a hood as a wedding gift and a new black silk bonnet. There were no flowers but Ellis had given her a prayer-book to carry that he'd told her had belonged to his mother.

The chapel felt even colder than the frosty air

outside as she walked in, her legs trembling at each step. With Edmund beside her, she walked towards the altar where the minister and her future husband were waiting for her. Ellis Duxbury smiled encouragingly as she approached, and even though Hannah felt that it was wrong and that she was being unfaithful to Jack, she knew she had no choice if she was to rescue her daughters and provide for them and Edmund.

May and her husband had come to witness the marriage and to hold Florence during the ceremony, and there were a handful of other neighbours driven by curiosity in the pews behind them. Reverend Jones gabbled through the words in his prayerbook at speed, barely pausing to hear Hannah's responses and didn't even seem to notice when she stumbled and hesitated over the vows. He seemed intent on getting the wedding completed before anyone could make an objection.

'I now pronounce you man and wife,' he said and Ellis took Hannah's hand in his. She glanced down at the wedding ring he had put on her finger. It would never be as precious to her as the one Jack had given her, which was now hanging on a string that was concealed by her neckcloth.

Ellis briefly brushed his lips over her cheek. May came forward to return Florence to them and there were a few murmured congratulations, but apart from the Reverend Jones shaking her new husband by the hand at the church door there was no fuss and within five minutes they were back in their own kitchen, Hannah taking off her new bonnet and Ellis hanging up his jacket and rolling up his shirt sleeves to add more coal to the fire.

'Is that it?' asked Edmund as he watched them. He had clearly expected more.

'Aye, that's it,' Hannah told him.

'What about my daddy?' he asked.

Hannah shook her head and turned away to wipe a stray tear from her face. 'Mr Duxbury will be your father now,' she told him. She glanced at Ellis to gain his approval. He nodded.

'I'll look after thee,' he told Edmund before sitting down on his chair and waiting for Hannah to put the dinner on the table. He'd already told her that he needed to be back at his work by one o' clock.

When he'd gone, and Florence was asleep, Hannah tried to explain to Edmund that he would probably never see his father again.

'Is he dead?' asked Edmund.

'Everyone says that he is. And we've heard nothing. We've had no letters from him.'

'I don't believe it,' said Edmund.

Hannah reached out a hand to cup his face in her palm. He was so small and thin, although he was cleaner than when she'd seen him at the Grundys' house. She'd asked Ellis to carry in the tin bath that hung outside in the yard and she'd filled it with hot water and scrubbed every vestige of coal dust and grime from her son's emaciated body. But she didn't reply to Edmund because she didn't believe that Jack was dead either, even though she'd begun to admit that she would never see him again. She hoped that he was well and that he was happy and that he could make a life for himself on the other side of the world. He deserved that even if he didn't deserve to be sent there in the first place.

'Mr Duxbury will be kind to us,' she told her son. 'He'll find thee work at his mill and he's promised that he'll take us to see Ruth and Kitty, and we'll bring them home if we can. We'll be a family again,' she promised.

Edmund shrugged his bony shoulders. 'It won't be the same,' he replied and Hannah knew that he was right, but it was the best she could offer him and she hoped that as he grew up and understood their situation better, he would realise that she had done the right thing.

She began to wash the dinner pots and Edmund sat brooding by the fire. Hannah wished that she could distract him, but it had begun to pour down with rain outside and he still didn't have a proper coat to wear. She knew that he would love to sit and look at some of the books that Ellis had in his parlour but she didn't want to make her husband angry by going in there to borrow one. She might be his wife now, but she didn't feel any closer to him and not much had changed in their relationship.

That night, after she'd settled the children to sleep in her bedroom, she went downstairs to find

Ellis sitting by the fire. He smiled at her. 'Come and sit down,' he said.

Hannah settled uneasily onto the chair opposite to him, wondering what he wanted to say.

'I won't press you to come to my bed, Hannah,' he told her. 'I know it's all been a bit . . . sudden.' He reached across and took her hand. 'I know you don't love me,' he said, 'but I hope that some affection may grow between us and I'll not spoil it by imposing myself on you.'

Hannah let out the breath that she'd been holding. She thought she'd probably been holding it for a week or more, dreading the moment when her wedding night would come. She fought back her tears of relief.

Ellis squeezed her hand. 'Don't cry,' he said. 'I've made us a pot of tea,' he added.

Hannah leaned back against her cushion and clasped her hot drink between her cold fingers. The rain had turned to sleet outside and it was bitterly cold with a keen northerly wind making an unwelcome incursion beneath the door and blowing down the lobby. How on earth would she have managed on a night like this if she'd taken her children onto the streets, she wondered. They would probably have been frozen stiff in some doorway by morning. As it was she was sitting by a good fire and her face was warm even if her back was still cold. And Edmund was safe upstairs, tucked under adequate blankets. Her daughters would be out of the weather too.

‘I hope they have warm beds at Quarry Bank,’ she said, voicing her thoughts.

‘I’m sure they have. We will go,’ Ellis promised her. ‘I haven’t forgotten. And in the meantime I’ll set Edmund on as a little piecer. There’s a Mr Mather at the mill who could do with a lad, and he’s kindly and patient and he’ll teach him.’

‘Jack wanted him to go to school,’ said Hannah.

‘Then I’ll see about him spending an hour or two in school,’ said Ellis. ‘A bit of book learning will do him no harm.’

Hannah thought again about the books in the parlour and how she wanted to show them to Edmund, but she didn’t feel brave enough to ask Ellis’s permission yet. It was early days, she thought, but perhaps she could learn to accept him – maybe go to his bed one night. But not tonight. She was tired and she wanted to be alone with her thoughts, because her thoughts were all of Jack.

CHAPTER TWENTY

Snow fell heavily that night and was piled high against the walls the next morning. Ellis got up early and dug a narrow path down to the privy and threw some ashes on it to stop it freezing over. Hannah was grateful. She hadn't wanted to use the pot with Edmund in the same room and she was bursting for a wee.

It was Edmund's first morning at the mill and he seemed excited to be going. Hannah was glad that he had boots but she had to wrap an old blanket around him to keep him warm.

'We'll get him a coat and a cap from the market,' said Ellis as they set off. 'I'll not have it said that a lad of mine isn't decently clad.' Hannah felt a rush of pleasure at his words, at his acceptance of Edmund as his responsibility, but she was aware that she owed him a huge debt for what he was doing for her and that before too long she would have to overcome her reticence and be a proper wife to him.

She spent the morning doing her usual chores. She hung some washing to dry on the rack over the fire and pegged the rest up in the outhouse, but it was so cold in there that Ellis's shirts froze, hanging stiffly as if they were being worn by some invisible being. Hannah kept Florence close to the fire on the rag rug, but watched the child carefully to make sure she didn't try to touch the flames that fascinated her. She'd forgotten how much a baby needed watching once they began to crawl about on their own, and Florence was curious about everything.

'Come to Hannah,' she told the child after a while, picking her up and sitting her in the little chair with the tray attached. It was a useful contraption, she thought, that kept her in one place. Florence laughed and grabbed hold of a stray strand of Hannah's hair. Hannah prised her strong little fingers away and kissed the child's head, wondering if she ought to teach the baby to call her something else now that she was her step-mother. Perhaps she should speak to Ellis about it. She didn't want to offend him or the memory of his first wife.

A little after noon, Ellis and Edmund came back for their dinner. Hannah heard them knocking the snow off their boots at the front door before they came in. Edmund's cheeks looked pink and his eyes were bright even though his hands were ice-cold when she touched them.

'Was it all right?' she asked. She didn't tell him that she'd been fretting about him all morning, wondering if he'd had to scurry in under the moving machinery like the children she'd seen.

'Aye, it were all right,' he said as he eyed the pan of stew that was bubbling on the hob, filling the house with an appetising smell. 'I have to mend the cotton threads when they break. It's not hard,' he added.

'I've fetched the milk so there's no need to take Florence out in this,' said Ellis as he took the kit into the pantry and put it on the stone shelf. There was no need to worry about it turning bad in this weather, thought Hannah as she spooned the stew onto plates for them to sit down and eat together. It still seemed a bit odd and she had to keep reminding herself that she was Ellis's wife now and not his housekeeper.

'The lad did well,' he told her. 'Mr Mather's pleased with him. He says he's a quick learner and good with his hands.'

Edmund grinned as he ate and Hannah felt a rush of pride in her son, and relief that he had not proved a disappointment. If he worked hard and behaved himself then Ellis would not be sorry that he had taken him in.

It was a relief to Hannah to have her son taken care of, but she remained desperately worried about her daughters. The winter weather would do Kitty's chest no good and Hannah wished she could have her lasses here as well. But the bad weather showed no sign of letting up. The snow kept coming down and adding layer upon layer to what was already lying on the ground before it had time to melt, and the path down to the privy was now bordered on either side by a wall of black speckled ice.

As he'd promised, Ellis bought a coat and cap for Edmund, and her son began to put on some weight and lose the hollow-faced look that Hannah had grown used to over the years. Florence thrived in her care and Ellis continued to be kind and made no demands of her, although on some evenings he still retreated to his parlour and on Sunday afternoons, after chapel, he would stand and gaze out of the window at the falling flurries of snow and sigh about not being able to go for his walk on the moors. Hannah was surprised by how much he missed the outings.

'You can go when the weather improves,' she ventured one Sunday. 'Perhaps we could all go.'

'No!' Hannah looked up in surprise at the dismay in his voice. 'No,' he said again, more softly. 'I like to walk alone.'

Hannah didn't reply. She presumed that she was right in her assumption that he went to visit his wife's grave and it was something he was not willing to share with her.

'Can we go to Quarry Bank once the snow melts?' she asked, her thoughts turning to Ruth and Kitty as she wondered how they were spending their afternoon. She was desperate to see them and worried that if more snowfalls came and Christmas approached, it could be months before they went. 'I worry about them,' she added. 'I need to know that they're being properly cared for.'

'Yes.' He frowned. 'I know how it feels,' he remarked, though Hannah doubted that he did.

Another week passed before the thaw set in and the roads, although slushy, were passable and Ellis agreed that they could go to Quarry Bank.

'I'll hire a horse and cart from the stables,' he said as they sat beside the fire, listening to the steady drip of the meltwater outside the house, 'because I'm not sure how agreeable the minister will be to lending us his trap when I tell him that we'll have to set off very early on Sunday morning and miss chapel. Besides,' he went on, 'it may be the better option. The trap would be too small to fetch both thy lasses home in.'

Relief flooded through Hannah at hearing that Ellis did intend to bring Ruth and Kitty back with them. She'd been afraid that he would think a visit was enough to reassure her of their well-being.

'They might as well earn their keep here as work for Mr Greg,' he said. 'Besides, I want you to be happy Hannah. I truly do.' He reached out for her hand and clasped it. 'I think it's time you were a true wife to me,' he told her. 'I've been patient for long enough.'

So this was his bargain, thought Hannah as she felt the intense pressure of his strong hand around hers.

‘Come to my bed tonight, Hannah,’ he said and although she thought that he may have intended to make it sound like a request, Hannah knew it was a command.

When she took her candle upstairs she looked in on Florence and Edmund. Both were sleeping soundly. Downstairs, she could hear Ellis drawing the bolts on the doors and moments later his steps came up and he paused on the landing.

‘Hannah?’

‘I’m coming,’ she said as she gently closed the door to her bedroom. She stepped across the landing and into Ellis’s room. It was familiar enough. She came in most days to dust around and once a month she changed the bedding.

He was undressing quickly. There was no fire up here and she could see his breath on the cold air. He got into bed wearing his shirt and pulled the blankets around him as he watched her. Hannah took off her apron and gown and her stays. She peeled off her stockings and tucked them into her boots, then got in beside him wearing nothing but a red flannel petticoat.

‘It’ll be nice to have the warmth of another body on a night like this,’ he told her as he put an arm around her. ‘I’ve missed the warmth of it.’

Hannah found it hard to respond to him, but she made no protest. Think of Kitty, think of Ruth, she chanted to herself in her head. She was doing this for them.

It wasn’t like it had been with Jack. Ellis was

gentle with her but she took no pleasure in it and was relieved when it was over and he settled down beside her with a sigh. Hannah lay still so as not to disturb him. Her feet were like ice and if she had been in bed with Jack, she would have put them on his legs to warm them. He would have protested and they would have laughed and he would have pulled her close so that they could sleep in one another's arms. With Ellis, she gradually moved away towards the edge of the bed so that they weren't touching. He said nothing and Hannah thought that he was already asleep, but she lay awake for a while longer in the unfamiliar bed and listened to the wind howling around the eaves. He would expect her to sleep here every night from now on, she realised, so she had better get used to it.

Hannah was up before him the next morning. She dressed without disturbing him, went carefully down the slippery path to the privy and then began to make a pot of tea before waking Edmund. When Ellis came down, he didn't mention the night before. He didn't kiss her cheek or pinch her bottom like Jack would have. It was as if nothing had changed between them.

It was Saturday and when he came in at dinner time he told her that the roads looked passable and that he had arranged to collect a cart early on Sunday morning.

'Thank you,' said Hannah. She could barely believe that she had only another day to wait until she saw Ruth and Kitty again; one more day before she could bring them home.

It was still dark on the Sunday morning when Hannah heard the cart wheels outside the door. She picked up the parcel of food she'd wrapped in a cloth so that they could eat on the way. Ellis had warned her that it was a long journey, but she didn't care. She would have travelled to the edge of the earth to bring her children home.

Edmund was yawning beside her. She felt sorry for him. He'd worked hard all week and it was a shame he needed to get up so early. She had suggested he stay behind with May, who'd agreed to mind Florence, but he wouldn't hear of it. He was as keen to see his sisters as she was.

When she went to the door she saw there was a piebald horse between the shafts with a long mane and feathered feet. He tossed his head and turned to look at her from behind his blinkers. He looked strong and eager. The cart looked sturdy too. There was a long bench seat and plenty of room in the back. Ellis was standing beside it with a lamp on the end of the long pole.

'You and Edmund will have to take turns holding this,' he told her, 'until there's enough daylight to see safely.'

He locked the door and they climbed up, Edmund sitting between them and eagerly taking the first turn with the lamp.

'What's the horse called?' he asked.

'Patch,' replied Ellis. It wasn't very imaginative, thought Hannah as they set off with a creaking of harness and grinding of wheels. She wondered how many of the neighbours had been woken by their noise and had slipped from their warm beds to peep out at them, curious as to what they were up to and where they were going. She quelled a sudden urge to wave.

The moon was up and frost glinted on what remained of the ice at the sides of the road. It would give a hard surface for the wheels and as long as they didn't slip it was better than the weather warming and turning the roads to mud.

Daylight came slowly as they drove through Bolton and headed south. She didn't ask if Ellis knew the way but he seemed confident of which road to take. She relieved Edmund of the lantern and turned to put it in the back of the cart as the monochrome dawn turned to day. Hints of colour appeared here and there as the sky lightened to an icy blue and they passed by farmhouses where dogs barked at them and farmers' wives glanced out from their doorways to see who was passing by so early on a Sunday morning.

After a while she unwrapped the bread and cheese and they ate as Patch pulled them along. There was no sign of snow as they drove around the outskirts of Manchester and down into Cheshire, the sun rising as high on the horizon in front of them as it would go before dipping away again to plunge the country into another long, dark night.

'We won't have time to linger,' warned Ellis. 'I'll ask them to feed Patch and let him rest for a while, but it'll be a difficult journey back if we leave it too late.'

Hannah nodded. She had no intention of lingering at Quarry Bank. All she wanted was to get Ruth and Kitty away from there.

At last, with the help of a man they passed walking in the opposite direction, they found the lane that led down to the mill. At the end of it, nestled in the valley, was a tall, brick-built building, with row upon row of windows. Beyond it there was a field where a group of lads were laughing and shouting as they kicked a football. Hannah stared around, trying to see if Ruth and Kitty were about, but there was no sign of them or any other girls and Hannah hoped that they'd arrived at the right place.

Ellis pulled up the cart in the mill yard as some of the children crowded curiously around.

'Where can I find Mr Greg?' he asked them.

'Up at th' 'ouse,' said one with a jerk of his thumb. Hannah looked up at the mansion that overlooked the riverbank. 'Tha should 'ave taken t' other road,' he told them. 'This 'ere's t' mill.'

'Do you know Ruth and Kitty?' Hannah asked him.

He shrugged. 'There's loads o' lasses,' he said. 'I dunno what they're all called.'

'Can I help you?' asked a voice and Hannah saw a man approaching them with a look of consternation on his face. 'What are you doing here?' he asked.

It was clear from his assessment of them and their cart that he had not mistaken them for visitors to the Gregs.

'Have you brought this lad as an apprentice?' he asked, eyeing Edmund. Hannah put an arm protectively around her son.

'No,' she told him.

Ellis handed the reins to Hannah and got down from the cart. 'My name's Ellis Duxbury,' he said. 'I'm manager of a mill at Egerton.' He held out a hand and the man regarded it suspiciously.

'What do you want?' he asked.

'We've come for my wife's daughters,' said Ellis. 'Ruth Fisher and Kitty Fisher.'

The man frowned. 'No one's told me,' he replied. 'Is Mr Greg expecting you?'

'No,' admitted Ellis and Hannah wondered if it would have been better if they'd sent a letter first. 'Are those lasses here?' he asked.

The man scratched his head in reply for a moment then said, 'My wife, Mrs Shawcross, will know more about it. 'Appen you'd better come inside,' he said, glaring at the increasing crowd of children who were gathered around them. 'Get away with ye!' he bellowed at them and they quickly dispersed to continue their ball game.

Ellis asked about somewhere to leave Patch and

the man called one of the older boys back and instructed him to tend to the horse. Then he led them up the lane, past a large and well-tended kitchen garden where winter vegetables were beginning to sprout, to a large whitewashed house.

'Mrs Greg teaches the lasses some bible stories on a Sunday afternoon,' he said as he took them in through the door. 'Best not disturb her,' he added. 'Come through 'ere and I'll fetch Mrs Shawcross.' He led them to a room with a large desk and a chair and left them standing whilst he tapped on another door in the hallway and called to his wife. A moment later a woman came bustling in with a scowl on her face. She was obviously annoyed to have her Sunday afternoon disturbed.

'I were havin' a sit down,' she complained. 'What is it you want?'

Ellis explained again and she agreed that there were two lasses by those names in her care. 'I don't know nowt about any parents though,' she told them, looking them up and down with obvious doubts. 'They came from a workhouse in Bolton.'

'I never gave my permission,' Hannah told her, speaking for the first time. 'Where are they?' she asked. 'I'm their mother.'

'All the lasses are in the schoolroom with Mrs Greg. I'll not disturb them,' said Mrs Shawcross.

'How long will they be?' asked Hannah. She was worried that it would be growing dark again soon.

'There's no telling,' Mrs Shawcross replied, unhelpfully.

'Can I speak with Mr Greg?' Ellis asked her.

She shook her head again. 'We'll not disturb him on a Sunday,' she replied.

'Then we'll have to wait for the Sunday School to finish,' replied Ellis.

'You can't wait in here,' said Mrs Shawcross.

Hannah glanced across at Ellis, praying that he wouldn't give up and simply take her home. The welcome, or lack of it, was not what she'd envisaged. She'd been hoping for a chair beside a fire and a cup of tea at the very least. Ellis nodded his head to Mrs Shawcross and told her that he was sorry to have disturbed her, then he took Hannah's arm and ushered her back outside.

'We can't just go!' she protested as she heard the door close behind them. It was clear that the woman hadn't believed a word they'd said.

'We're not going,' said Ellis. 'Come on.'

'Where to?' asked Hannah, hurrying to keep up as he strode away.

'To the house,' replied Ellis as if the answer was obvious. 'To see Mr Greg.'

The house was built from a pale yellow sandstone with a grey tiled roof. It stood on high ground overlooking the river and was surrounded by trees. From the mill they crossed a footbridge to reach it and then followed the gravelled path around to the front door.

Ellis tugged on the chain that rang the doorbell

and stepped back to wait. Hannah held Edmund's hand and looked at the huge curtained windows with trepidation. She was sure they would be sent away and all chance of rescuing Ruth and Kitty would be gone.

When the door was opened, a maid in a pristine white apron and cap peeped out.

'I'm here to see Mr Greg,' said Ellis in a tone that brooked no argument.

'I'll see if he's at home,' said the maid. 'Do you have a card?' she asked.

Ellis shook his head. 'Tell him its Mr Ellis Duxbury from the Eagle Mill at Egerton,' he said.

The maid left them waiting on the step, but Hannah could see that Ellis was irritated by the Shawcrosses and determined not to be thwarted by the Gregs. A few minutes later the maid came back and asked them to step inside the tiled hallway.

'May I take your hats and coats?'

Ellis, who already had his hat in his hand, gave it to her. Hannah whipped Edmund's cap off his head and told him to take off his coat before she removed her cloak and added it to the heap of clothing on the maid's arm.

'This way,' said the maid approaching a door.

'Good afternoon!' said Mr Greg, standing up when they came into the parlour. 'Come and warm yourselves by the fire. You look frozen. Bring some tea,' he instructed the maid.

Hannah felt ill at ease in the fine room. She'd

never set foot in such a place before, but Ellis seemed quite at home as he shook the mill owner's hand and introduced himself.

'And have you travelled all the way from Egerton today?' asked Mr Greg as they all sat down on the beautifully upholstered chairs that were arranged around the fireplace.

'We have,' Ellis said. 'We're here about my wife's daughters. Ruth Fisher and Kitty Fisher. They were sent here from the workhouse at Bolton against my wife's wishes.'

'From the workhouse?' Mr Greg sounded puzzled. He looked from Ellis to Hannah and back again.

'My wife and her daughters were forced to enter the workhouse when they fell on hard times through no fault of their own,' explained Ellis. 'Mrs Duxbury left her daughters behind when she took employment as my housekeeper. But now we are married and I want to take Ruth and Kitty home.'

'I see.' Mr Greg kept silent as the maid brought tea and poured it for them. 'My wife is better acquainted with the children than I am,' he told them when they all had tea in their hands, Hannah praying that Edmund wouldn't drop the delicate porcelain cup and saucer decorated with birds that he was staring at in fascination. 'She takes a great interest in their welfare,' went on Mr Greg. 'In fact she's teaching in the schoolroom at the present.'

Ellis nodded and explained that they had already been to the apprentice house.

'So you aren't the father of these girls?' asked Mr Greg as he set his cup and saucer on a side table and gave his full attention to Ellis.

'I'm their stepfather now.'

'I take it then that their father is dead. I think that's what we were told when we took them in, but I would need to check.'

'That's correct,' said Ellis, with a warning glance at Hannah not to contradict him.

'It's not often we have parents come to claim their children,' said Mr Greg. Hannah's heart was thumping. She was terrified he was going to make some excuse and say that her daughters couldn't leave.

'Mr Cartwright at the workhouse was mistaken to send them,' explained Ellis. 'He ought to have known that my wife would return for them once she was able.'

'Everything was done properly,' Mr Greg told him. 'The indentures were signed.' He glanced up as they heard the sound of carriage wheels on the drive outside. 'Here is my wife now,' he said. 'Excuse me.'

He got up and went out into the hallway to greet Mrs Greg.

'What if he refuses to let them go?' Hannah asked Ellis as they waited.

'Leave it to me,' he told her. 'Don't say anything.' Hannah frowned. She hated having to stay silent when it was her children that were being discussed.

They sat and listened to the sound of the clock ticking until Mr Greg returned, accompanied by his wife.

'I've sent a message for the girls to be brought,' he told them after the introductions had been made. 'We'll see what they have to say.'

Mrs Greg sat down with them and poured her own tea. She had handed her fur-trimmed overcoat to the maid and sat in a gown of iris-blue that fell to her ankles and had a high waist in the latest fashion. She wore no apron or bonnet and Hannah thought that she was beautiful. But the silence was strained and awkward as they waited for Ruth and Kitty to arrive.

At last, Hannah heard voices and she stood up as the door was opened. For a moment Kitty stared at her as if she couldn't believe what she was seeing.

'Mam?' she whispered. Hannah held out her arms and her younger daughter ran across the room and clung to her. Hannah hugged her close and kissed her.

'It's all right,' she said. 'It's all right.' She reached out to Ruth to hug and kiss her too. Hannah was relieved to see that both of her lasses looked clean and they had adequate clothing, even though Kitty seemed weary and sank onto her mother's lap as she sat back down.

Ruth hugged her little brother. Then stared at Ellis Duxbury. 'What's goin' on, Mam?' she asked.

'I've come to fetch thee,' said Hannah, with a

glance at the Gregs, challenging them to contradict her. 'Kitty and thee should never have been sent here. It were Mr Cartwright's doin'. I never gave him permission.'

'Where will we go?' asked Ruth. She looked from her mother to Ellis Duxbury again, clearly puzzled. 'How did tha find us?' she asked.

'Mr Duxbury here brought me – and he'll take us home. I'm married to him now,' she explained to her daughter.

'Married to him?' Ruth was obviously shocked. 'But what about my dad?'

Hannah shook her head, wishing that Ruth would be quiet, wishing that she'd had an opportunity to explain things to her without the Gregs listening.

'Where is your father, Ruth?' asked Mrs Greg.

'I don't know. I think he's in New South Wales, but my Mam always told us he would come back.'

'Was he a convict?'

'My husband isn't a bad man,' protested Hannah. 'He never stole or hurt anyone. He was protesting about the way workers are treated. He did nothing wrong!'

'Hannah,' interrupted Ellis and she could see he was exasperated that she hadn't heeded his advice to keep quiet.

'My wife's first husband was sent away many years ago,' Ellis told the Gregs. 'No one has heard of him since. These girls are my responsibility now.'

Hannah wanted to plead with the Gregs to allow

her to take her children home, but she was afraid of making matters worse.

'Ruth,' said Mrs Greg. 'Do you know this man who says he is your mother's husband?'

Ruth shook her head. 'No,' she admitted. 'I've never seen him before.'

'And do you believe your father is still alive?'

Ruth hesitated then said, 'I don't know.'

Mrs Greg looked to her husband for guidance. 'What are we to do?' she asked him.

'I think it needs to be looked into,' he replied.

'But they're my children!' cried Hannah, unable to keep silent any longer. She tightened her arms around Kitty. 'Tell them, Ruth. Tell them I'm thy mother.'

'She is my mother,' nodded Ruth looking bewildered.

'I don't dispute that,' agreed Mr Greg, 'but it's the whereabouts of your father that I need to ascertain.' He turned to his wife. 'I'll have to write to Mr Cartwright to get to the bottom of this,' he said. 'I can't just let them go with this man.' He turned to Ellis. 'I'm sorry, Mr Duxbury,' he said and he sounded genuinely apologetic, 'but you've put me in an awkward spot. I'm sure you understand. The truth is I don't know you and although you seem genuine, these girls are *my* responsibility, for now at least, and I must be sure that this is all above board before I allow you to take them away from here. I'm sorry,' he repeated.

Hannah held on tightly to Kitty. It was too cruel,

she thought. She'd come all this way and found her lasses and now she was going to be forced to leave them behind again. She didn't know how she would bear it.

'We should have written first,' Ellis said to Hannah. 'I'm sorry. It was my error.'

'If you can provide some evidence,' began Mr Greg, 'it would help me to decide what's for the best. A letter from Mr Cartwright at the workhouse perhaps, or from your employer that will show that you are who you say you are, and proof of your marriage.' He looked at Hannah who was still clasping Kitty. 'I'm sorry, Mrs . . . er . . . Duxbury,' he said. 'It's obvious that you are the mother of these girls and that they know you, but I cannot risk allowing you to take them if there is any chance that their father may come to claim them.'

CHAPTER TWENTY-ONE

Hannah had sobbed as her daughters were taken out of the room by Mrs Greg and Mr Greg had shown them to the door. As she and Ellis and Edmund had walked back across the bridge to the mill yard she'd seen Ruth and Kitty going back into the apprentice house. She'd wanted to follow them and plead again for them to be allowed to go with her, but she knew it would do no good.

'We should have come better prepared,' said Ellis as their cart was brought out and Patch harnessed up. 'I never thought they'd be so difficult about it.'

'But we can get the proof they're asking for, can't we?' Hannah asked, feeling desperate. 'We can come back for them?'

'I'll speak to Mr Cartwright and ask if he will vouch for me,' Ellis promised, 'but there's nothing more we can do now and we need to get going,' he told her, as he glanced at the setting sun.

It was a long and arduous journey back to Egerton. Darkness fell soon after they'd set off. Edmund was tired and kept falling asleep, so it was left to Hannah to hold the lantern as her son lay sprawled across her lap. She kept wishing that Ellis would say they should look for an inn but he kept urging Patch on even as the weather worsened. By the time they reached the outskirts of Bolton it had begun to snow again and Hannah was afraid that they would become stuck. But Patch pulled bravely and just as the church clock was striking midnight they took the road for Egerton. The snow was beginning to stick now as the temperature fell below freezing and at times the wheels spun on the ice. Ellis got down to lead the horse through the worst of it as Hannah shifted the lantern from hand to hand, her arms and shoulders burning with pain and tiredness.

At long last they reached home. Hannah gently woke Edmund and he got down, sleepy, cold and disoriented. Ellis took the lantern to return Patch and the cart to the stable.

'Poor horse,' said Hannah as she patted his neck. 'He's done us proud. Tell them to let him rest tomorrow.'

As Ellis led the horse away, Hannah hurried Edmund inside, out of the cold. The fire had gone out and she laid it with fresh coals and paper and blew at the first flames until they took hold.

'Tha must be hungry,' she said to her son as she began to get bread and treacle down from the shelf.

'Just tired,' he said as he sat listlessly in the chair. 'I want to go to bed.'

'Come on then,' she said as she lit a candle. 'Let's get thee settled.'

He let her help him get undressed – something he hadn't done since he was a baby – and then she tucked him into the little bed in the smallest room. He was asleep before she'd even blown out the candle and she closed the door quietly on her way out so as not to waken him. She went into the second bedroom and looked at the big bed that she made ready for Ruth and Kitty to sleep in. Its emptiness made her tears flow again. She'd been so sure that her daughters would be sleeping in it tonight, and having to leave them behind again was breaking her heart; she was desperate to find a way to convince Mr Greg to allow them to take the lasses away from Quarry Bank. Though she couldn't altogether blame the mill owner, thought Hannah. Kitty and Ruth had had no idea who Ellis was and it had looked suspicious.

She went back downstairs and left the candle burning and the door on the latch whilst she ran across the street to May's house. It was all in darkness and she hesitated to knock them up. May would have put Florence to bed, she realised and, deciding it was probably better to leave the child there until morning, she slithered back across the icy street and shook the snowflakes from her cloak before hanging it up.

'I've left Florence across the road,' she told Ellis when he came in. 'They've gone to bed. I'll fetch her tomorrow.'

He nodded. He looked tired too. They both were.

They ate a cold supper and drank some tea then climbed the stairs to their bedroom.

'I'm sorry it didn't turn out better,' said Ellis just after he'd blown out the candle. 'But at least you saw your daughters.'

Hannah didn't answer. She was relieved to know that Kitty and Ruth were in good health but leaving them behind had been so hard, especially when she didn't know when she would see them again. It had been a long journey and she wasn't sure when Ellis would want to give up another Sunday and pay for the horse and cart again, especially as the weather could only continue to get worse and the days shorter as Christmas approached. She'd been planning the celebration they would have together in her head. A family Christmas, although one without Jack, but now it looked like her daughters would spend theirs far away from her.

Even though she was tired out, Hannah couldn't sleep. The events of the day played over and over in her mind and her body felt as if it was still jolting along on the cart. Her bottom was sore from the hard seat and her back and arms ached from holding the lantern.

Beside her she could hear Ellis breathing softly. She was grateful to him for trying to help her, but she couldn't get Ruth's words out of her mind. *What about my dad?* How Hannah wished it was Jack lying beside her. If he hadn't been sent away she would never have been in this mess.

* * *

Still feeling weary, Hannah forced herself up from the warm bed at her usual time the next morning and went downstairs by the light of a candle to coax the fire into a blaze. Thankfully, it had stayed lit overnight and the kitchen wasn't as icy cold as it would have been if it had gone out. But the chill from the stone floor struck up through the soles of her boots and made her legs ache even more.

The water had a thick layer of ice on the top of it and Hannah had to break it to fill the kettle. She yawned and wiped at her eyes as she spooned tea into the pot. Moments later she heard the creaking of the bed springs in the room above her, followed by Ellis's footsteps as he retrieved his outer clothing and dressed himself. He looked tired too when he came down and she felt a momentary pang of guilt for having put him to so much trouble.

'I'd better go and wake Edmund,' she said.

'Leave him,' said Ellis. 'He'll be no good to Mr Mather this morning. I'll say he's sickly.'

'Thank you,' said Hannah, glad that Ellis wasn't going to insist that Edmund went to work. She knew that it was when children were tired that accidents happened.

Her son was still sleeping soundly when she went up after Ellis had gone, so she left him and went across to collect Florence. May opened the door with a look of relief.

'What time did tha get back?' she asked Hannah as she let her into the cottage.

'Gone midnight.'

'And are thy lasses well?'

'They are, but they wouldn't let them leave,' said Hannah and related the story of what the Gregs had said.

'That's a shame,' agreed May as she bundled Florence into a blanket for Hannah to carry her home. 'Tha were so excited about them coming home. What will tha do now?'

'I hope Mr Duxbury will find a way to persuade them,' said Hannah as she took Florence into her arms. 'It was hard to leave them behind.'

When the following Sunday came around, Hannah wondered if Ellis would go out for his walk after chapel or if he would go to see Mr Cartwright. She hoped he would see the workhouse master and ask if he would write to Mr Greg at Quarry Bank. But when he stood up after finishing his dinner he pulled on his overcoat and boots and said that he might be late back and she should go to bed if he wasn't home by ten o' clock.

'Is the weather fit for you to walk on the moors?' she asked. A look of irritation flitted across his face and Hannah hoped she hadn't spoken out of turn. 'It's just that I'm worried,' she explained.

'I know what I'm doing,' he told her. 'Lock up before you go to bed, but don't draw the bolts or I'll have to wake you.'

Hannah watched him go – head down as he hurried up the street towards the track that led over the moorland towards Darwen. She sat down opposite Edmund.

'Where has he gone?' asked her son.

'I don't know,' Hannah admitted, wondering if she should go to see Mr Cartwright herself, although she doubted that he would do anything for her. Perhaps it would be better to approach the Reverend Jones. He would be able to vouch for their marriage, but whether that would be enough to persuade Mr Greg to release Ruth and Kitty she wasn't sure. She understood that what he'd really wanted was proof that Jack was dead and had no claim on his daughters, and there was no way she could produce that, despite her marriage. She worried that it might make matters worse. But what was worrying her more than anything was the thought that Ruth and Kitty would be expecting her to return for them. The thought of them looking out for her and hoping that she would come, only to be disappointed, gnawed at her as she picked up some mending from the basket by the fire. She knew she would never rest until she had her daughters back with her.

CHAPTER TWENTY-TWO

It was a few days before Christmas and Ellis had taken Hannah to market to buy a goose for their dinner. It was a long time since she'd had one and she was looking forward to choosing a meaty bird to cook with roast potatoes and vegetables. She'd already made a pudding and a cake, and even though she was looking forward to the feast, Hannah was sad that Ruth and Kitty wouldn't be sharing it. She was finding it hard to be without them. She thought about them all the time and hoped that they were well. The Gregs had seemed kindly people, which was a blessing, but she knew that mill lasses were expected to work hard and for long hours and Kitty's fragile health was a constant worry to her.

She hated to nag Ellis about it because she knew how busy he was with his work at the mill – and he'd already done far more than she could have expected by giving Edmund a home and a job. On the one occasion she had dared to raise the subject he'd been quick to apologise for his neglect and told her that he would see Mr Cartwright as soon as he could and ask him to write to Mr Greg about the matter. But the December days had crept by, each darker than the last, and Hannah knew that even if Mr Greg did allow her daughters to leave Quarry Bank it would be impossible to go for them until there was more daylight. A journey in the dark in the unpredictable weather would be dangerous.

'Hannah Sharples?'

Hannah turned at the sound of her name and saw it was an elderly neighbour from Hill Fold.

'I thought it were thee,' said Mrs Cooper. 'Did thy Jack find thee all right?'

Hannah stared at her, not understanding what she was talking about.

'My Jack?' she asked, wondering if the woman was becoming confused in her old age and had forgotten that Jack had been sent away.

'Aye,' she said. 'He were lookin' for thee, up at t' cottage where tha used to live. I told 'im tha'd gone away.'

Hannah's heart was beating fast with excitement, but she was telling herself that it couldn't possibly be true and that the woman was rambling. 'Did tha tell him I'd gone in the workhouse?' she asked.

'Did tha go there?' Mrs Cooper looked puzzled. 'I didn't know. I knew tha'd gone and taken t' childer. I told him I weren't sure where tha were and he said not to mind that he'd keep on lookin'.' She paused. 'Did he not find thee then?'

'No.' Hannah shook her head. 'When was this?' she asked.

'I don't rightly recall.' Mrs Cooper sucked in her lips over her toothless gums. 'It weren't today or yesterday. Longer ago than that.'

'Did anyone else see him?' asked Hannah.

'Couldn't say,' replied Mrs Cooper. 'Mr Cooper were out.'

'Well, thanks for telling me,' said Hannah, trying to quell her hopes. It was most likely to be something the old woman had dreamt or imagined. She counselled herself to give it no credence so she wouldn't be disappointed when it turned out not to be true.

She gave her attention to the birds hanging on the market stall and pointed out the one she wished to purchase.

'Merry Christmas!' said the stallholder as he handed her the bulky parcel.

Hannah thanked him and hurried away. She'd arranged to meet Ellis at the Golden Lion and she didn't want to be late.

'Did you get everything?' he asked as she squeezed in through the throng of people and sat down beside him.

'I think so.' She put the goose on the table and he unwrapped a corner to take a look.

'It's a nice one,' he agreed. 'Ale?'

'Please.'

Ellis called the barmaid to bring her jug and a cup.

'Stew?' he asked Hannah.

'Aye.'

'You look a bit flustered,' he commented. 'Is anything wrong?'

'No. No. I just bumped into a woman who used to be a neighbour, that's all.'

Hannah decided it was best not to tell Ellis what Mrs Cooper had said. It probably wasn't true and there was no point stirring up trouble where there was none. But what if it was true? She couldn't dismiss the thought. After all, Thomas Holden had come home, so why not Jack?

They rode back to Egerton with the carrier and Hannah fetched Florence from May's house. Ellis had gone back to the mill and so she set to cleaning the goose and preparing it for cooking in the oven beside the hearth.

As she worked she wondered if it would be possible for her to find an opportunity to walk down to Hill Fold and ask if anyone else had seen Jack. Surely if he'd been looking for her he would have asked more people about her whereabouts. The trouble was she needed to do it secretly. Ellis must never know and she didn't want to raise Edmund's hopes either. Florence was another problem. If she left her with May she would have to make an excuse about where she was going and then it might get back to Ellis. It would be better to take the child with her, she decided, even if it would make her trip more difficult.

The next day was Christmas Eve. Ellis and Edmund went off to the mill as usual and as soon as they were out of sight, Hannah put on the red cloak and, with Florence in her arms, she hurried down the road towards Bolton.

A thaw had set in and, although it was still cold, the roads were puddled and mist clung to the hillsides. The mud built up on Hannah's boots as she walked and crept up around the edges of her cloak. She would have to try to clean them before Ellis saw them and asked where she'd been.

It took her the best part of an hour to reach Hill Fold. Her cottage looked just the same, but the familiar green door was shut against her. She imagined Jack arriving home, weary from his long journey and knocking on it, only to find that there was nobody there. The thought brought tears to her eyes.

She walked across the yard to where her nearest neighbours, Gracie and Sam, lived and tapped on their door. Gracie opened it.

'Hannah!' she cried. 'Hast tha come home? Who's this' she asked as her gaze settled on Florence. 'Is she thine?'

'No. I'm just minding her,' she replied. 'I saw Mrs Cooper on t' market yesterday,' she explained, 'and she said someone had been round lookin' for me.'

'Aye,' agreed Gracie. 'It were thy Jack. Did tha not know?'

Her friend reached out to snatch Florence from her arms as Hannah swayed on her feet.

'Tha'd best come in and have a sit down,' Gracie told her.

‘I’d no idea until Mrs Cooper told me, and even then I thought she were mistaken,’ explained Hannah when a cup of Gracie’s hot, sweet tea had revived her.

‘Everybody round here knows,’ said Gracie, ‘but we didn’t know where tha’d gone. I thought tha were in t’ workhouse.’

‘I’m livin’ up at Egerton,’ said Hannah. ‘I got a job mindin’ this child.’

‘Who does she belong to?’ asked Gracie as Florence played on the rug with the other children.

‘She’s daughter to a Mr Duxbury. He’s the mill manager. Her mother died,’ explained Hannah, being careful to tell the truth, but not all of it.

‘And are thine own childer with thee?’

‘Just Edmund. Ruth and Kitty are apprenticed at Quarry Bank Mill.’ She took another drink of her tea. ‘Dost tha know where my Jack is now?’ she asked.

‘I don’t. I’m sorry,’ said Gracie. ‘When it was clear thy house weren’t being lived in he went on his way. He must still be lookin’ for thee. If I see him again, I’ll tell him that tha’s at Egerton.’

‘No!’ Hannah almost spilled the dregs of her tea. ‘No,’ she said again. ‘It might make trouble if he goes there. Mr Duxbury thinks I were a widow. I’ll look for him myself, now that I know he’s home.’

‘Aye. Well, I’ll be right glad to see thee reunited,’ said Gracie. ‘It were a damned shame what happened to thy Jack and Thomas Holden and the others. They never deserved it.’

Hannah thanked Gracie for the tea and told her that she must get on.

'I hope tha finds him in time for Christmas,' said Gracie as Hannah left.

Hannah also wished that she could be with her husband for the holiday, but she realised that it wouldn't be possible. She needed to hurry straight back to Egerton to get Ellis's dinner on the table before he came in from the mill. She couldn't risk him coming home to find her and Florence missing. She didn't want him to raise a hue and cry.

She trudged back up the hill with a mixture of emotions. Part of her was overjoyed by the news that Jack was alive and had come home, but part of her was fearful about how the situation she found herself in could be resolved. How would she explain it to Ellis? And what about Florence. She kissed the child as she shifted her weight to her other hip. She'd grown to love this baby and it would be hard to leave the little motherless child behind when she returned to her husband.

In the afternoon she put the goose to roast slowly in the oven so that it would be ready for the following day. They would have to attend chapel in the morning and when they came back she would cook the vegetables for them to eat late in the afternoon. It seemed an odd time of day for a meal, but Ellis had said it was what he was used to.

She'd asked about decorations, but he'd told her that he didn't want a fuss, so she'd simply gathered some holly with a profusion of bright red berries and put it in a jar in the middle of the table. The question of gifts had perplexed her too. She would have liked to buy something for him and the children, but even though she was now Ellis's wife she still had no money of her own and she wasn't sure that he would be pleased if she kept back any of the shopping money he gave her to buy presents. She'd sewn some new clothes for Edmund and Florence and those would have to suffice. She'd puzzled about what she could give Ellis. He liked books but she certainly couldn't afford one of those, so in the end she'd used a few pennies to get him a twist of tobacco. It seemed inadequate, but at least it was a gesture, she thought.

She woke at her usual time on Christmas morning and lay in the comfort of her warm bed for a while, wondering what sort of a day Ruth and Kitty would have. The mill would be closed and she hoped that they would be given a good dinner at least. There might even be some singing and some games if the Gregs allowed it after church.

Hannah wondered where Jack was. Where would he have gone when he found their home empty and locked against him? Surely he would have turned to the man who he'd nursed back to health onboard the *Fortune* – Thomas Holden. Hannah knew that he hadn't been close friends with

Thomas before they were both sent away, but where else was there for him to go? He'd lost both his parents and his brothers to disease and starvation long since.

She turned as Ellis woke and yawned and stretched himself. He reached out for her, and Hannah saw that he was eager to have relations with her, so she flung the covers aside and reached for her stays and gown. He sighed as he watched her dress, disappointment clouding his face. But it was one Christmas gift that Hannah was unwilling to give now that she knew her husband Jack was waiting for her.

After sitting through another tedious sermon from the Reverend Jones they walked back to the house through the drizzle that had melted the snowfall leaving the moors dark and dreary beyond the village. Even though it was approaching noon the sun seemed to have barely crept into the sky and within another few hours darkness would have fallen again. Hannah hated the wintertime. The brightness of the Christmases she'd known as a child had more than made up for it, but this one was bringing her no joy at all, not whilst she was separated from most of the people she loved.

Hannah tried to make the day a happy one, for Edmund's sake. He thanked her for the new shirt but she knew that he would have preferred a hoop or a toy theatre. Florence knew no different and was excited to be brought up to the table where Ellis lifted her from her chair and sat her on his knee until it was time for him to carve the goose and share out generous portions onto their plates. The potatoes came crisp from the oven, the peas were tasty and the gravy was thick. They ate the pudding smothered in brandy sauce and later they cut into the cake with a pot of strong tea. Hannah ate more than she had in a long time, but still it didn't fill the void of loneliness that she felt; all the time she wished that her daughters and her husband were there to share it with her.

CHAPTER TWENTY-THREE

Boxing Day was fine with a pale blue sky and wispy clouds high over the moors. Hannah hoped that the change in the weather was a good omen. She'd made her plan and as soon as Ellis and Edmund left for the mill she set off with Florence.

'Where's tha off to so early?' called May as she came out to shake a rug at the front door. Hannah wondered if she'd been watching out for her.

'I'm visitin' family,' she replied.

'I can have Florence for a while if it'll make things easier,' she offered. May was always eager to look after the child. 'She's gettin' heavy to carry,' she added.

It was true, thought Hannah. And now that May had seen her going out it made little difference because she might talk about it anyway.

'I'll not be long,' she told May as she handed Florence over. 'I'll be back before dinner time.'

Without the burden of the baby she was able to strike out at a quicker pace. As she approached Hag End Fold, Hannah felt the lightness of every step and broke into a run as she neared the cluster of cottages. She was breathless by the time she knocked on the Holdens' door, waiting impatiently for her husband to take her in his arms again.

'Hannah! It's Hannah!' Molly Holden pulled her inside and there was Jack, staring at her as if she was an apparition. He looked familiar, but it wasn't the same Jack who'd left her almost seven years ago. This man had skin that was bronzed and weathered by the sun. He had creases around his eyes that hadn't been there before, and he looked healthy and well fed.

'Jack?' she whispered his name. She'd lived this moment over and over in her imagination so many times, but this was nothing like her dreams. She felt awkward and unsure. The man standing in front of her was almost a stranger and she didn't know what to say to him.

'Hannah,' he said, grasping her hands in his. 'I've been searchin' for thee. I couldn't find thee anywhere.'

'How long has tha been back?' she asked.

'A few weeks. I went to our cottage, but it were empty.'

'They put me out.'

'I'm sorry,' he said. 'I'm sorry for all t' trouble I brought on thee.' He studied her carefully. 'But tha looks well,' he said, noting her cloak and her boots.

'I got work as a housekeeper,' she explained.

'And the childer? Where are they?' he asked anxiously.

'Edmund's with me. He's working as a little piecer at t' mill. But they sent Ruth and Kitty away.' She had to pause whilst she overcame her emotions. 'They sent them as apprentices to Quarry Bank. It's a long way off, down in Cheshire—'

'But they're all right? They're well?'

'Aye. I've been to see them once. I tried to bring them home but they wouldn't allow it.'

She couldn't hold back her sobs any longer and it was only then that he put his arms around her and held her close to him.

'I've missed thee so much,' he told her.

Hannah rested her cheek against his chest. She could hear his heart thumping and his quick breathing. She pressed her palms against his back, urging him closer, savouring the moment she'd waited so long for.

Molly made them a pot of tea and took her daughter, Annie, down to the cellar to watch Thomas working at his loom. Hannah was grateful to her for seeing that she and Jack needed some time alone to get to know one another again. They sat down by the hearth and Hannah asked Jack what it had been like in New South Wales and how he'd got back. She learned that he'd had a hard time at first, that the sea journey to the colony had been long and difficult and the work when he arrived even more awful. She sensed that he was sparing her the worst of it and part of her didn't want to know. He was here. He was alive. Hannah thought it was a miracle.

‘I worked my passage back after I was given my pardon,’ he told her. ‘So many of the sailors on the *Atlas* had died of fever on the outbound journey that they were short of hands. I’d no experience but they were takin’ anyone who were willing and allowed to leave. It were hard,’ he admitted, ‘and we didn’t come straight home. I went sailin’ around the world for a year or more and I’ve seen all sorts, but it were the thought of seein’ thee again as kept me goin’.’

As Jack talked, Hannah lost track of the time and it wasn’t until Molly came back up the stairs and began to set the table that she realised it must be nearly dinnertime.

‘I’ll have to go!’ she exclaimed feeling panic mounting inside her.

‘Nay. Sit thee down. Tha’s only just got ’ere,’ protested Jack when she reached for her cloak. ‘Besides, it’s started to pour down outside. Tha’ll get soaked through if tha sets off in this.’

‘Stay for some dinner at least,’ urged Molly. ‘Tha can’t go off hungry.’

‘But Edmund’ll be back from the mill and wanting summat to eat. He’ll wonder where I am,’ she said. ‘I didn’t tell him I was coming here. I didn’t want him to be disappointed if it wasn’t true.’

‘Then I’ll walk back with thee,’ said Jack. ‘It’ll be good to see the lad. He were just a babe in arms when I left.’

‘No.’ Hannah was becoming afraid. She hadn’t

thought through what would happen after she'd found Jack.

'Why? What's troublin' thee?' asked Jack. 'Tha looks scared to death. If it's thy employer that tha's afraid of then tha needn't worry. I'll deal with 'im,' he told her, sounding as if he was ready to roll up his sleeves for a fight. 'Tha can't stay there anyroad. Tha's my wife and tha belongs with me. As soon as I've sorted out t' payment of t' rent on our cottage we'll move back in and I can take up my weavin' again.'

Hannah was shaking her head in desperation. 'There's no loom,' she told him. 'I had to sell it. I had to sell everything to buy food.'

Jack stared at her in disbelief. 'My loom? Sold?'

'Aye. I had no choice.' Hannah wanted to weep at the look of loss and horror on her husband's face.

'Hannah was in desperate straits,' Molly told him. 'She had nothing to feed the children and the parish would do nowt to help her until she'd sold everything, and even then they never gave her enough.'

'I struggled,' Hannah told her husband. 'It's not been easy, managin' on my own. I did petition to come to thee,' she added in case he wasn't aware. 'Me and Molly and the other wives. We begged them to give us a free passage, but they turned us down.'

'Aye. Some wives came,' Jack said. 'But they were mostly the lifers.'

'They told us seven years wasn't long enough. I'd have come if I'd been able. I had to throw myself on the mercy of the parish in the end,' she explained. 'Then, when the children were old enough to be employed, they turned us out and we were forced to go in t' workhouse. It were a stark place.'

Jack remained silent but she could see him clenching and unclenching his fists. 'I'll make 'em pay,' he vowed.

'No.' Hannah reached out to put a restraining hand on his arm. 'Don't make trouble,' she pleaded, hoping that he wouldn't take up with the reformers again. 'I couldn't bear to lose thee a second time.' She put on her cloak. 'Rain's easin' off,' she said. 'I need to get back to our Edmund.'

'I'm coming with thee,' said Jack in a tone that left Hannah with no option but to agree.

She walked beside him in silence for a while. He seemed different to the Jack she'd known before. The experiences he'd had over the last six years had changed him. It was only to be expected, thought Hannah. Perhaps he found her changed as well. It would take time for them to get to know one another again.

'We need to talk,' she said at last. She knew she had to tell him about Ellis Duxbury and her marriage, but she wasn't sure where to begin. 'There's a lot tha doesn't know.'

'I suppose that's only to be expected given we've been parted for so long,' he agreed.

'Mr Cartwright, the workhouse master sent me to work for Ellis Duxbury,' she told him. 'He were a widower with a baby daughter and needed someone to keep house for him. He's manager at t' mill at Egerton. Jack.' Hannah pulled on his arm. 'Stop a minute,' she said. 'There's summat I have to tell thee. It's important.'

'What is it?' he asked, turning to her with a worried look. 'What's wrong?'

'I didn't think tha'd come back,' she admitted. 'I hoped tha would. I prayed for it every night. But I'd had no word. When Thomas Holden came home and said he'd seen nowt of thee I thought that tha must have died. And I were desperate to get our Ruth and Kitty out of that place at Quarry Bank. And they sent our Edmund to work in the pit and I couldn't bear that so I had no choice in the matter . . .'

'What's tha talkin' about?' asked Jack, looking at her with a puzzled expression on his face. 'Tha's makin no sense.'

'Ellis Duxbury asked me to marry him. He said he'd help me get the childer back.' Hannah gazed at her husband, willing him to understand and not be angry with her.

'But tha told him no? Tha told him tha were already wed?'

'I told him about thee. Of course I did. But I were left with no choice,' she insisted. 'Not if I wanted to have the childer with me. I did it for them.'

Jack continued to stare at her. It was clear that he didn't understand. 'How could tha marry when tha were already wed to me?' he asked, looking genuinely perplexed. He glanced down at her hand and saw the ring for the first time. 'Did he give thee this?' he asked, grasping her by the wrist. 'Where's the one I wed thee with?'

'I have it here.' She fumbled under her cloak with her free hand and pulled out the ring on its string.

Jack stared it, then looked back at her finger. 'Put it on,' he told her. 'Take that off and put my ring on thy finger where it belongs. Here. I'll do it for thee.' He pulled at the string.

'Wait!' cried Hannah. 'Tha's hurtin' me. Let me unfasten it.'

Her fingers shook as she struggled with the tight knot but eventually she got it undone and put her ring in Jack's hand. Then she twisted off the ring that Ellis had placed on her third finger. It took a moment to get it free before she held out her hand for her husband to replace her original wedding band.

'There, that's better,' he told her when it was done. 'Don't go takin' it off again!'

'I won't,' she promised. 'But what will we tell Ellis Duxbury?'

'We'll tell him that tha's not his wife. That tha's my wife.'

He made it sound so simple, thought Hannah, dreading the conversation that lay ahead of her.

Ellis had been so kind. He'd thought she was free to marry him. And so had Mr Jones or he wouldn't have insisted on it otherwise. She didn't know about the law, so she couldn't be certain which man she was really married to and she wasn't sure how it could be resolved.

They walked on towards Egerton. The clock had already chimed noon before they reached the door of the house and Hannah pushed it open anxiously, wondering what Ellis would say when he saw Jack.

She hurried in first, down the tiled lobby and into the kitchen. Ellis was slicing bread and Edmund was sitting at the table.

'Hannah! Where have you been? I was worried. Where's Florence?' The anxiety on his face was clear. 'Who's this?' he asked as Jack followed her in. 'What's going on?'

Ellis was still holding the bread knife in his hand and Hannah wished that he would put it down.

'It's Jack,' she said. 'He's come home.'

Ellis continued to stare at Jack, but her husband had eyes for nobody but his son.

'Edmund? Tha must be Edmund. Tha won't remember me. I'm thy father.'

Edmund looked from one adult to another as he struggled to make any sense of what was happening. 'Mam?' he said.

Hannah went to her son and took his hand to pull him up from the chair. 'Aye, it's right,' she told him. 'This is thy father, come home to us.'

Edmund stared at the stranger in front of him.

Jack held out his arms, but the boy didn't move. He gripped Hannah's hand tightly and looked to Ellis for guidance.

'He doesn't know thee,' Hannah told Jack. 'Tha can't expect him to run to thee.'

'He's a fine lad. He has a look of my mother,' said Jack. 'I hear tha's workin' in t' mill?' he said to Edmund.

The boy nodded. 'I'm workin' with Mr Mather. I'm his little piecer. I fasten the threads back together when they break.'

Jack nodded. 'I'll teach thee to weave when we get home,' he said. 'That's a proper trade.'

'Are we going home?' Edmund asked Hannah. 'Back to where we used to live?'

'I'm not sure. Thy father's going to try to get the cottage back.'

'And will Ruth and Kitty come home?'

'They will!' Jack told him.

'Will we go for them? When will we go?' asked Edmund excitedly.

'Soon,' Hannah told him. 'There's a lot to sort out.'

'So tha's not married to Ellis any more?' Edmund asked her.

Hannah looked across at Ellis Duxbury who was still holding the knife, his knuckles white with tension. 'Put that down,' she said to him and he glanced at it, unaware that it was still in his grasp, before placing it beside the loaf he'd been cutting.

'Are you sure?' he asked Hannah.

'Sure of what?'

'Sure that this is thy husband . . . former husband . . .'

'Aye. This is Jack Fisher and no mistake.'

'Hannah is *my* wife,' Jack told him. 'She's coming with me – and the lad.' He turned to Hannah. 'Get thy things,' he told her.

'Now?' she asked. She hadn't expected him to insist on her leaving straight away, although she quickly realised that it was impossible for her to stay. 'But where will we go?' she asked, wondering if it would be asking too much to expect the Holdens to take them all in.

'We'll go to see Fletcher and get our keys back,' said Jack with the tone of a man who wasn't going to be thwarted.

Hannah headed towards the stairs, but Ellis put out a hand to restrain her.

'Don't be hasty,' he said. 'We need to be sure about this.'

'There's nowt to be sure of,' Jack told him. 'Hannah and the lad are coming with me.'

Hannah watched as the expression changed on Ellis's face.

'You can't just walk back in here and claim her!' he told Jack. His eyes were glinting with anger. 'She's married to me now.'

'How can she be?' asked Jack. 'When she were wed to me first?'

Ellis seemed flustered. Like Hannah, he seemed unsure about which man was legally her husband.

He appealed to her. 'Hannah,' he said, 'do you really want to go with this man when he has no house, no job, no money?'

'I've money,' Jack told him. 'Not that it's any business of thine!'

'Hannah?' Ellis appealed to her again. 'What about Florence?'

'She's with May. May will care for her,' she told him even though the truth was that she would find it hard to be parted from the child. Florence had become a daughter to her. She loved the little lass and she knew it would be hard to give her up – harder than giving up the life she had here with Ellis where she had warmth and food in abundance. Jack said he had money, but Hannah wasn't sure it was true. And even if they got back the keys to their cottage it was empty of furniture, and with no loom she wasn't sure how Jack would provide for them if he couldn't afford to buy another. On the other hand, he was her real husband and she was sure that he would be able to bring Ruth and Kitty home. Mr Greg couldn't be stubborn if their father went for them.

'Florence thinks of you as her mother,' Ellis told Hannah in an effort to persuade her to stay. 'She'll be inconsolable if you suddenly disappear.'

Hannah didn't answer. She felt the guilt and remorse that Ellis intended her to. She looked from one man to the other, not knowing what to do. She'd prayed and prayed for Jack to come home, but the man who was standing beside her seemed a stranger, and Ellis was the more familiar choice and she knew that he could provide for her. But how could she deny her son the right to know his father? How could she even consider leaving Ruth and Kitty at Quarry Bank? Mr Greg would never allow her and Ellis to take them now that Jack had returned.

'I must go with Jack,' she told Ellis after a moment. 'I'm sorry,' she added as she began to make her way to the stairs again to collect her things.

'It's your choice, Hannah, but you'll not leave with anything that belongs to me,' Ellis warned her as he bristled with anger at her decision. 'Not that cloak, nor those boots nor anything you're wearing. Same goes for the lad. You take what you came with, nothing more.'

'Ellis, be reasonable,' she pleaded. 'The clothes we came in went for rags. Dost tha expect us to walk out naked?'

'If this man is really your husband then he can clothe you,' said Ellis with a hostile stare at Jack.

Hannah looked from one man to the other. She saw the hatred and distrust on both their faces and she began to fear that it would come to blows.

'Don't be ridiculous!' she said to Ellis then stepped back in alarm as he thumped a fist on the table making the plates jump and rattle.

'You can't expect to take what's rightfully mine!'

'Tha's scarin' the child,' said Hannah as she saw tears welling in Edmund's eyes. She turned back to Jack. 'Tha'd better go,' she told him. 'I'll sort it out with Ellis. It's best if I talk to him alone.'

'Dost tha think I'm going to leave my wife and child alone with this madman?' raged Jack. 'I'd rather take thee naked than let thee stay here with him.' He spat the last words. 'Tha's not safe,' he insisted and Hannah wondered if he was right. The Ellis she'd known was usually calm and reasonable, but the man standing on the other side of the table had taken on the look of a lunatic. His eyes were filled with hatred for Jack and he looked ready to snatch up the knife again at any moment.

Making her decision, Hannah unfastened the cloak and threw it onto the table, sending plates and cups crashing to the floor. Then she sat down to take off her boots and threw them as well, followed by her stockings, as Edmund watched her in astonishment. She'd thought that Ellis would relent when she began to undress, but he simply watched as she pulled off her cap, unfastened her apron and began to wriggle out of her gown. Jack pulled off his coat and put it around her.

'That's enough!' he said. 'We'll send the rest back in a parcel!' he shouted at Ellis.

Barefoot, Hannah reached for Edmund's hand. 'Come on,' she urged him. 'Let's go.' Bewildered, the boy followed her to the front door and out onto the street where the shock of what had happened and the cold of the winter's day overcame

Hannah all at once and she began to sob. 'I never thought he'd do this,' she wept as the icy cold began to turn her feet blue.

Jack pulled off his own boots and bent to put them on her feet. They were much too big. She pulled the coat around Edmund and looked up at Jack, hoping he might have some solution to their plight.

'Is there a stables nearby?' he asked. 'I'll hire a horse.'

'Hast tha really got money?' Hannah asked, surprised.

'Aye. They paid me off when I left t' ship,' he said. 'I can spare a little and I'll not let thee and Edmund walk back like this.'

Hannah wondered if it wouldn't have been simpler to offer Ellis the money for her clothing, but she realised that he would probably have refused. His ruse had been to stop her leaving.

She walked up the street with Jack, struggling to keep his boots on her feet, and worrying about who was watching them. Edmund clung to her and looked on the verge of tears. It wasn't the best way for him to be reunited with his father, thought Hannah.

Jack asked at the stables for a pony and trap and the stableman brought out Patch and a small cart. Her husband paid for the hire and promised he would return them later that day. Then he helped her and Edmund up and urged Patch out of the yard, towards Bolton. Hannah held her son close as they drove away, but almost called for her husband to stop when she saw May come to her front door with little Florence in her arms and confusion written across her face. She longed to gather the baby in her arms and take her with them, but Florence was not hers to keep she realised, and the loss hit her harder than she expected as she fought back tears of regret.

CHAPTER TWENTY-FOUR

'Where are we going?' Hannah asked Jack as they approached the outskirts of Bolton. She was worried about imposing on the Holdens.

'We're going to see Fletcher to get our keys,' he said.

'Right now?' she asked. 'I can't go like this!' Hannah told him, wondering what the colonel would say if she appeared before him with only Jack's coat covering her underwear and Jack in his shirtsleeves and no boots.

'I suppose not,' he replied with a frown. 'We'd better tidy ourselves up.'

Jack drove them back to the Holdens' house where Thomas and Molly came out at the sound of the hooves and the wheels. Patch snorted as Jack tied his reins to a fence then helped Hannah to get down.

'Whatever's happened? Has there been an accident?' asked Molly when she saw Hannah. 'What's happened to thy clothes?'

'Let's go inside,' said Jack ushering the women

towards the doorway as curious onlookers came to their windows to see what was going on.

Molly guided Hannah to a chair by the fire before running upstairs to fetch a blanket to wrap around her.

'Yon bloke's a madman,' Jack told the Holdens. 'He made Hannah take off all her clothing, said it belonged to him and he wouldn't let her leave wearing it. It's lucky I came back when I did,' he said to Hannah. 'I hate to think what would've become of thee, livin' in that house.'

Hannah felt she ought to say that Ellis had always been good to her in the past, but she was still shocked at his outburst. She'd known it would be hard to tell him that Jack was back, but she'd never imagined that he would react as he had.

'Hast tha got owt tha can lend our Hannah to wear?' Jack asked Molly. 'She can't go to see Fletcher wi' nowt on.'

'Tha'd best come upstairs and look at what there is,' she said to Hannah. 'But I've nowt as fancy as that cloak tha were wearin' earlier,' she added as they went up.

'I'll be grateful for owt tha can spare,' Hannah told her, wishing that she hadn't had to part with the cosy red cloak that she'd loved wearing.

They went into the bedroom and Molly found a grey gown that was patched at one of the elbows and a frayed shawl that had once been a much brighter green. 'Will these do?' she asked. 'I know they're not much but they'll cover thee and help to keep thee warm.' Molly glanced at Hannah's feet. 'Tha'd best borrow these as well,' she said, proffering a pair of faded slippers. 'Jack will want his boots back.'

'Thank you. I'm grateful,' Hannah told her as she pulled the gown over her petticoat and squeezed her feet into the slippers, realising that they were much too small and would be little use in the winter weather. 'I'll take good care of them and tha'll get them back as soon as I can get some things of my own,' she promised, hoping that Jack had enough money for her to buy a few things from the market.

'Did he really make thee take off thy clothes?' Molly asked. 'That Mr Duxbury?'

Hannah nodded. 'I think he would have seen me leave stark naked if Jack hadn't stepped in to prevent it,' she said. 'He were furious.'

Molly shook her head in disbelief. 'But surely he didn't expect thee to keep workin' there now that thy husband's come home?' she said. 'I think Jack were right when he said he were a madman. Tha's best off well away from him,' she added.

It was clear that she hadn't heard about Hannah's wedding and Hannah decided not to confide in her. The fewer people who knew, the better she thought, hoping that it would all blow over before long and that she would never have to set foot in Egerton again.

They went back downstairs and Molly insisted

that they had something to eat before they went to see Colonel Fletcher about the cottage.

'What about Edmund?' asked Hannah when they were ready to go. 'He's got no jacket or cap to wear.'

'He can stop here where's it's warm,' said Molly. 'You can pick him up later.'

'Colonel Fletcher will be at his pit at this time,' Hannah told Jack as they headed towards the Hollins.

'Best check at his house first. We don't want a wasted journey.'

Jack trotted the horse up to the front door, passed the reins to Hannah and jumped down to pull the bell. The maid answered the door and Hannah saw her shaking her head before closing it firmly.

'The pit it is then,' said Jack as he got back up and they headed out towards where the winding gear stood starkly on the horizon.

The pit manager seemed doubtful when Jack insisted he had come to see the colonel himself on a matter of the greatest importance, but at Jack's insistence he went to ask whether Colonel Fletcher was available. Hannah was surprised when they were shown inside and taken to an office that looked more like a parlour than a workplace, with a roaring fire and leather chairs as well as a huge oak desk.

The colonel, standing with his back to the fire,

his newspaper tossed aside, looked them up and down with contempt, obviously regretting allowing them to come in.

'What can I do for you?' he asked Jack.

'I've come about the cottage I were rentin' afore I were sent away.'

'Sent away?' The colonel frowned. 'To prison?' he asked, with a look towards his clerk who scurried from the room, possibly to fetch a constable, thought Hannah, feeling uncomfortable and hoping that Jack would remember his place and not antagonise the man.

'Nay. To New South Wales. Seven years I got, for fightin' for my rights. Well, I'm back!' he told Colonel Fletcher. 'And I've come about the cottage that my wife and children were put out of.'

The colonel stared at Jack as if he could scarcely believe his boldness. Then he began to shake his head. 'I know nothing about it,' he said. 'You've come to the wrong person.'

'No, I haven't. Tha owns the cottages at Hill Fold, doesn't tha?'

Hannah was horrified at the way Jack was speaking to the colonel. It was true that he was widely disliked by the working men and women, but she'd never thought any of them would dare to address him in such familiar tones. She reached out to tug on Jack's arm, to try to warn him to be careful, but he shrugged her off. It was clear his hatred for this man had been brewing for over seven years and now that he had the chance to speak plainly, he wasn't going to let the opportunity pass him by.

'Yes. I own Hill Fold,' replied the colonel. His glance towards the door betrayed that he was anxious. Jack's life at sea had made him a powerful man and even Hannah could see that he appeared threatening.

'What sort of man puts a woman and children on the streets?' he asked.

The colonel braced his shoulders and stood square on to Jack. 'If tenants can't pay their rent, they get put out. That's how it works.'

'Even women with small children, whose husbands have been sent away found guilty of summat they never did?' demanded Jack.

The colonel looked at Hannah for a moment. 'There's parish relief for those in need,' he said. 'And failing that the workhouse. No one is left on the streets, except by choice.' He moved to put the width of his desk between Jack and himself. 'I'll bid you good afternoon if that's all you've come to say.'

'Nay. I'm not finished yet,' Jack told him. 'I want it back – my cottage. I want my keys. And don't tell me it's let, because I've been up to look and it's standin' empty.'

'I don't deal with such things,' protested Colonel Fletcher. 'You'll have to speak to the clerk.' A look of relief crossed his face as he heard voices outside and the clerk came back in accompanied by a man Hannah recognised as Mr Booth – one of the constables.

'Are these people botherin' you, sir?' he asked.

'They're just leaving,' replied Colonel Fletcher.

'Not until I have my keys to my cottage, I'm not,' replied Jack. 'Number two, Hill Fold,' he added, holding out his hand, palm up.

'Look it up in the ledger will you,' the exasperated colonel asked the clerk. 'See who it's rented to.'

There was a tense silence, broken only by the sound of the turning pages, until the clerk cleared his throat. 'It was let to a Mr John Fisher. Then to his wife after he was convicted and sent to the penal colony in New South Wales. Mrs Fisher was evicted for non-payment of the rent in August last year.'

'There you have it,' said Colonel Fletcher with a satisfied smile. He had regained his composure since the other men had joined them.

'So it's available for rent then?' asked Jack, addressing the clerk.

He began to nod, but Colonel Fletcher spoke first. 'If you are Mr Fisher, then you're not a suitable tenant for a property of mine,' he said. 'Mr Booth, will you remove these people from my office. Arrest them if you must.' He paused as he saw the constable studying Hannah. 'Is something troubling you?' he asked him.

'I know this woman,' said Mr Booth. 'She's wife of the mill manager up at Egerton if I'm not mistaken – a Mrs Duxbury.'

'She's my wife,' growled Jack. 'And I'll not have

it said otherwise! And tha can keep thy cottage!' he added to Colonel Fletcher. 'I'll find one elsewhere.'

'There aren't many cottages to rent that aren't owned by the colonel,' said Hannah as they left. 'Especially not with a cellar for a loom.'

'We'll find one,' muttered Jack. 'I'll not be beholden to that man. I've given him a piece of my mind, so let that be the end of it. Come on.' He untied Patch's reins and waited for Hannah to get into the trap. 'I'll take thee back to the Holdens' and then I'll return this horse. They'll charge me double if it's not back afore sunset.'

Patch trotted eagerly enough and Jack dropped Hannah off at the cottage at Hag End Fold. As she watched him turn the trap around and head off again to Egerton, Hannah hoped he would return the horse and come straight back. She had a fear that he would go in to see Ellis Duxbury and give him *a piece of his mind*, or worse.

She went inside, grateful for the hospitality, but wishing that she could go to a home of her own with a full larder, a roaring fire and a comfortable feather bed. She'd become used to such comforts during her time as Ellis's wife and although she was overjoyed that Jack had come home, the prospect of not being able to find anywhere to live filled her with dread.

Inside she accepted Molly's offer of a cup of tea. Thomas had gone back to his work and from below she could hear the thud of his loom. Things had worked out all right for the Holdens, she reminded herself, noticing the swell of pregnancy below Molly's apron. Hopefully they would turn out well for her and Jack as well, once they found a place to live.

Edmund was sitting on a stool looking lost. He kept glancing at her, obviously worried about what his future held – and he had been so happy that morning when he'd set out for his work at the mill with Ellis. Hannah felt guilty that she'd deprived him of that security.

'Are we going to stay here?' he whispered to her when she beckoned him to come to her.

'We're going to get a cottage of our own,' she told him, 'but it won't be the one we had before.'

He looked sad. She knew he'd been looking forward to going home.

'Did Jack not get the keys then?' asked Molly, who was kneading dough at the other end of the table.

'Colonel Fletcher said he wouldn't have Jack as a tenant, not after what happened.'

'I can't say as I'm surprised,' she replied. 'He's not one to do a favour unless it benefits him.'

'Dost tha know of any other cottages that are available?'

Molly shook her head. 'Nowt springs to mind,' she said.

'We need to find one. We can't impose on thee,' she told her friend.

'Tha's welcome to stop as long as tha needs to,' Molly told her.

Hannah was grateful, but she felt despair settle over her. If they couldn't find somewhere to rent she wasn't sure where they would go, because although the Holdens were welcoming she knew that they couldn't stay with them for ever.

Hannah was surprised about an hour later when the sound of hooves and wheels stopped outside the door and Jack hurried in looking alarmed.

'Whatever's the matter?' she asked, jumping up from her chair. Her first thought was always that something had happened to one of the children.

'They're lookin' for thee!' he burst out, reaching out to take hold of her arm. 'We've got to go!' he told her. 'Come on! Quickly!' he insisted as he glanced behind him, as if he thought he was being followed.

'Ellis?' she asked, thinking that he was coming to claim her back by force. After his outburst earlier she wouldn't have been surprised by anything he did.

'No. Not him. The constable. They've raised a hue and cry to have thee arrested!'

'Arrested? What for?' asked Hannah, doubting for a moment that it was true. Jack had a wild look and she wondered, for a moment, if his time in New South Wales had affected his mind and he was imaging it all.

'Bigamy,' he told her. 'Come on. We must get going afore they find thee.'

Hannah stared at him. 'Bigamy?' she repeated, not sure what he was talking about.

'Aye. I bet it were Fletcher's doing. That man Booth said he recognised thee as the wife of Ellis Duxbury.'

'But . . .' Hannah was finding it difficult to make any sense of the situation, although the panic on Jack's face was real enough.

'What's the matter? What's wrong?' asked Molly as she came hurrying up from the cellar with Thomas behind her.

'Jack says as t' constable is lookin' to arrest me!' Hannah told her, feeling bewildered by the turn of events.

'Whatever for?' asked Molly.

'Bigamy,' repeated Jack as he tried to urge Hannah towards the cart. 'Bein' married to two men at t' same time. It's not legal.'

'But that can't be right,' said Molly, glancing at Thomas in disbelief.

'I married Ellis Duxbury,' Hannah admitted, feeling that she had done something shameful. 'I never wanted to,' she added, quietly, hoping that her friend wouldn't judge her too harshly for not having the courage to wait for Jack to come home.

'Hannah's my wife!' said Jack. 'And I'll not have her taken because of this. We need to get away!'

'Mam?' said Edmund, confused by the sudden alarm.

'We'll have to take him with us,' said Hannah as Jack urged her out through the door.

'Aye, come on, lad, thee an all!' urged Jack and he lifted Edmund into the cart before turning to help Hannah up.

'Here!' Molly came running out with the shawl and an old jacket of Thomas's for Edmund to wear. 'Take these!' she urged.

'Thank you,' said Hannah as Jack shook the reins and they lurched forward.

'Don't tell 'em that tha's seen us,' called Jack over his shoulder to the Holdens. 'If they come, tell 'em nowt!'

'Where are we going?' asked Hannah as Jack urged the horse to a gallop on the slippery cobbled streets. She clung to the seat thinking that they were all going to be killed if he didn't slow down.

'Far away from 'ere!' he replied. His face was grim with determination, but it was clear to Hannah that he didn't have a plan. He just knew that they had to run.

She put an arm around Edmund and tried to comfort him. How had it come to this? She'd been so relieved when she'd found Jack. But her situation seemed more precarious now than it had ever been.

At last, when they'd passed out of the boundary of the town, Jack slowed the panting, sweating horse to a walk and she was able to speak to him.

'How did tha find out?' she asked him.

'I were goin' up towards t' Egerton road when I heard someone call to me,' he explained. 'I saw it were Old Frank from up at Hill Fold. I'd spoken to him t' other day when I went to look at yon cottage. He said as t' constable had been up there enquirin' about your whereabouts and thought he should warn me that they were set on arrestin' thee for bigamy.' He turned to look at her. 'It's a serious charge, our Hannah,' he warned her.

'I know,' she said as she gathered the faded shawl more tightly around herself. She didn't want to say much in front of Edmund for fear of making him even more worried, but she knew that being found guilty could mean a prison sentence at the worst and at best a branding. She found herself rubbing her thumbs together as she imagined having her hand locked into the metal holdfast in the court dock and the red hot iron burning a letter 'M' into her flesh.

'What shall we do?' she asked Jack, hoping that he could offer her some hope that the accusation could be refuted. 'It wasn't done on purpose,' she added, although she suspected that Colonel Fletcher would not allow that as an excuse.

'I'll keep thee safe,' Jack promised. But he didn't say how and it was growing dark and Hannah was cold and hungry and she had no idea how much money he had or if it would be safe to take a room somewhere or if they would have to sleep as best they could in the cart.

They were forced to stop when it grew too dark to see. They had no lantern and if the horse turned a leg in a pothole they would be stranded. Jack got down and led Patch along, seeking somewhere for the night.

When he saw a light burning in a window ahead of them, he made towards it and they found it was a small wayside inn.

'Wait there,' he told her. 'I'll enquire about a bed. I doubt news of us will have reached this far. We should be safe enough.'

Hannah hoped that he was right, but she was so tired that she knew she couldn't go on and Edmund had already fallen asleep in her arms.

The landlord came out with a lantern and took Patch round the back to stable him. Jack had lifted his sleeping son down and Hannah followed them inside to a small snug with a fire blazing in the hearth. A man moved aside with his cup of ale to allow her a seat by the fire and the landlady brought out a pot of rabbit stew and some bread. Hannah thought that she was too tired to eat, but when she took a mouthful she found she couldn't stop and Jack had to stay her hand.

'Tha'll give thyself a belly ache,' he warned.

Edmund woke and Hannah made sure he ate as well, then the landlady showed them up to the attic room where there was an iron bed for them all to share. Hannah tucked Edmund in first, in his shirt, and hung up his trousers and the borrowed jacket on a hook before putting his boots neatly side by side. Then she hung up the shawl, eased the too-small slippers from her painful feet in relief and hesitated before unfastening the gown.

She'd schooled herself to appear willing when she'd gone to Ellis's bed. It had been difficult at first. She'd known no other man before except Jack. But Ellis had been kind in his way and she'd accustomed herself to his attentions. Hannah had always thought that when Jack came home she would be overjoyed to renew the intimacies of their marriage with him, but now, in this chilly garret, by the light of one flickering candle she felt shy and unsure. It had been a long time since they'd been together.

He was sitting on the edge of the bed, pulling off his boots. He threw them aside, as he always had. Hannah remembered how it used to drive her mad that he never stood them straight. She watched as he pulled off his trousers and then his shirt. There were scars across his back that hadn't been there before and the sight shocked her, but she didn't like to ask how he'd come by them.

'Come to bed,' he told her, holding up the blankets for her to clamber in beside him.

'Perhaps we'd best lie either side of Edmund,' she suggested. 'I don't want him to tumble out.'

'Aye,' agreed Jack. 'Tha's probably for t' best.'

Thankfully, Hannah lay down next to her son feeling exhausted. When she'd prayed and hoped for Jack to come home she'd never envisaged it being like this, she thought. Although, as she reached across the sleeping lad to grasp her husband's hand, she knew that she would never regret his return, no matter what new challenges it brought.

CHAPTER TWENTY-FIVE

Hannah woke with a start the next morning and for a moment wondered where she was. Then memories of the previous day surfaced and as the fear of being found guilty of the charge of bigamy took hold of her once again, she found herself trembling.

'Is tha awake?' whispered Jack.

'Aye,' Hannah looked around for the shawl. 'What are we going to do?' she asked, hoping that, during the night, Jack might have thought of some plan or solution that would save her.

'We'll get it sorted out,' he promised.

'I doubt Ellis Duxbury will speak up for me after what he said yesterday,' whispered Hannah, glancing at Edmund who was still sleeping. She wanted to ask Jack what would happen if it was found that she was Ellis's legal wife. Could she be forced to go back to him? Would she have to try to seek an annulment? A divorce would be impossible. It would cost too much – and the shame it would bring was unthinkable. 'Dost tha think we need to talk to someone who knows about these things?' she asked, wondering if Jack had enough money to pay for the advice of a lawyer.

'Aye, 'appen so, if it comes to that,' he said. 'But we've more pressing concerns to deal with first.'

'What concerns?' she asked, not able to consider what might be more important to him than saving her from a prison cell or the excruciating pain of a branding.

'We need to get our lasses,' he said.

'Aye, of course we do,' agreed Hannah, feeling guilty that her own fears had made her forget her daughters for the moment. 'But will it be safe to go for them?' she asked. Hannah didn't know how far the hue and cry for her arrest had spread. Quarry Bank was some distance away, but what if Mr Greg had heard that the constable was looking for her? To walk into his mill might be a dangerous thing to do. 'It might be for the best if tha went in and asked for them alone,' she told Jack. 'I told them I was Mrs Duxbury last time I were there.'

He nodded. 'Aye. It might be for the best,' he agreed. 'I can leave thee and Edmund nearby to wait.'

'Where will we go after?' asked Hannah. It was difficult enough being on the run with one child. How much harder would it be when Ruth and Kitty were with them as well. She knew that Jack couldn't keep paying for beds at inns, especially when he wasn't earning any money. He might have a bit put by, but it wouldn't last long if it was squandered. He needed to find work and a place for them to live.

'Don't worry,' he told her. 'We'll find a safe place.'

He leaned to kiss her forehead to reassure her, but Hannah was unconvinced by his confident words. She thought he was only saying it to prevent her worrying.

After they were dressed they went down to the parlour and Jack paid for tea and bread whilst the horse and cart was brought round for them. There was payment for the stabling too and he bought a net of hay to take with them so Patch could be fed. The horse was another thing that was worrying Hannah. The stables at Egerton had been expecting him back yesterday and she worried that they would be accused of stealing to add to their problems.

They headed south in a light drizzle. Edmund was excited at the prospect of fetching his sisters and seemed to be warming towards his father. Jack let him take a turn with the reins, showing how to guide the horse and instruct him to go faster or slow down. From the smile on her son's face Hannah could see that he was enjoying himself and she tried to return his grin with enthusiasm every time he turned to her. It wouldn't help to allow Edmund to see how frightened she was.

By early afternoon they were approaching Quarry Bank.

‘There it is!’ cried Edmund, pointing out the mill to his father. ‘That’s it, over there.’

At the next inn they came to, set back on the side of the road, Jack reined in the horse. ‘Whoa!’ he called to Patch as they rumbled to a halt.

‘Why are we stopping?’ asked Edmund. Hannah could see his disappointment. They were so near and he was eager to be reunited with Ruth and Kitty.

‘We need to wait here so that thy father can go on alone,’ explained Hannah. ‘He’ll not be long. He’ll bring Ruth and Kitty to us soon,’ she promised.

They went inside and Jack asked for tea and bread again. The landlord seemed unimpressed by Hannah’s worn clothes and her son’s oversized jacket, but he saw that her husband looked respectable enough and agreed to provide her with a seat beside the hearth until Jack returned. Hannah worried what the man must think of her. She could see that he was curious, but she kept her eyes averted and refused to be drawn into conversation once Jack had gone. She just hoped that it wouldn’t take him too long and that once her daughters came, things would seem better.

Hannah’s wait seemed interminable. The bread was long since eaten and the tea drunk and she sensed that the landlord was wondering what he would do if Jack didn’t return. She wanted to plead with him to be patient and not turn them out, but the inn was growing busy and she could hear the grumbles of the paying guests who were unable to seat themselves nearer to the fire.

Every time she heard hooves outside she wanted to jump up and see if it was Jack with their daughters, but she was reluctant to relinquish her seat so she sent Edmund again and again to look out of the door and every time he returned with a glum expression to tell her that Ruth and Kitty weren't here yet. Then, when she'd given up hope, he came back in with Jack and Hannah got up to greet them.

'Where are they?' she asked, realising that Jack was alone.

He was shaking his head. 'They kept making difficulties,' he said.

'Did tha see them?' she asked.

'Aye.' Hannah could see that something was wrong. 'They fetched 'em from t' mill, but they were unsure.'

'How dost tha mean?'

'They asked 'em if I were their father. Ruth looked at me keenly enough and said she thought so, but Kitty hung back, all shy, and Mr Greg said he weren't convinced and needed to be certain – that he couldn't just let 'em leave with anyone. Tha'll have to come with me tomorrow,' he said. 'We'll have to chance it, or we'll never get them lasses back.'

Hannah wanted to weep. All through the afternoon she'd been longing for the moment that her daughters would walk through the door and now she felt as if something had been stolen from her.

'Can we afford to stay here for the night?' she asked. She half-turned to see that the chair by the fire had been taken. 'We could sleep in the back of the cart I suppose.'

'Don't talk nonsense. We've no blankets.' Hannah watched as he pulled some coins from his pocket and began to count them. 'I'll ask how much he wants for a room, or a bed,' he told her with a nod of his head towards the landlord.

The man took three shillings from them. Hannah thought it was too much for the one bed in the small room that he showed them too, but the landlord had a gleam in his eye. He knew that they were desperate and had nowhere else to go. He'd overcharge for the stabling as well, thought Hannah, and the dishes of the pot-luck stew that they ate sitting on stools in the coldest part of the parlour.

'What if Mr Greg still refuses to let Ruth and Kitty go?' asked Hannah when they'd gone upstairs and were growing warmer in the bed.

'It'll be all right,' said Jack once more. She had to believe him, trust him, thought Hannah. Surely a man who could get himself home from the other side of the world could manage to reclaim his family and find them somewhere to live.

'I'm worried that tha's spendin' all thy money,' she whispered, not wanting to be overheard.

'I've enough,' he told her.

Realising he didn't want to discuss it, Hannah snuggled against him, the familiarity of his body reacquainting itself with hers.

Morning dawned, and after another paltry meal of bread and tea, they backed Patch into the shafts of the cart and set off the short distance down to Quarry Bank.

The mill was already working. Hannah could hear the thud of the mill wheel as they approached, and children were fetching and carrying tubs of cotton and bobbins to and fro across the busy yard.

She wondered if they should have gone to the house, but after Patch had been secured, she followed Jack to the mill office and found that Mr Greg was expecting them.

'Mrs . . .' He hesitated and glanced at something that was written in a ledger on his desk. 'Mrs Fisher?'

She nodded. 'Aye, that's right,' she told him. 'I am Mrs Fisher. This is my husband come back from New South Wales.'

'You called yourself by a different name the last time you came here. You were with a Mr . . .?'

'Mr Duxbury,' she confirmed.

'I was given the impression that you were the other man's wife. He said he was taking responsibility for your children.'

'Aye. And you said as we couldn't take them in case their father came back. And now he has.'

'It seems rather . . . convenient.'

'It's true!' Hannah told him, seeing that the mill owner was suspicious. 'This is my husband. Jack Fisher!'

'Your daughters weren't certain this man is their father.'

'Well, it's been a long time since they've seen him. He's changed,' admitted Hannah. 'And our Kitty was only very young when he was sent away.'

She looked at Jack, hoping that he wouldn't accept a refusal from Mr Greg. She was determined not to leave Quarry Bank again without her daughters.

'You must understand that I have a responsibility for these girls,' said Mr Greg, repeating what he'd said on Hannah's first visit. 'I can't allow them to leave with just anyone who claims to be their parent.'

'I'm their mother,' Hannah told him. 'There was no question about that last time I came.'

Mr Greg nodded. 'That's true,' he agreed. He looked at Jack again, taking in his swarthy appearance where he'd been tanned by the sun. It was true that he didn't look like an English weaver any more.

'I would need proof that this man is indeed your husband before I can allow you to take the girls away from here,' he told her.

'Well, if it's proof tha's after, tha should have said so yesterday,' Jack told him as he reached into the pocket of his jacket and took out a folded piece of crumpled paper. He opened it up and slapped it down on the desk in front of Mr Greg. 'This here's my certificate of freedom,' he told him. 'There's my name,' he added, pointing with a grubby finger. 'Will that do thee?' Hannah wished that he would be less aggressive and remember his manners. A confrontation would help nobody.

Mr Greg looked at the piece of paper carefully and then back at Jack who was towering over him with his arms folded across his ample chest. 'It seems legitimate,' he agreed, hesitantly. Then he seemed to make a decision. He turned to the mill manager. 'Get the girls,' he told him. 'Take them to the apprentice house to collect their belongings and then they can go with their parents.'

Hannah felt a flood of relief at the man's words. 'Thank you, sir,' she told him, trying to make up for her husband's brusque manner. 'They should never have been sent here in the first place,' she added.

Moments later they were back in the yard and Jack led the horse and cart up to the door of the apprentice house to wait for Ruth and Kitty to come out. Hannah was still unsure where they were going to go. Mr Greg seemed unaware that she was wanted by the constable, but word would reach him soon, she was sure. She hoped that they could get far away before it did.

It wasn't long before the door opened and her daughters ran out. Hannah opened her arms wide and then hugged the lasses to her as relief nearly overwhelmed her.

'You're safe now,' she told them, trying not to cry and hoping that it was true. 'Let's go!' she urged Jack, eager to get away from the mill.

Ruth and Kitty threw their bags into the back of the cart and climbed in. Edmund insisted that he wanted to sit with them and they made room for him. They both looked pale and Kitty had cotton fluff in her hair, but their faces were beaming and there was the atmosphere of a holiday as Jack clicked his tongue and Patch pulled them up the driveway towards the turnpike road.

'Kitty wasn't sure if it was really our dad,' explained Ruth as they trotted along. 'I knew it was, even though he looks different.' She exchanged a smile with Jack.

'Kitty were too young to remember me,' he agreed, although Hannah could hear the disappointment in his voice.

'Is tha sure tha doesn't remember him?' Hannah asked her younger daughter.

'I think I do. But Mr Greg wouldn't give me time to recall,' she explained. 'But I'm glad he's come home and that you came for us. I hated that mill,' she told her mother.

The child looked worn out, thought Hannah, and it wasn't long before Kitty had fallen asleep, her head resting on her sister's shoulder.

'Mam?' said Ruth after a while. 'Who was that other man who came with thee last time? The one tha said that tha was married to?'

'His name was Ellis Duxbury.'

'But tha's not really married to him?' asked Ruth. 'Tha's still wed to my dad?'

'Aye, of course I am. Mr Duxbury were just helpin' me out so's I could get thee back from yon mill.'

'Why did he do that? He said we were to go and live with him.'

'It's complicated, our Ruth,' Hannah told her, wishing that her daughter would stop asking questions. 'It's different now that thy father's come home. We'll be livin' with him now, like we used to. We'll be a family again.'

'So are we going back home? Back to Hill Fold?' she asked.

'No. We'll be finding somewhere new to live,' she said.

'Where?' asked Ruth. 'Where are we going?'

Hannah turned back to look at her husband. 'Where are we going, Jack?' she asked him. The sun was high overhead and she wasn't sure of their direction of travel. He didn't answer her straight away and she suspected that he was uncertain himself.

'We could go to London,' said Jack after a moment. 'We could disappear there. They'd never find us in a big city like that.'

'But it's such a long way,' protested Hannah, horrified by the thought of it.

'Not that far,' he replied.

Hannah thought that having travelled all around the world, the journey from Lancashire to London was nothing to Jack, but to her it seemed an unimaginable distance.

'Where would we live? What work would tha do?' she asked. 'All tha knows is cotton.'

'I know more than that,' he told her. 'I've worked at all sorts these past years.'

'Tha's not thinkin' of goin' back to sea?' she asked, suddenly alarmed that she might be left alone with the children again if he got work on board a ship.

'No. I'll not do that. But there'll be work on the docks down there. We'll find a little place to rent.'

'I'm not sure,' admitted Hannah. She didn't want to leave her home town and everything that was familiar to her to start over in some strange place.

'Perhaps tha should leave us somewhere and take the horse and cart back to Egerton,' she suggested as it reached mid-afternoon and the children grew restless, picking up her anxiety. She knew that they were hungry too, but Jack had driven them past two inns where they could have stopped for food. 'It won't help us if tha gets arrested for stealing,' she reasoned with him. Her worst fear was the constable would find them and they would both be sent to prison. And what would happen to the children then? They would be no better off if they were returned to the workhouse or the mill or, heaven forbid, Edmund was sent down the pit again. 'Hast tha got enough money to pay for the extra time we've had the cart?' she ventured.

Jack let out a sigh. 'I just want to get away – to keep us safe,' he said at last.

'But it's no good just travelling on and on,' Hannah said. 'We need to have a plan.'

'Aye. I suppose so,' he admitted.

They fell silent and the tired horse clopped on. 'Should we just go back and try to sort it out?' asked Hannah after a while.

The thought of going back and being arrested frightened her, but she'd decided that she would prefer to get things sorted out than just keep running. She needed to know where she stood, and which man she was married to or she would never have any peace of mind. 'Let's go back,' she said again. 'Return the horse and cart at least so tha can't be accused of being dishonest. It'll do us no good to start a new life as thieves. Please, Jack!'

She saw him hesitate at her words, but then he shook his head. 'I'll not take thee back whilst Fletcher has yon constable lookin' for thee,' he said.

'But I'm sure I've done nowt wrong,' she protested. 'It were a mistake. That's all. Everyone said I were a widow. Let's go back. Let's try to make things right,' she said again. 'I don't want to go all the way to London.'

Hannah was aware that the children were sitting silently, listening, as she argued with him.

'I'll talk to Ellis Duxbury again,' she promised. 'I'll get him to say that it was a misunderstanding.

They can't find me guilty of anything if he says I'm not his wife.'

Jack shook his head again. 'I'll not take thee back to that madman.'

'He's not like that. Not really,' persuaded Hannah. 'I think he were just shocked. I'll talk to him. Make him see reason. And tha can take this horse and cart back. Pay for the extra days. Then we can neither of us be accused of owt, and we can find a cottage and settle down rather than goin' off to somewhere strange at t' other end of the country.' She waited as he drove on in silence. 'It'll be better for the children,' she added. 'You want to go home, don't you?' she asked, turning to include them in her pleading.

Kitty was still asleep and Ruth looked away as if she was afraid of saying anything.

'Tell thy father tha wants to go home,' Hannah encouraged her.

'I do,' she said, quietly. 'But why do they want to arrest thee?' she asked her mother.

'They think I was wed to two men at the same time,' explained Hannah. 'But I never was.'

'But tha said tha were wed to that Mr Duxbury,' persisted Ruth.

'I know. I thought I was, but I wasn't. I'm wed to thy father. Always have been.'

Ruth nodded, but she looked confused. It was confusing, thought Hannah. That's why it needed to be sorted out.

At Hannah's insistence, Jack eventually agreed

to turn the cart around and go back to Bolton. She thought it was the threat of being arrested himself for the theft of the horse and cart that persuaded him in the end.

'Tha doesn't want to be sent back to New South Wales,' she'd told him. 'They'll send thee for life this time. There'll be no comin' back.'

He agreed to stop off at the same inn where they'd slept the previous night. The landlord raised his eyebrows at the addition of Ruth and Kitty to their party, but he said nothing except to tell them the price for two rooms – seven and sixpence. Hannah knew it was daylight robbery, but Patch was exhausted from pulling the heavily laden cart and if they allowed the horse to become ill or injured or, heaven forbid, die, their situation would be even worse. So they saw him safely stabled, ate some stew and went to try to get some sleep before rising early the next morning to go back to Egerton.

CHAPTER TWENTY-SIX

It was mid-afternoon as they came up the rise into the village.

'Let me down here,' said Hannah as they reached the end of the lane that led down to the Eagle Mill. Go on to the stable and I'll meet thee there in a bit, when I've had a word with Ellis.'

'I'd rather come with thee,' said Jack.

'No.' Hannah jumped down from the cart. 'It's better if I go alone,' she said. 'He'll not harm me down there where all the millhands are. It's not like I'll be seeing him alone.'

She knew that Jack wasn't happy about her decision, but she thought that she stood more chance of reasoning with Ellis if she went alone. He'd been shocked when he'd first discovered that Jack had returned, she realised that – shocked and angry. But now that he'd had time to consider what had happened, she hoped that he would listen to her and help her to get the charge of bigamy dropped and the constable called off so that she and Jack could sort out a cottage and a job and get on with their lives.

Hannah walked down the path that followed the

flow of the brook until she came to the yard where the main doors to the mill stood open. She quailed as she approached them. Her last visit here had been difficult enough, with the men watching her as she took Ellis his dinner, but she knew that this one would be worse. She just hoped that he wouldn't shout or lose his temper, or worse, refuse to speak to her at all.

With a deep breath to steady her nerves, Hannah went inside. The noise of the machinery made speech impossible and she was forced to wait until one of the men noticed her.

'I've come to see Mr Duxbury!' she shouted above the din of the spinning machines.

The man stared at her for a moment. Hannah wasn't sure if he recognised her from her last visit or knew who she was. Then he began to shake his head.

'He's not here!' he shouted back.

Puzzled, Hannah watched the man return to his work leaving her with no option other than to step out of the mill, with her ears ringing, and head back up the track towards the village.

She wondered if Ellis had fallen ill, and if so, who was caring for him and Florence. With concerns for the baby at the forefront of her mind she increased her pace, thinking that May might know something. But she decided to go and knock on the door of his house first to see if he was at home.

Hannah raised the knocker on the familiar green

door and gently rapped it. If Florence was at home and asleep, Ellis wouldn't thank her for waking the child. But no one came to answer it. Hannah listened at the door but it seemed quiet inside. She knocked again, more forcefully this time, and when the door still wasn't answered she went to the window and tried to peer through the net curtains into Ellis's front parlour.

'Hannah?' She turned around to see that May had come to her door. 'Oh it is thee,' she continued. 'I wasn't sure,' she added.

Hannah pulled at her shawl, realising that it was her poor clothing that had made May doubt herself.

'I'm looking for Ellis,' she said as May crossed the street to join her.

'He's gone,' said May. 'I saw them loading his things onto a cart early one morning and then off he went.'

'What about Florence?' asked Hannah, suddenly concerned about who was caring for the little girl.

'Took her with 'im,' said May.

'Dost tha know where he's gone?'

May shook her head. 'He didn't say nowt to me,' she complained. 'But I'm right worried about that little lass,' she confessed. 'He's no idea how to care for her on his own.' Hannah was beset by a feeling of guilt and she suddenly felt desperate to see Florence to reassure herself about the child's welfare. 'I thought tha might know summat about it,' May continued. 'Hast tha left 'im?' she asked. 'I saw thee goin' away on a cart with another man.'

'That was my husband, Jack. He's come back,' Hannah told her.

'But I thought tha were married to Ellis,' replied May, looking puzzled.

Hannah shook her head. 'No. I'm Jack's wife,' she said.

'Is that why Ellis went away?'

'I don't know,' Hannah told her. 'He was angry when he found out. I've come back to try to make it right with him. I need to find him,' she said, realising that her situation could never be resolved if she couldn't find Ellis Duxbury. 'I'm worried about him now,' she added. 'And Florence.'

'Aye. Poor little Florence.' May wiped away a stray tear and Hannah saw how much she was going to miss the child.

She turned as footsteps approached and saw her family coming down the street.

'There tha is!' exclaimed Jack. 'I thought tha were goin' to meet us at t' stables. Hast seen him? What did he say?'

'He's gone,' Hannah explained. 'May here's just been tellin' me. He went in the middle of the night and nobody knows where.'

'Are we going in?' asked Edmund when he reached the doorstep. Hannah saw him look longingly at the door.

'Not now. Mr Duxbury has gone away,' she told him gently, hoping that Jack wouldn't see the disappointment on the lad's face.

'This is the house,' Edmund told his sisters. 'This is where we were going to live.'

Ruth and Kitty gazed at the house longingly, and Hannah hoped they wouldn't say anything that might upset their father. The life she'd promised them on her first visit to Quarry Bank was no longer possible and they would have to make the best of what Jack could offer.

'We shouldn't have come back,' Jack grumbled. 'We should have gone on as we were.'

Hannah wondered if he was right. She hated having to turn away from the house that had sheltered her these past months. She would have liked nothing better than to go inside and light a fire and sit down beside it in a comfortable chair. If only she could have Jack and her children beside her it would be perfect. For a moment she wondered if it would be possible for them to rent it, but she quickly realised that it would cost too much money for such a fine place.

'Where will I find thee, if I hear owt?' May asked her.

'I'm not sure. Send word to Thomas and Molly Holden,' Hannah told her, giving her the address.

'I will,' May promised as Jack urged them on their way. Hannah knew it was a long walk back into Bolton and they needed to get across the open countryside before night fell.

As they walked, she worried about where Ellis had gone. He'd been angry with her for leaving with Jack, but surely that wasn't what had prompted him to leave his house and his job and disappear? And who was taking care of Florence? Her arms ached for the child who had become a daughter to her.

'Where are we to go?' she ventured to ask Jack at last as the outskirts of the town came into sight. 'Shall we go back to the Holdens'?'

'No. We'll go home,' he replied.

'But . . . we don't have a home,' she whispered hoping that the children wouldn't overhear their conversation.

'Yon cottage is standin' empty,' he replied. 'It were our home and there's no one else livin' there.'

'But it's all locked up.'

'I'll get in,' he replied. 'We'll sleep there tonight.'

'We can't!' protested Hannah. 'It's breakin' the law!' She was desperately worried that Jack seemed intent on getting himself into trouble again.

'Dost tha have a better idea?' he asked her. 'We can't expect the Holdens to put us all up.'

'I know,' said Hannah. 'But it can only be just for tonight. We'll have to find a proper place tomorrow.'

'Aye,' he agreed as they turned up the track towards Hill Fold. 'We'll just shelter there for tonight, and tomorrow we'll be on our way again. It were stupid to come back here,' he told her.

CHAPTER TWENTY-SEVEN

It was dark by the time they approached Hill Fold and it was only the familiarity of the well-trodden path that led them safely to what had been for many years their own front door. Jack warned them to be quiet.

'Folk'll be asleep,' he told the children. 'We don't want to wake 'em.'

The door was locked against them so Jack led them around the edge of the row of cottages and they approached it from the back. Hannah knew the small window that lit the pantry didn't close properly because the wood swelled in damp weather. She hoped that the people who'd locked up the house hadn't noticed that it wasn't secure.

She heard Jack swear quietly as he fumbled with it.

'I should have thought to bring a lantern,' he muttered. 'There! That's got it.' He turned and spoke to Edmund. 'Dost tha think tha can get through there, lad, if I give thee a leg up?' he whispered.

Hannah couldn't see her son's face, but she sensed his reluctance.

‘It’s all right,’ she told him. ‘Do as thy father says.’

Jack pushed the boy forward and made a step with his hands to get Edmund high enough.

‘Unlock the back door when tha’s inside,’ said Hannah, hoping that he would fit through the narrow window. It seemed very small.

‘Put one arm in and then get thy head through,’ advised Jack as Edmund struggled to balance and get a grip on the sill. ‘Don’t mess about!’

‘He’s not messing,’ protested Hannah. ‘He’s doin’ his best. But what if he can’t get through?’ She wanted to ask what they would do if he got stuck, but she didn’t want to frighten the lad. She wished that she could see him better, but there was only a sliver of moon and from time to time that was obscured by cloud.

She was suddenly startled by a sound from the cottage next door. It was only Sam coughing, she realised, but Hannah knew that if anyone heard them breaking in they might call for the night watch.

Hannah turned back as she heard a bump.

‘He’s in!’ said Jack.

A moment later she heard the squeak of the bolt on the back door as it was eased back and Edmund opened it.

‘Quickly!’ Jack said as Ruth and Kitty went in ahead of them. They all hurried into the kitchen and her husband re-bolted the door behind them.

Hannah breathed a sigh of relief. She knew that

what they were doing was wrong, but this was their home and it felt right that they should be safely inside it. Without the need for a lantern or candle to guide her, Hannah went through to the parlour. As far as she could tell nothing had been changed since the day she left it. She knew that there had been a few rushlights left over and she cautiously made her way towards the fireplace and reached for the tin that held them and the flint.

'Close the curtains, Ruth,' she instructed her daughter. 'And make sure there's no gap. We don't want anyone to see the light.'

She struck the flint and managed to get the rushlight to take hold of the spark. It spluttered into a faint glow and Hannah held it up to look around the room. Everything was as she'd left it. The damp straw mattresses lay in the corner with the threadbare blanket folded on top of them. They were hardly fit to sleep on, she thought as she went to look more closely and startled a mouse that scurried away from the nest it had made. 'Oh!' she exclaimed.

'What's wrong?' asked Jack.

'Just a mouse. It made me jump,' she told him as she moved back towards the hearth and saw the four bowls and spoons and her kettle still hanging from its chain in the fireplace. But the scuttle that had held coal was empty. There was no chance of kindling a fire to keep them warm and even if there had been, the smoke from their chimney would have given them away.

‘I’m hungry,’ said Edmund.

‘I know. We all are,’ Hannah told him.

‘Are we going to eat?’ he asked hopefully.

‘In a bit,’ she told him. She knew that she’d left nothing in the pantry and they’d had no chance to buy any provisions.

‘Are we going to stay here?’ asked Ruth. She didn’t say it was worse than the mill, worse even than the workhouse, but Hannah wondered if that was what she was thinking.

‘Only for tonight,’ Hannah told her.

‘We’ll get a bit of sleep,’ said Jack as the sound of rain began to pitter patter on the window. ‘At least we’ll be dry. Then in t’ mornin’ we’ll get on our way.’

They did their best with what was left of the straw mattresses. Hannah put the blanket over Ruth and Kitty, wrapped Edmund in the shawl and allowed Jack to spread his coat over her when she lay down beside him on the freezing cold floor. She thought it seemed even colder than being outside; the only advantage was that she was dry.

She lay awake for a long time, listening to the storm beat on the roof and the windows. Jack’s steady breathing told her that he had fallen asleep. He must have grown used to sleeping anywhere, she thought. Edmund was awake. She could tell, but she didn’t speak to him, hoping that he would eventually doze off. Kitty had fallen asleep straight away. She still didn’t look strong and Hannah worried that the damp straw would set her coughing off again. Ruth sighed and turned restlessly. Goodness knows what she was thinking. Hannah just hoped that they could find a way to make everything all right again. It wasn't the joyous homecoming that she'd dreamed of.

When daylight crept around the edges of the curtains, Hannah eased herself up from the floor and crept to the back door. She tried to open it quietly but Jack woke as she struggled with the bolt.

'Where's tha goin?' he asked.

'Just down t' yard.'

As she made her way to the privy she shivered. The sun was rising and at least the rain had cleared, but it was very cold. She wished that they could get a fire going to warm the cottage and fetch water from the pump. But none of it could be done without their neighbours seeing them and although Gracie and Sam were good friends, Hannah was unsure if she could completely trust some of the others. Like Isaac Crompton, who'd given evidence against the weavers who were his own folk; she knew that there were some who would turn spies for Colonel Fletcher in return for a favour.

The children were all awake when she slipped back inside. They looked at her expectantly.

'The childer need to eat,' she reminded Jack, feeling her own stomach ache with hunger. They'd not eaten since the morning before. 'Hast tha got any more money?'

Hannah still had no idea how much Jack had left. Up until now she'd watched as he'd pulled coins from his pocket, but he'd never said whether there were any more and she knew that paying for the horse and cart, and a little extra to keep the stableman sweet so's he wouldn't report them as thieves, must have cost him dearly.

'Don't worry. I've enough,' he told her. 'Dost t' pieman still come round?'

'I don't know. But there's no point sitting here waiting for him,' she replied. 'If we set off towards t' market we might meet him on the way. Then perhaps we should go to see Fletcher again,' she suggested. 'If we tell him that Ellis Duxbury has gone he might call t' constable off. I'll not rest easy whilst I keep thinking they might come for me.'

As if conjured by her worst fears, Hannah started at the sound of several pairs of footsteps approaching the cottage.

'Let's go!' she urged Jack. 'Out the back way! Come on! Someone must have seen us.'

Her heart was racing with fear as she tried to grasp hold of all three of her children at once. Edmund looked terrified and Kitty, having just woken, was confused.

'Will they arrest us for sleeping here?' Ruth asked anxiously.

'We'll not wait to find out,' Hannah told her as she pushed them towards the back door. She wrenched it open, glancing back to see if Jack was following them. She hoped he wouldn't stay behind to try to give them time to escape. If he was arrested she would be no better off than when he was away, worse in fact, she thought.

'Hannah Fisher!'

She saw Constable Booth too late to be able to close the door again. He closed his hand firmly around her wrist. 'I'm arresting thee on suspicion of bigamy,' he told her. 'Tha'll have to come with me.'

'Where to? Where's tha taking me!' protested Hannah. 'What about these childer?'

'They looks old enough to fend for themselves,' observed the constable as he pulled her out of the doorway.

'Where are we going?' she asked again, looking frantically around for any sign of Jack. Surely he would come to help her and rescue her from this man, she thought as she saw the faces of her scared and bewildered children watching as she was dragged towards a horse and cart that was waiting at the end of the lane.

'I'm taking thee to the lock up,' the constable told her. 'Then tha'll come up afore the magistrate.'

'Colonel Fletcher?'

'Aye. That's right. He'll not have behaviour like it!' warned the constable. 'He'll not have such goings on in this town.'

'I've done nowt wrong!'

'Aye, well, tell that to the colonel. My orders are to take thee in. That's all I know.'

Hannah had no choice but to get up onto the cart. Her hands were bound in front of her and her cheeks blazed with shame as all her former neighbours came to their doors to see what the fuss was all about. As they lurched off, she tried to turn to acknowledge the children, hoping that their father would take good care of them until she was released. Surely she would be released? The charge against her was ridiculous.

The lock up was situated near to the workhouse, but when the constable unlocked the high metal gate and pushed her down the worn steps to the stone building that held the cells, Hannah saw that it was a far, far worse place. It stank to high heaven of human waste and goodness only knows what else. The smell made her retch and she tried to cover her mouth and nose with her hands.

The constable shoved her inside the dark, drab building. Water was dripping in from a leak in the roof and the floor was slick with moss and moisture. He unlocked the gate of the middle of three cells and she was forced to step inside and wait as it clanged shut behind her and the key grated in the lock. There was a wooden bench down one side of the cell and a tiny window high up in the wall. When the outside door was closed, Hannah was left alone in near darkness, water pooling around the flimsy ill-fitting slippers that she wore. Her hands had been untied; she was thankful for that as she tried to warm herself by rubbing her arms.

Hannah sat down on the bench. She was thirsty and hungry as well as very afraid. She hoped that she wouldn't be held here for very long and that she would soon have the opportunity to explain to Colonel Fletcher that Ellis Duxbury had disappeared and she had no other husband than Jack Fisher.

CHAPTER TWENTY-EIGHT

Hannah had expected the constable to come back quite soon, but it seemed hours before she heard his footsteps and the door to her cell was unlocked.

'Come along,' he told her taking a tight hold of her upper arm.

'Where are we going?' she asked. 'I need a drink of water,' she protested. 'I need summat to eat. I've had nowt since yesterday.'

The constable shrugged. 'Nothing to do with me,' he told her as he pushed her ahead of him, back up the steps to where the horse and cart was waiting. Hannah considered trying to twist free and make a run for it, but she knew she couldn't run in the tight slippers and that the constable was probably quicker than her anyway.

'Where are we going,' she asked again as he picked up the reins.

'To the petty sessions,' he said. 'Colonel Fletcher's come from his pit office to hear evidence.'

Hannah hung her head to hide the shame she felt as they drove through the streets of Bolton.

She wanted to lift her shawl to hide her face, but it was impossible with her hands bound.

Their progress was slow as they threaded their way through a crowd that had assembled to watch her arrival. It was a pity some folk had nothing better to do, thought Hannah.

She scanned the faces, looking for Jack and the children, but didn't catch sight of them until they reached the door of the court room where they were waiting outside. She tried to speak to them but Constable Booth pushed her past before they could exchange a word.

Inside, Colonel Fletcher had spread his ample girth across a straight-backed wooden chair behind a polished table. He looked at her with contempt as she was brought in and Hannah was aware that she presented a sorry spectacle with her clothing dirty from the lock-up and nothing covering her hair.

'Name?' he demanded.

'Hannah Fisher, sir.'

'Fisher is it?' he asked, leaning forward to intimidate her. 'Not Mrs Duxbury then?'

Hannah held his gaze. 'No, sir,' she told him. 'I'm the wife of Jack Fisher.'

'Yes. I think that much is true,' replied Colonel Fletcher. 'Do you know what you are accused of, Mrs Fisher?'

Hannah nodded. 'Aye. Bigamy,' she whispered.

'I didn't hear you, Mrs Fisher.'

'Bigamy,' she repeated.

'And do you know what that means, Mrs Fisher?'

Hannah nodded. She could feel herself trembling and wished that she could sit down. The room seemed to be spinning slightly around her and she felt as if she were watching the proceedings from afar, as an interested onlooker, removed from her own body.

'Answer me!' shouted the colonel, making her flinch.

'Aye. I know what it means. But it isn't true,' she told him.

'Not true?' The colonel gave a slight snigger. 'So you deny that you married a Mr Ellis Duxbury from Egerton in the knowledge that you were already the wife of another man?'

Hannah wasn't sure what to say. She was finding it difficult to explain her situation to this man who showed her no sympathy.

'I thought I was a widow,' she said after a moment. 'Everyone said I was a widow.'

'And what made you believe you were a widow, Mrs Fisher?' asked the colonel, leaning back on the chair and making it creak. Hannah wondered if it might collapse under his weight.

'My husband was sent to New South Wales, sir. I'd heard nothing from him. Everyone said he must have died. Even Mr Cartwright at the workhouse had me down as a widow.'

'But your husband wasn't dead, was he?' asked

the colonel. 'Was he?' he repeated in a louder voice when Hannah didn't immediately respond.

'No, sir,' she admitted. 'He came back, but it was only after.'

'After you had married Ellis Duxbury?'

'Aye, that's right.'

'Well,' said the colonel with an air of satisfaction. 'There we have it – a clear admission that you married Ellis Duxbury when you were already the wife of Jack Fisher. There is irrefutable evidence here,' he said to his clerk who was scratching at his paper with a badly shaped pen. 'You'll be remanded to the gaol at Lancaster to await trial,' said the colonel, addressing Hannah. 'But it's obvious that the verdict will be one of guilt. Take her out,' he instructed the constable.

'Ellis Duxbury has disappeared!' shouted Hannah. Her heart was beating wildly as Constable Booth approached her. But Colonel Fletcher ignored her and she was grasped once again by her already bruised arm and taken from the courtroom.

It had grown dark in the short time that Hannah had been inside. The streetlamps had been lit and the crowd had dispersed into the surrounding inns and beerhouses. She saw Jack, waiting anxiously with the children.

'Hannah?' He began to approach her, but the constable threatened him with his nightstick.

'Get back!'

'Where's tha takin' 'er?' Hannah heard Jack ask him.

'Back to the lock-up. Then she'll be put on the cart to Lancaster at first light.'

'Lancaster? What for?'

'To be tried for bigamy.'

'Jack!' called Hannah as she stumbled against the constable, feeling faint. 'Help me. Please help me.'

'I'll get thee out,' he promised. 'Don't fret, our Hannah. I'll not let 'em harm thee. Here! Take this.' He pushed in front of the constable and thrust a pie into her hands. Hannah took a bite quickly in case it was snatched from her. It was still warm and the potatoes and onions were soft and tasty.

'Find Ellis Duxbury,' she pleaded with her husband. 'Ask him to speak up for me.'

'I will,' promised Jack.

'Come on now,' said Constable Booth, short of patience. 'Time to go.'

Back in the lock-up, Hannah shivered uncontrollably as she sat huddled on the wooden bench in total darkness. She felt a little better with the pie inside her and, although she hadn't been given a drink, she'd managed to cup her hands together and gather a little of the rainwater where it was dripping through the roof again.

Jack had been right when he'd said they'd been stupid to come back, she thought. She'd believed that it was the right thing to do and that it would be easy to sort out the misunderstanding about her marriage to Ellis Duxbury. But now she knew that she'd been wrong. They should have kept the horse and cart and gone to London like Jack wanted. She should never have persuaded him otherwise.

What was going to happen to her now? she wondered. She hoped it wouldn't be a prison sentence. She thought she'd rather bear the pain of a branding if it meant she could be released to be with her husband and children again. Then, if Jack still wanted to go to London, she wouldn't try to talk him out of it. Even if he went back to sea, he would return with money. And she'd already managed to care for the children on her own so it wouldn't be that hard, especially now that Ruth was almost grown up.

She tugged at the borrowed shawl, but there was little warmth in it. The slippers were ruined. She'd taken them off and put them on the bench to try to keep them dry, but they would never be fit to return to Molly. She would have to send her some money in payment, thought Hannah.

Although she was tired, she couldn't sleep. The bench was hard and she was shivering with the cold, and with fear. She couldn't remember ever having been alone like this before. All she wanted was her husband and her children and a place to make a home. Surely it wasn't too much to ask?

Hannah kept thinking about Florence too. Hannah had no idea where Ellis might have taken her, and although he'd begun to show some interest in his daughter, Hannah knew that he wasn't capable of caring for her properly. The thought of Florence being hungry and wet and crying for her, gnawed at her. She wished she knew that the baby was safe.

Hannah didn't know if was dawn or not when she heard the constable coming for her. Part of her was relieved to be getting out of the lock-up, but she didn't dare to consider what awaited her when she reached Lancaster. She just hoped and prayed that Jack would find a way to get her freed.

Constable Booth took her out to where a few other prisoners, hands bound, were sitting disconsolately on the benches that ran down either side of a cart. They were mostly men, but there was one other woman and Hannah briefly met her bleak stare as she climbed up. The sun was just rising as they left Bolton on their long journey. No one spoke and even though Hannah looked about for Jack there was no sign of him. She hoped he and the children were safe and had found somewhere to pass the night. And whilst she wasn't sorry that the children weren't witnessing her being taken away like this, she wished she could see them to reassure herself that they were well.

The journey up to Lancaster was long and arduous. Snow had fallen on the hills during the night and the roads were slick with ice making it hard for the horses to keep purchase on the slippery surface. They stopped a couple of times and were given water to drink and some stale bread to eat. Yet even though Hannah had been so hungry the previous day, she found she had little appetite now and her stomach was aching with worry.

It was dark again before they reached their destination. The horses had been changed twice, but even the last pair seemed weary as they hauled their load up the steep cobbled street towards the imposing castle gates. The huge doors opened as they approached and the cart came to a halt in the outer yard as they closed again behind them with an ominous thud followed by the grating of keys in locks and the drawing of bolts.

Hannah looked around as best she could, but could see little. The four towers that surrounded them seemed menacing and all that there was of the sky was a clear patch directly above their heads, where the cloud had finally cleared and Hannah could make out some bright stars.

The flap on the back of the wagon was lowered and the prisoners climbed down, stiff and aching from the hours on the road. Hannah stood, shivering with fright, wondering what awaited her and if she would ever find a way out of this fortress.

'Women this way!' said a voice and Hannah and the other woman prisoner stumbled towards the sound of it.

Someone was jangling keys on a ring and Hannah followed the sound across the uneven cobbles, trying not to stumble and fall. They were taken to some buildings that nestled under the huge stones of the castle wall. A studded wooden door was unlocked and they were led inside, following a woman who held a lantern high to light their way.

Hannah heard the murmur of interested voices and saw the ghosts of faces in the gloom, pressing against the bars of their cells to see who was being brought in. She and the other woman were taken to a dim room with a small fire smoking in the grate. A couple of cheap tallow candles were filling the air with the stench of pig fat and Hannah gagged and hoped she wasn't going to disgrace herself by being sick on the floor.

'Strip off your clothes,' instructed the wardress.

It was like the workhouse all over again, thought Hannah as she handed over what she was wearing and put on the prison issue dress.

'This way,' said the wardress and they followed her down the shadowy passageway to a door which was unlocked for them. The cell was tiny, and already crowded with women. The lucky ones had a board to sleep on, raised above the floor, but others were lying on straw on the ground. Hannah didn't think there was room for any more people, but the occupants were made to move closer together, grumbling as they did, so that the two new prisoners could be pushed inside. Then the cell door was closed and the key turned in the lock.

'There's a bucket in the corner if tha's caught short,' the wardress told her before walking away with her lantern, leaving the women in total darkness.

Weary and afraid, Hannah sank down to the floor and tucked her hands under her head to serve as a pillow. She closed her eyes, but when she opened them again at the sound of some creature scurrying close to her, she found that it was just as dark. Women around her were sighing and coughing and shifting in their sleep, but no one spoke. Although Hannah was tired out, anxiety kept her awake for many hours as she hoped for the new day and release from her torment.

At last a faint light illuminated the cell from the windows and Hannah was able to see that she was in a chamber that must have formed part of the original castle. The walls were hewn from stone and the windows were slits that narrowed to the outside wall. In the distance she could hear voices and footsteps and one or two of the women were awake and pulling on their gowns over their petticoats.

The wardress came back and the door to the cell was unlocked so that the women could file out into their exercise yard to use the privy. Hannah saw that the prisoners were wearing two colours of dress. Some red, and some blue like her own. After they had been taken to a room with tables and benches and issued with a bowl of gruel for their breakfast, the women in the red gowns were marched out and the ones in blue were taken to a day room where a meagre fire burned and there were some benches against the wall to sit on.

'New?' asked a woman who came to sit beside her.

'Aye,' nodded Hannah.

'I'm waiting to be tried,' said the woman. 'Everyone here is. That's why we wear blue. Them that's found guilty wear red, and they have to work, but t' rest of us just sits 'ere, waitin',' she explained. 'I sometimes envy them as goes to work,' she went on. 'T' days are long wi' nowt to do.'

'Hast tha been here long?' asked Hannah. She'd expected to be given the chance to explain herself that day, but now it seemed she would have to wait.

'A week, maybe two. I loses track of time when all t' days are t' same,' she told Hannah. 'I think it might be two,' she went on. 'Sunday we're taken to church and I've been twice. But it's not Sunday today, is it?'

'No,' agreed Hannah. 'I think it might be Friday, but I couldn't say with certainty.'

'What's tha accused of?' asked the woman. 'I'm in for stealin' from my employer. I'm pleadin' innocent though.'

Hannah hesitated. Bigamy seemed a worse sin than stealing and she was embarrassed to say, but the other woman was waiting eagerly to hear her charge. Someone new must be the only relief from the tedium, thought Hannah as she realised that all the others in the room were listening with interest to the conversation.

'They say as I married a man when I were already wed to another. I'm accused of bigamy,' admitted Hannah.

She was surprised by the murmurs of admiration from her companions.

'And is it true?' asked one.

'No,' Hannah told them. 'They said I was a widow. But then my husband came back.'

The other women began to move closer to hear the story and although Hannah was reluctant to tell it, she saw that there was no choice. It seemed to bring her some esteem and she was urged to a seat closer to the fire as they clamoured for more details.

CHAPTER TWENTY-NINE

Several days passed before Hannah was told that she had a visitor. Jack was allowed into the day room to see her and became the object of close attention from the other women. But he only had eyes for Hannah and gathered her in a fierce embrace.

'Is tha well?' he asked. 'Is tha bein' treated proper?'

'Aye. I'm well,' she reassured him. 'The food's plain, but there's enough of it and I've managed to sleep a bit at night. But it's thee and the childer that worry me,' she went on. 'How's tha managing?'

'Thomas and Molly are lookin' to the childer,' he explained. 'And I've been askin' about for folk who'll speak up for thee at thy trial.'

'Hast tha found Ellis?' she asked him, hopefully. She wanted to know that Florence was safe.

Jack shook his head. 'No,' he told her. 'There's no sign of 'im. I went up to Egerton to ask about at t' mill, but no one knows where he's gone. I called on yon parson as well, Mr Jones. He weren't very helpful either. Bit shifty if tha asks me.'

'He were the one as insisted that I were wed to

Ellis Duxbury,' said Hannah. 'He came to warn me about livin' in sin, even though Ellis never laid a finger on me – not until after we were wed any road.' A blush of shame suffused her cheeks and she couldn't look Jack in the eye. Hannah hated to admit that she'd been unfaithful to him and found it impossible to explain that it hadn't really been her choice. 'Will he come and give testimony at my trial?' she asked Jack.

He shrugged his shoulders. 'I don't know,' he replied. 'He wouldn't say owt to me.'

'What if he comes and says he married me and Ellis? What if I'm found guilty?' asked Hannah. 'What if they say I'm to be branded?'

'Don't fret about that, our Hannah,' said her husband. He leaned closer so that they wouldn't be overheard. 'I'll slip a couple of bob to yon gaoler to make sure t' irons are cold. Tha'll feel nowt,' he reassured her.

Hannah wasn't convinced. Half of her wished that she would be called up to the courtroom for her trial soon so that it would be done and over with, but the other half of her lived in terror that the case wouldn't be dismissed and that she would be found guilty.

'What about the Reverend Brocklehurst?' she suggested. 'He married us. Would he speak for us?'

The man owed her a favour, thought Hannah, remembering the day he had given her the letter to enter the workhouse. Maybe, if he'd pleaded harder on her behalf and persuaded the guardians to keep paying her rent, she wouldn't be in this mess.

'I'll go and speak to him,' promised Jack. 'I wish I had the money to pay a fancy lawyer to come and argue on your behalf, but . . .' His voice tailed off and Hannah realised that her fears had come true and he'd spent nearly everything he'd been paid on the ship.

'We can't afford that,' she agreed. 'We'll have to pay the gaol fees though,' she reminded him, hoping that he'd kept something back for that.

'Aye, I know,' he said. 'Don't fret. I'll not let thee stay in here a moment longer than necessary.'

'Jack,' she said after a moment, not sure how to broach the subject of her not being released. 'What if they give me a prison sentence. What will tha do?' she asked. 'Tha won't go away again?' she asked, worried that he might be tempted to return to sea if there was no other work for him. 'Tha wouldn't go off to London and leave the childer?' she asked.

'No, of course I wouldn't. But don't worry about it, our Hannah. It'll all get sorted out soon and tha'll get out of here.'

'Time's up!' announced the wardress, jangling her keys.

Hannah grasped hold of Jack's hand as he stood up to leave her.

'Do everything tha can,' she asked him.

'I will,' he promised and bent to kiss her. 'I will, Hannah.'

She cried after he'd gone and the iron gate had clanged shut behind him. She wished she could have seen her children as well, though she wouldn't have wanted them to see her in this place. Hannah was thankful that her friend Molly Holden was caring for them, but she knew they couldn't stay there for ever. And then there was Florence. Her arms ached for the baby and she longed to see her bonny little face and her sweet smile.

It was three more days before Hannah was told that the time had come for her trial. She tried to tidy her hair and make herself look respectable before she was taken up the stairs that led to the courtroom. A wooden door was opened in front of her and she stepped through, straight into the dock with the turmoil of the court all around her. Hannah felt as if it were all unreal and that she was disconnected from it as she watched the clerks in their wigs, the men of the jury taking their seats on the benches and the sparse crowd of interested onlookers who had come in out of the rain for some entertainment.

A door opened at the back of the courtroom and a clerk demanded silence as the judge entered in his robes and long curly wig. He looked over the wire spectacles that sat on the end of his nose and glared at everyone who was present, daring them to make a sound. Then, with a flourish of his robes, he seated himself on the immense carved chair and nodded his permission for the session to begin.

'What is the prisoner accused of?' he asked, scowling at Hannah as if her guilt was a foregone conclusion.

She saw Constable Booth rise from his chair at the table below her and move forward.

'The accusation is of bigamy, my lord,' he explained.

'Bigamy!' exclaimed the judge. He seemed more interested now that the trial wasn't to be about the usual indictments of stealing or fighting. 'What is the evidence?' he asked.

'The prisoner came to see Colonel Fletcher of Bolton, asking about the rental on a cottage she had previously lived in with a man named Jack Fisher who is her legal husband. However, I recognised the prisoner as a Mrs Duxbury from Egerton, the supposed wife of the mill manager there, an Ellis Duxbury, my lord.'

'I see.' The judge turned his attention to Hannah and she gripped the edges of the box she was standing in, trying to quell the shaking that it was impossible for her to control. 'How do you plead?' he asked her.

'I'm not guilty,' she whispered.

'Speak up, woman!'

'Not guilty,' she repeated as she felt her heart beating wildly at the prospect of this man disagreeing with her.

'I see. What witnesses do we have?' the judge asked.

'The woman's husband. Call Jack Fisher!'

Hannah was slightly reassured by the sight of Jack who managed to give her an encouraging smile before he took the bible in his hand and swore to tell the truth.

'Are you the husband of the prisoner?'

'I am. We were married in July 1806 at the parish church in Bolton.'

'And are there records of this marriage?'

'There are, my lord,' the clerk told the judge. 'The parish record clearly shows the marriage took place by banns on the third of July 1806 and was witnessed by the father of the bride, one John Halliwell, now deceased, and by the then curate of the church, a James Orrell.'

The judge nodded his approval and wrote something on the sheet of paper that was on the desk in front of him, then turned back to Constable Booth.

'And do you have evidence that this same woman, the prisoner in the dock, was married to Mr Ellis Duxbury of Egerton whilst her husband was still living?'

'I do, my lord,' agreed the constable. 'I have witnesses who were present at the marriage of the prisoner to Mr Duxbury in Egerton.'

'Call them forward!'

Hannah watched in horror and disbelief as all the curious onlookers who had been in the chapel that cold and frosty morning came forward to swear that she had indeed married Ellis Duxbury whilst still the wife of Jack Fisher.

'Were you present at the marriage of this woman to Ellis Duxbury of Egerton?'

'I was,' they all confirmed. 'It took place on the eighteenth of November at the chapel there. They were married by the Reverend Jones in front of me and other witnesses.'

'Is the Reverend Jones here to confirm this?' asked the judge.

'No, my lord,' replied Constable Booth. 'He was asked to attend but declined.'

'No matter,' said the judge as the last of the witnesses for the prosecution returned to their seats. 'It seems a straight forward case of bigamy. What can you offer in the way of a defence, Mrs Fisher?' he asked, as he took out his pocket watch to glance at the time, obviously hoping to have the case quickly concluded before his dinner hour.

'I didn't know it was wrong,' protested Hannah. 'They all said I was widow. Mr Cartwright at the workhouse and the Reverend Jones – they all said I was a widow.'

'But you were not a widow, were you?' asked the judge, taking off his spectacles to breathe on them and polish them with the edge of his robes. 'Were you?' he repeated, looking up at Hannah when she didn't immediately reply.

'No,' said Hannah as she wiped a stray tear from her face. 'But I'd heard nowt from Jack, not for years. Even Thomas Holden said as he thought Jack must be dead. I'd given up hope and Ellis

Duxbury said as he'd help me get my childer back from their apprenticeships if I were wed to him. I had no choice!'

There was murmuring throughout the court as the men around the table and those who were members of the jury exchanged views on what Hannah had said. The judge frowned at them and the clerk called for order.

'Why had your husband abandoned you?' asked the judge.

'He didn't abandon me!' protested Hannah. 'He was sent away to New South Wales.'

She saw the judge look more closely at Jack, and Hannah wondered if he was the same man who had found her husband guilty. If he was, the chance of her being found not guilty seemed to lessen.

'You were a convict?' he asked Jack.

'Aye. It's true, sir,' Jack told him, as he got to his feet and came forward again. 'I served my sentence and got my certificate of freedom.' He once again produced the crumpled paper from his pocket and the clerk laid it before the judge who studied it for a moment.

'You were sentenced in the year 1812,' he observed. 'Sent over the seas for seven years.' He looked again at the paper. 'This is dated 1817.'

'All prisoners had their sentences reduced by the king,' said Jack.

'Yes,' said the judge. 'Yes. That's correct. So seven years had not passed when your wife married again.'

'No, sir.'

'So the marriage cannot be annulled through desertion because not enough time had passed.' The judge sighed and turned back to Hannah. 'It is a pity Mrs Fisher that you did not wait a while longer to remarry,' he observed. 'As it is, I can only conclude that the charge of bigamy is upheld and that you are guilty.'

'No!' The cry came involuntarily from Hannah as her glance flickered from her husband to the judge and back again. She'd hardly had chance to say a word in her own defence. How could the man decide on her guilt so quickly?

'Sir!' called out Jack. 'We have another witness.'

'Who is it?' asked the judge, clearly irritated that he could not move on to the next case.

'The Reverend Brocklehurst, from the parish church in Bolton,' the clerk told him.

'Very well. Call him up,' agreed the judge.

Hannah watched as the vicar made his way towards the judge and took the bible in his hand to swear the oath. What help could he possibly be? Hannah didn't think there was anything else he could say that would make any difference at all.

'Do you know this woman?' the judge asked him, indicating Hannah.

'I do. She is Mrs Fisher, the wife of Jack Fisher.'

'And you officiated at their wedding?'

'I did, my lord.'

'So you agree that their marriage is legal?'

'I do, my lord.'

'I really don't see how this is helping your case,' the judge told Hannah.

'My lord,' implored the vicar. 'May I speak?'

'Go on.' The judge sat back on his chair and folded his arms.

'The marriage of Hannah and Jack Fisher is lawful,' explained the vicar. 'But the marriage of Hannah Fisher and Ellis Duxbury is not.'

'Well, I think that point has been amply made,' replied the judge. 'Do you have anything further to add?'

'I do, my lord,' continued the vicar. 'The truth is that there was no marriage between Hannah Fisher and Ellis Duxbury.'

'But that's nonsense! We have had witness after witness who were present at the wedding.'

Hannah watched as the Reverend Brocklehurst shook his head. She hoped that he was going to say something which might save her although she couldn't imagine what.

'There is no record of this second marriage in the parish register,' explained the vicar. 'As you well know, my lord, any marriage that does not take place in the parish church is not lawful. A ceremony conducted in the chapel at Egerton is not lawful unless the parties involved also attend the parish church to be wed according to the laws of this land.'

Hannah heard an excited burst of conversation from the assembled men. She exchanged a glance with Jack who was grinning up at her. He must have known he was about to play this trump card. Why on earth hadn't he told her sooner and saved her from the anguish she'd felt ever since she'd set foot in this dock?

'So there is no legal record of the marriage of Hannah Fisher and Ellis Duxbury?' asked the judge.

'None whatsoever, my lord.'

'Well.' It was clear to Hannah that the judge had had the wind taken from his sails and she almost began to laugh in delight at his face and that of Constable Booth. Her only regret was that Colonel Fletcher was not here to see it. 'Well,' repeated the judge, looking disappointed. 'The case is dismissed,' he announced. 'Mrs Fisher, you are free to go.'

Moments later, Hannah was in her husband's arms.

'Why didn't tha tell me?' she asked him. 'I were that terrified about what they were goin' to do to me!'

'I told thee not to fret. I told thee I'd make it right.' Jack couldn't keep the smile off his face.

'Did tha know when tha came to see me?' she demanded, thinking she'd never forgive him if he'd caused her all the unnecessary anxiety and torment she'd been through for the past few days.

'No, I didn't. I swear,' he told her. 'It was only after tha suggested askin' the Reverend Brocklehurst to help that I went to see him and he realised straight away that there was no case to answer.

I wanted to get word to thee, but there wasn't time. We only arrived on the coach early this morning.'

'Thank goodness,' said Hannah as she clung to Jack.

'Mrs Fisher?' said a voice behind her and she turned to find the vicar waiting to speak to her.

'Thank you!' she told him. 'Thank you for coming all this way to speak for me. I'm that grateful. More grateful than you'll ever know!'

'It was my pleasure,' Reverend Brocklehurst told her. 'And I'm glad that your husband has come home and that everything has worked out so well for you.' He hesitated. 'I always felt guilty about you having to go into the workhouse,' he said after a moment. 'I wish there was more I could have done then.'

Hannah nodded. 'It was hard,' she agreed, 'but now that Jack has come home I hope I never have to see the inside of a workhouse ward or a prison cell ever again.'

'I'm sure you won't,' said the vicar. 'A good day to both of you.'

As he walked away, Hannah put her hand in Jack's. 'What now?' she asked him. 'What are we going to do? I'm beginning to think that you were right when you said we should go away to London and make a fresh start,' she admitted.

CHAPTER THIRTY

'I think we should leave Bolton,' agreed Jack as they travelled back to the town later that day. 'I need to find work and there's none to be had here. I've not much savings left,' he admitted, 'and if we're to go to London or some other port then I need to keep enough on one side to buy tickets.'

'We should have walked back from Lancaster,' replied Hannah, clinging to his arm as the coach bounced over a pothole and nearly threw her down from the roof. 'It would have saved you some money.'

'It would have taken too long. We need to collect our childer and get on our way,' he told her.

'We should have gone before,' said Hannah, wishing that she'd never persuaded Jack to return the horse and cart.

'No, tha were right,' said Jack. 'It would have been no help to begin as thieves. At least now we can go without worryin' about yon constable comin' after us.'

'Unless he comes up with some other charge,' said Hannah. Even now that she was heading home she couldn't quite shake off her fears. Seeing all her former neighbours in the courtroom giving evidence that might have resulted in a branding or a prison sentence had shaken her.

'They'll not charge thee with owt else,' Jack reassured her. 'They were made fools of in yon courtroom. They'll not risk it again. But Fletcher won't make us welcome. It's another reason to get away and make a fresh start somewhere else. He'll do his best to make our lives difficult if we stay here.'

Hannah knew that Jack was right, but even so she knew she would find it hard to leave the place that had always been her home and the friends she had here – friends like the Holdens who had been so good to her whilst Jack was away.

It was growing dark by the time they got down from the coach on Churchgate and began to walk up to Hag End Fold. Hannah hoped that the Holdens wouldn't mind them all sleeping there for the night. It would be a squeeze and they would have to make do with some blankets on a chair, but at least it would be better than the prison cell.

Although she was tired, Hannah walked quickly, eager to be reunited with her children. If only she could be reunited with Florence as well, she thought. She knew that she would never rest easy until she was sure that the little lass was safe.

At last they saw the silhouette of the houses against the moonlit sky and they hurried up the slope towards them. There was a candle burning in the window of the Holden's home. Thomas and Molly must be expecting them, thought Hannah.

Jack had barely raised his hand to knock when the door was flung open and Molly peered out at him with a worried face.

'It's all right,' he told her. 'Our Hannah's with me. The case against her was dismissed.'

'Oh, thank goodness! Hannah!' Molly rushed forward as Hannah stepped into the light spilling from the doorway and wrapped her arms around her friend. 'I've been so worried,' she admitted.

Molly took her hand and pulled her inside. 'Shall we wake the childer to tell 'em tha's home?' she asked.

'No, let them sleep. But I'll look in on 'em if that's all right?'

'Aye. Of course. They're in the back room with our Annie.'

Molly picked up the candle that she'd left on the windowsill and Hannah followed her up the steps. Molly lifted the latch on the bedroom door, trying not to make any noise and Hannah stepped quietly into the room. She could see Ruth and Kitty sharing the bed with Annie. All three lasses were deep asleep, hair strewn across the pillows and arms around one another. Edmund was asleep at the foot of the bed on a mattress made of straw stuffed into sacking. He looked warm and comfortable and Hannah realised what a huge debt of gratitude she owed to the Holdens for caring for her children.

'I'm so thankful for what tha's done for us,' she told Molly as they came back down the stairs, 'and now I need to ask thee if Jack and me can stop the night an all. We've nowhere else to go.'

'Of course tha can stop!' exclaimed Molly. 'We'll not turn thee out at this time. Tha can sleep in our bed.'

'No!' exclaimed Hannah. 'We'll not take thy bed. We'll be grateful enough for a blanket to wrap ourselves in.'

'What did they say – at the court?' asked Molly as she brewed tea. 'I kept tellin' t' childer as tha'd soon be home, but I were worried they might find thee guilty – after what happened afore,' she added, meaning when Thomas and Jack had been sent to the colonies.

'They fetched witness after witness from up at Egerton to say as they'd seen me wed to Ellis Duxbury,' Hannah told her. 'But in the end I were saved by Reverend Brocklehurst. Thing was, the wedding were never legal because it should have taken place in t' parish church.'

'Aye, I've heard of such things before,' agreed Thomas. 'These non-conformists don't hold with the proper church and they conduct their own weddings and baptisms and such like. But none are legal in the eyes of the law. Oftentimes, it makes no difference, but it seems it's turned out the best for thee. What did Ellis Duxbury have to say for himself?' he asked.

'He never came,' Hannah told them. 'No one

knows where he's gone. He probably went into hiding when he heard I'd been arrested in case he was brought up before the court too.'

'Well, good riddance I say,' remarked Molly as she handed out slices of bread and cheese.

'Aye,' said Hannah, 'but I'd like to know that the little lass is safe. I'd grown fond of her.'

'That's not surprising, I suppose,' agreed Molly. 'But he's her father. She's not thy responsibility.'

'Even so,' said Hannah. 'I'm worried about her.'

Nothing more was said about Florence as the women listened to the men talking about the downturn in trade, the threat of growing industrialisation and how it might be possible to safeguard the work of the handloom weavers.

'I don't think there's any hope of it,' explained Jack to his friend. 'I've decided to go away from 'ere. There's work aplenty in the ports, so I'm thinking of takin' my family to London.'

'That's a long way to go,' interrupted Molly. 'What dost tha think of it, Hannah?'

'I'm not sure,' she admitted. 'But if Jack thinks it's the right thing to do, then we'll go with him.' She was about to add that she hadn't waited all this time for her husband to come home to have a falling out with him now. But she kept quiet. She didn't want to seem disloyal in any way because she knew it was only Jack's efforts to persuade Reverend Brocklehurst to speak up for her that had saved her from a far worse fate.

'When will tha go?' asked Molly.

'Tomorrow,' Jack answered for her. 'There's nowhere for us to live around here and we've taken advantage of thy hospitality for too long already. I reckon tha'll be glad to be shut of us,' he added.

'Tha's always welcome here,' Thomas told him. 'Tha were a good friend to me on board the *Fortune* and I'll not forget it.'

Jack nodded and with the discussion at an end, they made themselves ready to sleep. Thomas and Molly in their own bed and Hannah and Jack by the hearth, wrapped in a blanket each.

'Will we really go tomorrow?' Hannah asked her husband after a while. Exhausted as she was, she was finding it impossible to sleep when so many thoughts and worries were circling her mind.

'Aye. Is there any reason not to?' he asked her. Hannah was silent for a moment, not sure what to say. 'Hannah?' asked Jack. 'Surely tha's not thinkin' of stoppin' here? Not after everything that's happened. A fresh start is for t' best for all of us.'

'I know,' agreed Hannah. 'It's just that I'd be easier in my mind if I knew that Florence was safe.'

'Florence?' he asked. 'Who's Florence?'

'Ellis Duxbury's little lass. I'm worried about her.'

'Nowt to do with thee,' replied Jack. 'Give it no more thought. Get some sleep. We've another long day ahead of us come tomorrow.'

* * *

Hannah was woken the next morning by the cries of delight as her children came down the stairs and saw her. She hugged them all, shedding tears of relief that they were all together again. Her own children were her first concern, of course they were, and she could see how excited they were as their father explained that they were going to London.

'I'll get plenty of work there,' he promised them, 'and we'll get a nice house to live in. We'll be proper set up,' he said. 'We'll send Edmund to school and there'll be all manner of fine gentlemen comin' callin' on such fine lasses as you,' he told Ruth and Kitty.

After they'd eaten bowls of oatmeal and drunk some tea, they gathered their few belongings and, after hugging and thanking the Holdens, Jack and Hannah and their children set off to walk into Bolton to enquire about a coach that would take them south.

As they walked, Hannah looked at the children and wished that they were better dressed. Kitty and Ruth were wearing what had been returned to them by the workhouse. When she'd seen them at Quarry Bank they'd had ample clothing, but it had all been taken back when they left. She knew that she couldn't expect her daughters to be provided with clothing when they'd only worked there for a few months, but Kitty was already shivering in her thin gown and Ruth wrapped her shawl around her little sister as well as herself to try to keep them warm. Edmund had reluctantly given back the jacket that belonged to Thomas. The Holdens had wanted him to keep it, but Jack had said it was too generous and that he would clothe his own children. In the end they'd reached a compromise and Molly had fashioned an old blanket into a makeshift jacket for the lad and Jack had accepted a cap for him to wear. Hannah herself had had no option but to keep the gown and shawl that had once been Molly's – the slippers as well, although they'd been ruined by the water in the lock-up and were hardly fit to wear.

'I could do with getting a few things for the childer and myself,' said Hannah, as they approached the market that was growing busy now that more people were out and about, getting their shopping. 'We can't take our lasses to London barefoot, and these thin shawls'll not keep us warm on the outside seats. I don't want our Kitty taken badly again,' she added, looking at the lass who was huddled against her sister, her teeth chattering. 'I've no money though,' she reminded her husband.

'Aye, tha's right,' he agreed, looking at the children. 'We don't want 'em catchin' their death of cold afore we get there.'

Hannah watched as he reached into the pocket where he kept his money. He pulled out a handful of coins and frowned at them. 'How much dost tha think tha'll need?' he asked.

‘I don’t know,’ said Hannah, not wanting to ask for too much. ‘I’ll need to go and look at what’s on the stalls and haggle for a good price. But we can’t spend too much,’ she added, thinking that they would also need to buy food on the journey and pay for places to sleep when they stopped for the night. She didn’t even know how many days it would take to reach London.

‘Let’s go and see what’s to be had,’ suggested Jack. ‘It needn’t be fancy, just warm.’

Hannah called to the children and they crossed the road to the marketplace and Hannah approached the stall where Mrs Holt, the clothes dealer, was setting out her wares.

‘What’s tha needin’ today?’ asked Mrs Holt as Hannah began to look at the shawls that were on display.

‘I need something warm for myself and my daughters,’ Hannah replied, hoping that the woman wouldn’t remember the last time she’d come, when she’d been with Ellis Duxbury.

But Mrs Holt had a good memory for faces. ‘Tha didn’t fetch these lasses last time tha came,’ she observed. ‘Tha had a babe in arms then, if I remember rightly. Not brought her out today? Not that I can blame thee. It’s perishin’ cold,’ she said rubbing her mitten-clad hands together and blowing hot breath on them, as if to make her point.

‘No, I haven’t got the baby today,’ agreed Hannah. ‘She wasn’t mine. I was lookin’ after her.

How much is this one?' she asked, pointing to a thick woollen shawl woven in checks, to try to distract Mrs Holt's attention.

'I'd be wantin' two and six for that,' she said.

Hannah shook her head; although the shawl was lovely it was too expensive, unless she could talk Mrs Holt into reducing the price.

'I've a few special things kept aside for my regular customers,' Mrs Holt told Hannah, with a wink of her eye. 'Wait a minute and I'll show thee. Suit thee down to the ground this will.'

Hannah watched as she rummaged about in the sacks under her stall, then drew a sharp breath as Mrs Holt held up a red, woollen cloak, identical to the one that Ellis had given her for their wedding day.

'I bought this from a gentleman who'd lost his wife. Poor man,' she added. 'At least he said he'd lost his wife, but it were a funny thing because I saw him later with a young woman. She had a baby. Had a real look of that little lass tha said tha were mindin'. Gone back to her real mother, has she?'

Hannah was speechless for a moment. She wondered if what the woman was saying were true. Surely it would be too much of a coincidence for this to be the very same cloak that she had thrown back at Ellis?

'Can I take a closer look at it?' she asked, holding out her hand. She knew that she'd snagged the hem on the right hand side because she'd been upset about the damage and had tried to pull the loose thread back onto the wrong side of the garment.

Hannah took the cloak from Mrs Holt, who watched her shrewdly as she turned it around to examine it. Hannah heard herself gasp as she saw the loose thread.

'Where did you get this?' she asked, wanting more details that might give her a clue as to where Ellis and Florence were now. The woman had mentioned a baby being held by a woman. Did it mean that Ellis had found someone new to care for Florence?

The stallholder smirked. 'Like I said, it were sold to me by a gentleman. These boots an all,' she added, pulling out the sturdy boots that Hannah recognised as her own.

'Here in Bolton?' asked Hannah.

Mrs Holt shook her head. 'I take a stall on the market at Darwen some days,' she told her. 'It were there.'

Darwen, thought Hannah. That was where May had said she thought Ellis came from. He must have gone back.

'How much?' asked Hannah.

'I'd want five shillings for that cloak. It's like new. And a couple of bob for the boots.' Hannah frowned. It was a lot of money. She still needed to get clothes for the lasses as well, and she'd no idea how much Jack could afford.

'Come on, our Hannah,' said Jack impatiently,

coming up to stand beside her. 'There's no time to stand and chat. Just get on with choosin' what tha needs.'

'Who's this then?' asked Mrs Holt, looking Jack up and down and probably noting that he was fairly well dressed, better dressed than Hannah and the children at least. 'Hast tha got a different fancy man now?' she asked.

It was obvious that Mrs Holt was curious about her situation and was trying to find out more. Not that it was any of the woman's business. She was a gossip and Hannah wished she'd chosen another stall even though she knew that Mrs Holt's was the best place for clothing.

'This is my husband!' Hannah told her irritably. 'Can I just make my purchases, please?'

Mrs Holt raised an eyebrow at her outburst. 'Aye, don't mind me,' she bristled. 'I were only bein' friendly. Dost tha want this cloak, or no?'

Hannah watched in dismay as Mrs Holt began to fold the cloak away. Of course she wanted it. It was warm and cosy and she loved it – the boots as well. But it was no good her being warm and shod if her daughters weren't.

'Get it if tha wants it,' said Jack, clearly keen to get the shopping completed so that they could go on their way.

'It's too much money,' whispered Hannah.

'He looks as if he can afford it,' cajoled Mrs Holt. 'Don't sell thyself short lass. Take what tha can get,' she encouraged.

'How much?' asked Jack.

'Five shillings. And let's say one and six for the boots?'

Hannah watched as Jack counted the coins in his hand and the stallholder watched eagerly.

'It's too much,' Hannah told her husband. 'We need to get something for Ruth and Kitty as well.'

'Hast tha got any more cloaks?' Jack asked Mrs Holt.

'I've a couple. Not as good as this one though.' Seeing a good sale in prospect, Mrs Holt produced two more woollen cloaks from under her stall. They were worn and patched and looked a bit grubby, but they would be warm, thought Hannah.

'Then they'll be much cheaper,' replied Hannah.

In the end, they got the cloaks and Hannah's boots and another pair for Kitty, whilst Ruth agreed that she would have to make do with the slippers. They weren't sturdy but at least they fitted her. Mrs Holt added it all up and Jack managed to talk her down from twelve shilling to ten, but she wouldn't go any lower and in the end he paid up.

'How much hast tha left?' asked Hannah as they walked away from the stall, well wrapped up in their new purchases. 'Tha's kept enough back for tickets, hasn't tha?' she asked him.

He looked shame-faced as he shook his head. 'I don't think so,' he admitted as he counted the last of his coins.

'Then why did tha let me spend so much?' she

asked him, wondering if they should take something back and ask for a refund of their money.

'I weren't goin' to let yon woman think I couldn't afford to clothe my family,' he told her. 'Don't fret, our Hannah. I'll find some work and when I've earned enough we'll get on our way.'

'But what will we do in the meantime?' she asked. 'We don't even have anywhere to stay. We can't go and beg from the Holdens again. It wouldn't be fair on them. Tha should have kept some money back. I could have done without this,' she said, drawing the cloak around her, thankful for its warmth, but already regretting the purchase.

'I'll go and ask at yon mill,' said Jack. 'I'll ask if they're takin' on and if anyone knows of a cottage we can have for a short rental.'

'I've a better idea,' said Hannah as she realised this turn of events might be to her advantage. 'Let's go to another town. Tha's more likely to find work and a place for us to live if we're well away from the influence of Colonel Fletcher.'

'Aye,' agreed Jack. 'We could go to Manchester. There might be work there.'

'No,' said Hannah. 'They say there's a shortage of places to live in Manchester. We need to go where it'll be healthy, where's there's fresh air for our Kitty so she doesn't get poorly again, not squeezed into some damp cellar.' She hesitated, knowing that she needed to find the right words to make Jack agree to what she was planning without giving too much away.

‘Where was tha thinkin’ of?’ he asked her. ‘Not back to Egerton?’

Hannah shook her head. ‘No. Not there. But maybe in that direction. Maybe Darwen way?’ she ventured.

‘Darwen? Why there?’ he asked.

‘It’s near enough to walk in the day,’ suggested Hannah.

Jack sat down on a low stone wall and took off his cap to scratch his head. ‘Will there be work there?’ he asked. ‘I know nowt about where the work is now, havin’ been away so many years.’

‘I believe there is,’ replied Hannah, even though she wasn’t sure. ‘It may not be weavin’,’ she added. ‘But I heard they have a bleach works and a printing factory, and they’re building a new spinnin’ mill.’

‘Well,’ conceded Jack as he settled his cap back onto his head and stood up, ‘I suppose it’s as good as anywhere, and there’s no point sittin’ around here all day.’

‘Good.’ Hannah turned away so that her husband wouldn’t see her smile and be suspicious. She’d tell him the real reason she wanted to go to Darwen when they got there, she decided. It would be too late then for him to make any objections.

They set off walking on the road that would lead them through Egerton and out again onto the moors beyond.

‘Are we going back to Mr Duxbury’s house?’ asked Edmund hopefully.

'No.' Hannah took his hand and wished that he would stop talking about Ellis in front of his father. 'We're going on a bit further to a place called Darwen so thy father can get work and a house for us to live in.'

'I thought we were going to London?'

'We are. But not today. We need some more money first,' she explained.

As they reached the crest of the hill and she and her daughters gratefully raised the hoods on their cloaks against the fierce wind, Hannah wished that she'd had the foresight to buy some bread and cheese from the market to sustain them on the journey. She'd been so relieved that her plan had worked that she'd been anxious for them to set off before Jack changed his mind or began to ask too many questions. Her only hope was that they might meet the pieman with his tray of baked goods going door to door in the village, and that Jack had enough pennies left over to buy them some dinner.

There was no sign of him as they approached the main street. When they reached May's door, Hannah wondered if she should knock and try to have a word with her friend, but she didn't want to linger and Jack urged her on when she hesitated. She tried not to look at Ellis's house although she was aware of her children, and Jack as well, gazing at it as they passed.

'Still looks empty,' commented Jack.

'He'll not come back here,' replied Hannah.

Thankfully, they met the pieman on the far side of the village. His goods were still warm and plentiful and Jack paid for whatever she and the children wanted. They ate sitting on the roadside, and after the last crumbs were brushed from their clothes, they continued on their way, heads down against the weather until the road began to drop steeply down and they saw Darwen nestled in the valley below them.

'We'll have to find a place for the night,' said Jack.

'There's an inn,' ventured Hannah. 'The Grey Mare. Can we afford it?'

'Aye. Maybe just the one bed,' said Jack, trying to count what was left of his money in the twilight.

The landlord grudgingly agreed a price and included a bowl of pot luck, but told them they would have to pay for their ale. They ate hungrily and then tucked Edmund and Kitty into the bed first. Both children were white with exhaustion and Hannah felt guilty that she'd made them walk so far. Ruth was tired too, but sat up a while with them by the fire, even though Hannah was wishing she would fall asleep so that she could confess to her husband what had really brought them to this town.

Eventually, Ruth went to get into the bed with her brother and sister, and Hannah knew she had to be honest.

'That woman on the clothes stall at Bolton told me a curious thing,' she began, staring into the flames of the hearth to avoid looking directly at Jack.

'Oh aye. What were that then?' he asked as he drained the half pint of ale he'd been nursing all evening to the obvious displeasure of the landlord.

'She said that she'd bought this cloak in Darwen,' Hannah told him, fingering the garment that was hanging from the back of her chair. 'It looks a lot like the one I had before. The one Ellis Duxbury gave me.'

'They're common enough. Lots of women wear them,' replied Jack.

'I'm sure this is the same one. The boots too.'

'Well, that would be a coincidence,' he remarked.

'May once told me that she thought Ellis Duxbury came from Darwen.'

'What's this about, our Hannah?' asked Jack sitting up straight and turning to her. 'Tha's not tellin' me that tha's brought us here on some wild goose chase?'

'No,' she protested.

'Why would tha want to find him anyway?' asked Jack. 'After the way he treated thee, I would have thought tha'd never want to set eyes on 'im again.'

'I thought we could ask him for money,' confessed Hannah. 'I worked for him for all those months and he never paid me a penny. And because it turns out I was never his wife then I must have been his servant, and if so he should pay me wages.'

Jack considered her words for a moment then began to shake his head. 'And is that why tha's brought us all this way? He'll give thee nowt, Hannah, even if tha finds 'im,' went on Jack without waiting for her answer. 'I wish tha'd told me about thy hare-brained scheme afore we left Bolton. I'd never have agreed to it,' he told her.

'I know,' admitted Hannah. 'But there's another reason I want to find him. It's little Florence. She was like my own child and I'm that worried about her. I need to know she's safe and being cared for or I'll not have a minute's peace.'

'Aye, but she's not thy child to fret over,' Jack reminded her. 'I can understand that tha were fond of her, but she's not thy responsibility.' His face darkened. 'We shouldn't have come,' he said. 'We should have headed south if we were to start walkin'. We could have been on our way to London by now.'

'I'm sorry,' said Hannah, even though she wasn't.

'We'll not stop 'ere,' announced Jack. 'We'll go on our way at first light. I don't want thee to have anythin' more to do with that man.'

'But if he pays me some wages, we can get our tickets to ride on a carriage to London,' argued Hannah. 'Surely that's better than settin' off walkin'?'

'No!' said Jack emphatically. 'I forbid thee to see 'im again.'

With the conversation at an end, they went up to the bed in the attic room that they were sharing with the other travellers and squeezed in as best they could with their children. It was cramped and uncomfortable, but at least they were warm and dry, thought Hannah, hardly daring to sleep in case someone stole her boots in the night.

When dawn came, Jack woke the children and said they were going on their way, but wouldn't answer when they asked where to.

'Let's enquire about Ellis Duxbury at least,' pleaded Hannah as they ate some bread and butter for their breakfast. 'Let's ask if anyone knows where he is.'

Jack grumbled and shook his head, so Hannah knew she would have to defy him if she were to stand any chance of finding Ellis.

'I wonder if you know of an Ellis Duxbury?' she asked the landlord who was standing nearby obviously interested in their conversation and trying to listen to what they were saying.

'Ellis Duxbury? Dost tha mean the son of the cotton spinner?' he asked curiously.

'No,' replied a disappointed Hannah. 'The Ellis Duxbury I'm looking for told me he had no family.'

The landlord shook his head. 'I don't know another by the same name – and it's not a common one – Ellis. Non-conformists I think they are,' he added with a tone of disapproval.

'Do you know where he lives?' asked Hannah, wondering if it was worth checking. There were other things that Ellis had told her that weren't true – her being his wife for one. So he might have lied to her about his parents as well. She'd always been convinced that he was keeping secrets from her.

'I couldn't say,' replied the landlord. 'But his father's buildin' a new spinning mill down at Lower Darwen. They might be wantin' to employ folk if thy husband's lookin' for work,' he went on.

'Thank you,' said Hannah. 'We'll go to enquire.'

'There's no point chasin' after yon man,' Jack told her when they were outside. 'It's probably a different chap any road.'

'But it's worth a try,' insisted Hannah. 'If we can get some money from him, it'll make it easier for us to start again in a fresh place. And he owes me wages,' she persisted. 'He owes me that at the very least.'

In the end Jack gave in to her persuasion and they made their way to the mill. It wasn't difficult to find. The chimney stood stark on the horizon and the tall stone-built building, similar to the one at Quarry Bank, dwarfed the rows of small cottages clustered near to it.

'Wait outside,' Hannah told Jack and the children as they approached the open gates that led into the yard. 'It's no good us all going in, making a nuisance of ourselves.'

'Aye,' he agreed. 'We'll sit over there,' he told her indicating a low wall that was built along the side of the river that turned the waterwheel.

As Hannah approached the main door she saw that the mill was in the final stages of completion. Some men were busy dismantling the wooden scaffolding from one side of it and another was supervising the fitting of the final panes to the windows that ranged in tiers down both sides of the building. She was reminded once again of the drawings she'd seen inside the notebook in Ellis's parlour.

Recalling her visits to the mill at Egerton, Hannah felt the fluttering of nerves in her stomach as she opened the door. And sure enough she was met by the same looks of curiosity from the group of men who were standing around a desk studying what she took to be the plans for the construction. They all stared at her wordlessly for an uncomfortable moment before one spoke.

'Can I help thee?' asked a middle-aged man with whiskers. He had a familiar look about him, although Hannah was certain she'd never met him before.

'I'm looking for Mr Duxbury,' she said, glancing around for any sign of Ellis.

'Well, tha's found him,' replied the man. 'What can I do for thee? We're not takin' on any workers yet if that's what tha's come about.'

Hannah shook her head, disappointed. 'No,' she said. 'I was looking for a Mr Ellis Duxbury.'

The older man frowned again as if not sure what to say. 'What dost tha want with our Ellis?' he asked after a moment of hesitation.

'It's a private matter,' replied Hannah, her heart racing with a mixture of relief and trepidation. This man, presumably Ellis's father, hadn't denied that Ellis was there, but she wasn't sure how her former employer would act when he saw her again and she began to regret asking Jack to wait outside.

'What's thy name?' asked the man

'Tell him it's Hannah – Hannah Fisher. He knows me,' she added.

The elder Mr Duxbury glanced at the other men who were making no secret of their interest in the exchange. 'Come into the office,' he told her, turning to a door which he opened for her. Warily, Hannah went in and he followed her closing the door behind him so that they wouldn't be overheard. 'Sit down,' he said, pulling a chair forward. 'Tha says that tha knows my son, Ellis?'

'I think so,' replied Hannah, wondering if she'd made a mistake and this man's son was not the Ellis Duxbury she was looking for.

'How dost tha know him?'

Hannah hesitated. She wasn't sure how much to reveal to this man. 'I worked for him at Egerton,' she began. 'I cared for his daughter, Florence, and kept house for him. That is the Ellis Duxbury who's your son, isn't it?' she asked him, seeing from his face that it was true.

The man sat down himself and drummed his fingers on the table as he continued to study her. 'What is it tha wants?' he asked brusquely. 'Money? I've no money here,' he told her with a sigh. 'But if tha comes to my house this evening I'll give thee five pounds if tha promises to go on thy way and not bother us again.'

Hannah was tempted to agree to taking the money; it seemed a huge amount to her, but it wasn't all that she'd come for. 'I want to see

Florence,' she told him. 'I want to know that she's safe and being cared for.'

The man glanced towards the door through which the voices of his companions could be heard talking outside.

'I can't discuss this now,' he said. 'Tha'd better come to the house later. The Sycamores. Just down the road. Come this evening.'

'Will Ellis be there?' she asked.

'Aye,' replied his father. 'We'll hear what he has to say about this tale tha's tellin'.'

Hannah nodded although she was disappointed to be told to wait. She would have preferred to see Ellis straight away. She wanted to ask him why he'd left Egerton and whether he knew that she'd been arrested and taken to prison charged with bigamy. She wanted to ask him why he hadn't come forward to tell the magistrate that the marriage had been a sham and she was guilty of nothing, because it would have saved her all those desperate days in the gaol at Lancaster.

'Well?' said Jack when she rejoined him and the children by the river. 'Did tha see 'im? Did tha get some money?'

Hannah shook her head. 'He wasn't there. But I spoke to his father. I'm to go to his house this evening.'

'And will Ellis be there?'

'I hope so,' she replied, wondering if he was likely to run away again rather than face her. 'And his father offered me money,' she added. 'He said he keeps none here, but he'll give me five pounds later.'

'Five pounds!' Jack's eyes lit up in delight. 'We'll be able to travel like gentry with that,' he said. 'Inside seats and the best rooms at the inns.' He rubbed his hands together in anticipation.

It seemed a long time to wait and they wandered into the small town, attracting curious glances as they trooped along the narrow streets trying to pass the time. Hannah wished that they had the money already so that they could go inside the inn to warm themselves by the fire and get something to eat, rather than being forced to wander about cold and hungry. Jack asked about work in some places but he was told that there was nothing, at least not until the new spinning mill was finished, and even then Hannah doubted that Jack would be agreeable to working for the Duxburys.

At last, as the afternoon wore on and it began to grow darker, Hannah enquired where The Sycamores could be found and she was directed to the end of a quiet street on the outskirts of the town.

The house stood alone, surrounded by a small garden that seemed mostly given over to flowers and lawns at the front. Hannah was surprised that so much land was not put to better use growing fruit and vegetables, but she thought that maybe there were plots around the back, hidden from the view of an approaching visitor. She told Jack to wait again with the children, outside the gates. 'If I see him, I want to see him alone,' she told her husband, knowing that if Jack went in with her it might well end in a fight.

'Aye, well, don't stop in there too long,' he reminded her. 'Remember tha's got cold and hungry childer waiting out 'ere, so make sure tha gets the money so's we can pay for food and a bed for the night.'

Hannah nodded and walked up the gravelled driveway to the front door, telling herself that she had no reason to feel afraid. She'd done nothing wrong. It was Ellis Duxbury who'd treated her badly and there was no reason for her to hesitate if she was offered some wages as a recompense.

She rang the doorbell and stood back, pulling the red cloak tightly around herself, waiting to see if the man who had claimed to be her husband would acknowledge her. After a moment she heard footsteps and the door was opened by the man she'd spoken to earlier at the mill.

'Tha'd best come in,' he said standing aside to make room for her to pass him.

Hannah went in, out of the biting cold, to a tiled hallway with its own fireplace, although the fire that had been laid in the grate there hadn't yet been lit. 'This way,' said the elder Mr Duxbury and, after closing the door behind her and casting a worried glance towards the staircase that led to the upper rooms, he showed her into a small parlour at the opposite side of the hall.

Here, there was a good coal fire burning and Hannah longed to go nearer to warm her hands and face, but she stood just inside the doorway, glancing about in the faint light of the oil lamps as she recognised the two easy chairs that were turned towards the blaze and the polished table as the furniture that had once stood in the front parlour at Egerton.

Ellis Duxbury stood up from one of the armchairs and turned towards her. 'Hannah!' he said, glaring at her. 'What are you doing here? What do you want?'

'So tha does know her?' his father asked him.

'Yes, I do,' replied Ellis. 'She kept house for me at Egerton.'

It was a promising start at least, thought Hannah, who had wondered if Ellis would simply deny all knowledge of her.

'I need to talk to you,' she told him.

'I think everything was said the last time I saw you,' he replied. 'You made your choice then. Or are you here to beg me to take you back?'

'No! Of course not. But I've been worried about Florence. I want to see her. Where is she?'

'She's safe,' replied Ellis.

'But where is she?' repeated Hannah, thinking that she only had his word for it that the child was safe, and that his word meant nothing. 'I want to see her,' she insisted.

He was shaking his head. 'No, Hannah. I'm sorry. It isn't possible.'

‘Is she here? In this house?’

‘She’s upstairs, but she’s sleeping. I don’t want her woken.’

‘Can I just see her?’ pleaded Hannah. ‘I’ve been so worried about her since May told me you’d left Egerton.’

‘No.’ He was emphatic. ‘It’s for the best, Hannah. I don’t want Florence to be upset again. How did you find me?’ he asked her, changing the subject.

‘Because of this cloak.’

She watched as he looked at it more closely.

‘Is it the same one?’

‘Aye. It is. I bought it back from Mrs Holt on Bolton market. She told me she’d seen you here in Darwen, and the landlord at the Grey Mare told me to ask at the spinning mill. You were easy enough to find,’ she told him, enjoying having the upper hand for a moment. ‘And Mrs Holt told me that she’d seen you with a woman,’ went on Hannah. ‘Have you found a new nursemaid for Florence?’ she asked him.

Ellis shook his head.

‘Little Florence is being cared for by her mother now,’ interrupted the elder Mr Duxbury.

‘Her mother?’ asked Hannah, turning to him to check that she’d heard him correctly. ‘But I thought her mother was dead.’

‘Is that what he told thee?’ asked the elder Mr Duxbury with a scathing glance at his son. ‘Rose were never dead. She were unwell, that’s all.’

'Unwell?' Hannah felt her head spinning in confusion. She'd always suspected that Ellis had been keeping something secret from her, but she'd never expected this.

'Aye. It began after t' child were born. Puerperal insanity they called it and the doctor arranged for her to go to the asylum to be cared for.'

'Insanity?' repeated Hannah as she pictured some mad woman chained to the wall in a filthy straw-strewn cell, similar to ones she'd experienced in Lancaster. She couldn't bear to think of Florence being cared for by a woman who was a lunatic.

'My wife is as sane as you or I,' Ellis told her. 'It was the strain of the birth that made her ill. She's better now. I should never have allowed the doctor to persuade me to take her to that place.'

Suddenly, Hannah began to piece things together. 'Is that where you went every Sunday afternoon?' she asked Ellis. 'To see your wife?'

'Yes,' he nodded and began to look contrite. 'I'm sorry, Hannah. I'm so sorry for all of it,' he said.

'But I don't understand. Why did you keep it a secret? Why did you tell everyone your wife was dead?' she asked him.

'It was shameful,' he replied, 'having my wife in that place. I felt as if it was my fault.'

Ellis sank down on the chair and put his head in his hands. Hannah thought that he was crying and she had to stop herself from going to comfort him.

'Is that why you left Egerton so suddenly?' she

asked him as everything that had happened continued to fall into place. 'You weren't free to marry either,' she told him as her anger rose at the thought of what he'd done. 'You left me to carry the blame when you were the one who was guilty of bigamy!'

'Bigamy?' exclaimed the elder Mr Duxbury. 'What's tha talkin' about now?' he demanded of Hannah. 'What's tha tryin' to accuse my son of?'

'I'm accusin' him of being a bigamist! Of askin' me to marry him when he knew that he was already wed!'

Ellis's father turned to his son in bewilderment. 'What's this about?' he asked. 'Surely there's no truth in it?'

Hannah watched Ellis's face, wondering if he was going to deny it. He ran a hand through his hair. He was clearly agitated and looked much younger than she recalled. He'd always seemed so sure of himself at Egerton, but now under the interrogation of his father he seemed more a like a boy.

'I did ask her to marry me,' he admitted at last, not meeting his father's eyes, but looking down at the floor, clearly embarrassed to have been caught out.

'Tha did more than ask me!' burst out Hannah, unable to contain her anger any longer. 'Tha insisted on it. Thee and the Reverend Jones. I was left with no choice even though I told thee as my Jack might come back!'

'I did it to keep you safe!' retorted Ellis. 'What I did was for you and your children. I did it for your sake!' he insisted. 'I never meant to trick you or coerce you. I never thought your husband would come home.'

'So tha has a husband?' asked the elder Mr Duxbury, clearly perplexed by what was being revealed to him.

'Aye. But my husband was in New South Wales. I were alone with my childer and we'd been sent to t' workhouse. They all said as I should style myself a widow, though I never wanted to. I just wanted to keep my childer safe.'

'But tha must have known it were wrong?' said Ellis's father, turning to his son angrily. 'Tha must have known tha weren't in a position to be askin' anyone to wed thee.'

'I did it to protect Hannah and her children,' Ellis tried to explain. 'They were threatening to take her off to the asylum as well, and I couldn't bear it, not after seeing Rose in that place. And at the time I didn't think Rose would ever get better.'

His father stared at him. 'When did this happen? Where were tha wed?'

'In the chapel at Egerton.'

'Except it was never a real wedding,' Hannah told him. 'But you didn't know that, did you Ellis? You packed your bags and ran away as soon as you heard they'd sent the constables after me! You weren't that keen on protecting me when you thought it might land you in trouble! And you never came to speak for me!' she accused him. 'I could have been released straight away if you had, instead of spending nearly two weeks in the prison at Lancaster waiting for my trial. But you stayed away to save your own skin. It wasn't until the Reverend Brocklehurst told the court that there had never been a legal marriage, that I was set free!'

Ellis stared at her in amazement. 'They arrested you? And sent you to prison?' he asked, looking shocked. 'I didn't know. Hannah, I swear I didn't know,' he protested. 'I would have come and pleaded for you if I had. I'd have told them it was all my doing and that you weren't to blame.'

'Would you?' she asked. She wasn't sure that she believed him. 'I came looking for you to ask for help, but May said you'd left – that you'd run away.'

'I didn't run away,' he told her. 'After you'd gone I didn't know what to do at first. I knew I had to make provision for Florence. I knew that May would look after her, but it wasn't what I wanted. I wanted a proper family and it was clear from my visits to the asylum that Rose was getting better, so I decided to go and persuade them to release her into my care. The doctors were reluctant at first, but in the end they agreed and I brought my family home. I'd only gone to live at Egerton to be nearer to her, so that I could visit her,' he explained. 'There was no reason for me to stay there any longer.'

Hannah stared at him, not sure what to believe.

'So tha never were married to Ellis?' checked the elder Mr Duxbury, trying to make sense of what he'd heard.

'No,' agreed Hannah. 'Not legally. It was because we weren't married in the parish church, but I didn't know that at the time. I lived with Ellis as his wife. I believed I was his wife.'

'Even though tha had a husband?'

'They all told me Jack was dead. They gave me no choice,' persisted Hannah.

Mr Duxbury shook his head. 'I can scarce believe what I'm hearing,' he admitted. 'Where's tha husband now?' he asked Hannah. 'Has he come back?'

'He's outside waiting for me with our childer.'

'So what is that tha's come for? Money? Is that enough to persuade thee to go on thy way and never speak of this again?' he asked.

'I didn't come for money,' protested Hannah. 'I came to see Florence. Please let me see her!'

'No. I won't have her upset,' repeated Ellis. 'She sobbed for you for a long time after you left. She missed you. She screamed whenever her own mother took in her arms at first and it made her weep. But Florence is happier with her mother now, though it's been hard for both of them,' he said. 'You know what it's like to be parted from a child, Hannah. Just think how it might feel to be wrenched away from a newborn and told that you are mad.'

Hannah sympathised, remembering how distraught she'd been when Mr Cartwright had dragged her away from Kitty in the workhouse infirmary. She still wanted to be sure that Florence was safe and that her real mother was capable of caring for her, but she suspected that it wasn't going to be allowed.

Ellis's father sighed with impatience and picked up an envelope from the table. 'Here.' He thrust it at her. 'Take this. Never come back here again,' he warned her. 'Just take this and go. And don't come bothering us again.'

'I've done nothing wrong!' lashed out Hannah. 'I'm the one who's been wronged here,' she reminded them both.

Ellis's father shook his head, but he looked determined. 'Take the money,' he growled. 'My son was wrong and he's admitted that, so it's best if tha goes now. I'll not have shame brought on our family,' he told her.

Realising that her hopes of seeing Florence were not going to be fulfilled, Hannah had no other option than to take the envelope in her trembling hand. She wanted to look inside to check that it really did contain five pounds, but she resisted and tucked it into the pocket that was fastened beneath her gown. Then she looked at Ellis who had stood up again. He looked weary, she thought.

'I'm sorry,' he said again. 'I did what I thought was best.'

'What if my Jack hadn't come back?' she asked him. 'What would you have done then?'

'I don't know,' he said. 'But it was you that made me realise it was wrong to keep my wife separated from Florence and wrong to deprive my daughter of her real mother. It was when I saw how important your children were to you, when I realised that you'd do anything to keep them safe, that I knew I'd been mistaken in agreeing to Rose being taken to that place. I don't know what would have happened if Jack hadn't come back,' he admitted, 'but I'm glad he did. You have your husband; your children have their father and it gave me the opportunity to reunite Florence with her mother.'

Hannah nodded. Finding Ellis had not turned out as she'd expected. Although she'd been angry and raged at him for what he'd done, all she felt now was sorrow. 'I hope you'll be happy,' she told him, realising that he had never been happy with her at Egerton.

'Thank you, Hannah,' he said. 'Thank you for trying to understand.'

His father had already moved between them to usher her to the door and Hannah made no more objections. She crossed the tiled hallway, only for a moment being tempted to run up the stairs and look for Florence. Mr Duxbury opened the door and moments later she was standing on the step in the cold of a moonlit night, with her breath visible under the light of the lamp illuminating the front door of The Sycamores, which had been firmly closed behind her.

She saw Jack and the children waiting for her at the gate with anxious faces and hurried to meet them.

'Did tha get it?' asked her husband.

'I did,' she replied as she fumbled for the envelope, praying that she hadn't been tricked and that it did indeed contain money.

Jack took it from her and peered inside. 'Ten pounds!' he exclaimed.

'Ten? Really?' asked Hannah as she met his grinning face. She'd never expected Ellis's father to be so generous. It was twice as much as he'd promised. 'So we can eat and get a bed?' She felt relief wash over her as she realised that they could afford such luxuries.

'We'll have t' best meal ever and the warmest of feather beds!' said Jack as the children looked up at his delighted face in anticipation. 'And tomorrow we'll be on our way.'

'Aye.' Hannah thought that it would be for the best. She would be sorry to leave Lancashire, but it had taught her some harsh lessons, and perhaps things would be easier in a new place where there were opportunities rather than hardship.

She reached out and took Kitty's cold hand in hers, smiling back at her younger daughter's happy face. Then she tucked her other hand under Jack's arm. 'Come on,' she said as she watched Ruth take Edmund's hand. 'Let's go and get warm and fed. It's been a long day and we're all weary.'

They set off to look for the best inn, but before she turned away from The Sycamores, Hannah gazed up at the curtained windows and wondered behind which one little Florence lay sleeping in her crib. She was disappointed not to see the child again, but she agreed with one thing Ellis had said. There was nothing that could replace the love of a mother and she hoped he was right when he'd told her that his wife was recovering.

She drew Kitty closer and hugged her. 'I'll never be parted from thee or thy sister or brother again,' she promised her. 'Have no fears.'

Her daughter rested her head against Hannah's arm and Jack smiled at both of them.

'There were times when I thought I'd never see this day,' he said. 'All those years on t' other side of the world, hopin' that tha'd not forgotten me.'

'I never forgot thee, Jack Fisher,' Hannah told him. 'I always knew tha'd come back to us if tha possibly could. I never doubted that for a moment.'

The next morning dawned bright and sunny as if it was ripe with promise for the future. After rising reluctantly early from the comfort of the best feather beds and eating a hearty breakfast of fried bacon and soft fresh bread, Hannah and her family walked the short distance into Blackburn and Jack bought tickets for the coach to Manchester. They had the luxury of inside seats, out of the cold of the frosty morning, and it made Hannah feel like one of the gentry as they rode along the highway, her children happy and smiling as they watched houses and cottages then farmland go by. They were excited for their new adventure and even Hannah felt a flutter of anticipation. From Manchester, they planned to travel to London and find a nice house near to the river so that Jack could find work. Edmund would go to school where he could learn to read and write. And Hannah was determined that Ruth and Kitty would find an easier way to earn their living than toiling in the mill for sixteen hours every day. Maybe they could take in sewing or make sweets to sell on the streets – Hannah had lots of ideas for a better future for them all. One thing she was certain of: they would never darken the doors of the workhouse ever again.

ALSO BY LIBBY ASHWORTH
FROM CLIPPER LARGE PRINT

The Cotton Spinner
A Lancashire Lass
A Family Secret
The Convict's Wife

A Mother's Fight